LIBERTY

LIBERTY

A HISTORICAL NOVEL

———◆———

DEAN HUGHES

DESERET
BOOK

SALT LAKE CITY, UTAH

Visit us at deseretbook.com

Library of Congress Cataloging-in-Publication Data

CIP data on file

ISBN 978-1-63993-287-0

Printed in the United States of America
Publishers Printing, Salt Lake City, UT

10   9   8   7   6   5   4   3   2   1

For My Great-Grandson
Henry Hsiung Russell

PREFACE

Many Latter-day Saints visit the reconstructed county jail in Liberty, Missouri, where Joseph Smith and five other Church leaders were held during the winter of 1838–39. Most of us know the story of what happened there. The fact is, however, some of what we "know" has proven to be lore more than history. That creates a problem for me as a writer of historical fiction. If I don't say that the men in the jail were unable to stand up straight because of the low ceiling, some readers will conclude that I haven't done my research. That idea, however—that they couldn't raise themselves to full height—has proven, almost certainly, to be untrue. And that's only one of the myths about Liberty jail.

I've done my best to be accurate about history in this novel. I've read historical accounts, biographies, records, journals, letters, along with documents now published in *The Joseph Smith Papers*. I admit, it's tempting to include some of the traditionally believed versions of events, partly because they make good stories—and partly not to be doubted by readers—but I believe that readers of historical fiction want to trust that they are receiving an accurate picture. So let me list some of the commonly held folklore that hasn't held up under the scrutiny of careful historical research:

1. An early estimate of the height of the ceiling in the lower

part of the jail, sometimes called the "dungeon," placed it at six feet. Writers assumed that this estimate was accurate and concluded that Joseph and Hyrum would have bumped their heads on the ceiling and Alexander McRae would have had to bend low to walk around. But in the 1880s, Latter-day Saint historian Andrew Jensen visited the jail and offered more accurate dimensions. He measured the ceiling in the lower room at six feet and six inches, which would have given plenty of clearance to Joseph and Hyrum. McRae has been described as anywhere from six feet three to six feet seven, but such estimates were notoriously exaggerated in the nineteenth century. McRae wrote about his own experience in the jail and complained about the food and the miserable conditions, but he never once reported that he couldn't stand up straight. It would appear that he was not quite as tall as some had estimated, and even though the ceiling may not have given him much room, he surely would have described the misery of walking around hunched over all the time. So in my novel, the men all stand up when they're in the dungeon.

2. Another common belief is that the prisoners spent all, or at least most, of their time in the dungeon. Andrew Jensen, in speaking with a jailer who knew the situation firsthand, reported that the men did spend their nights in the lower room but were allowed to climb the ladder to the upper level for meals and for visits by relatives and Church members. Evidence now suggests that they probably spent most of their time upstairs in the daytime hours. Joseph's important letters were written at a table in the upper room, with his scribes sitting across from him. Alexander Baugh, the preeminent authority on Latter-day Saint history in Missouri, discovered evidence that there was also a stove in the upper room, so the men were certainly very cold at night, but they were probably able to warm themselves during the day.

3. The imprisoned men believed that they were poisoned by their guards and that they were offered human flesh—which they refused to eat. It's possible that this is true, but in recent years, careful historians have expressed serious doubts about both these matters. The food was less than satisfying to the prisoners, but there is no evidence of poisoning. I decided not to portray the men as being poisoned, but I do portray them *believing* that they were poisoned, and I left out the suspicion about the human flesh.

4. The accounts of the two escape attempts by the prisoners have not been widely told. But the attempts are well documented and reported by the men themselves, with Alexander McRae providing a full report published in the *Deseret News* after he reached Utah. I therefore included both of these accounts.

5. A story almost never told is that Joseph had his dog with him in the jail for at least part of the time he was incarcerated. Alexander Baugh has found evidence that the dog spent time in the jail, so when I report that in the novel, please don't accuse me of stretching the truth. Of course, I did have to decide when Old Major might have arrived and how long he stayed.

6. Most Latter-day Saints know that section 121 of the Doctrine and Covenants was written in the jail. They probably also know that sections 122 and 123 came from the same letter that Joseph wrote to the Saints. What most of us haven't known is that the material in those sections is a "highlights version" of the letter. The actual letter was very long and took Joseph two days to write. He stopped at one point and closed the letter and got up the next morning and added to it. Some of the passages not included in the Doctrine and Covenants are powerful, written in poetic language. I decided to include some of that material in my novel, and I quoted those passages as they were written, modernizing spelling

and punctuation but leaving sentence structure and word choice the same. When possible, I used the spelling and punctuation as found in the Doctrine and Covenants, but otherwise changed things as minimally as I could from the original letters to balance ease of reading and preservation of authenticity.

7. Alexander Doniphan, attorney for the Saints, said that when Sidney Rigdon spoke at a local hearing and was granted bail, "Such a burst of eloquence it was never my fortune to listen to, at its close there was not a dry eye in the room, all were moved to tears." (Even Doniphan, a lawyer, couldn't punctuate.) Sidney's speech must have been powerful. My problem, however, was that no one recorded what he said. I wanted the reader to feel Sidney's passion, but I couldn't make up the speech out of whole cloth, so I used an impassioned plea that Sidney made when he wrote an affidavit seeking redress from the federal government for the depredations against the Saints in the state of Missouri. I followed his logic and often his choice of words, and above all, his passion. I hope it was a way of creating that moment without "inventing" history.

This last example gets at another challenge of writing historical fiction. Some of what I've written is invention. What I set out to do was provide insight into what happened to all the men—Joseph and Hyrum Smith, Sidney Rigdon, Alexander McRae, Lyman Wight, and Caleb Baldwin—during the four months and one week they spent in the jail. But especially, I was interested in what happened inside the heart and mind of Joseph Smith that brought him to the point that he could write one of the most beautiful and insightful revelations ever recorded. And yet, I knew that if I wrote the novel from the point of view of Joseph himself, readers would struggle with my pretending to know what went on in his mind. Latter-day Saint historians have written that Joseph changed during that time, gained depth and compassion, and received doctrinal insights. So what happened to change the Prophet? I decided I could only create a sense of Joseph's inner life by viewing the events through the perception of the person most readers know the least about: Caleb Baldwin. True, I had to "invent" Caleb's mental and emotional experience, and I had to let the reader see Joseph through Caleb's eyes. But I felt safer doing that than entering the mind of the Prophet directly.

The main problem in writing historical fiction is always the same: filling in gaps in places where historical research hasn't provided the entire story. I try mightily to stay as close to reality as I know how. But in this novel, all the characters are real people. I couldn't plant a fictional character in the jail to observe what happened. So relatives of Caleb Baldwin will have to forgive me—if they can—for probing his mind on the basis of what I could learn about him.

Let me say too—for those historically sophisticated—that I left a few things out. For example, during one short period of time, another prisoner was kept in the jail. I could learn little about this man, and his presence seemed more a distraction to the story than a useful bit of knowledge. The men in the jail also wrote and received other letters than the ones I mentioned, and some of these letters are extant, but again, a novel has to stay with information that moves the story forward. (And let me add, nonfiction historians also have to decide what details to include and what is trivia unimportant to the account.)

Professional historians often relate various, sometimes conflicting, sources for the events they describe. This is an effective way to offer differing perspectives without taking a stand on which version is correct. As a writer of historical fiction, however, I am forced to choose one version of an event, but I search for reliable sources to guide me in my choice. For example, in the prologue to this novel, I report some intense verbal exchanges: Caleb Baldwin questioning Judge Austin King, and King's response; Joseph Smith's query directed to Samson Avard; and the statement of one of the guards before the Richmond hearing began. The exchange between Caleb Baldwin and Judge King is based on an affidavit written by Caleb Baldwin himself. He paraphrased the words, and I turned them into direct dialogue, but Baldwin is my source. The other two exchanges were recorded by eyewitnesses David Pettigrew and Ebenezer Robinson.

As I said before, I didn't try to report Joseph's thoughts, but some readers may wonder whether or not I should have made up dialogue for him to speak. There is simply no way to know exactly what Joseph said in certain situations, but I have made a careful attempt to quote him when I could and to base conjectured dialogue on descriptions of events, and upon his opinions, attitudes, anxieties, and even self-doubt. I read and took notes on every entry in all three volumes of his journals published in *The Joseph Smith Papers*, and I did my best to understand the man and the prophet he was. I've attempted to be certain that I can trace anything he says in my novel to a source or at least to an explanation as to why I think he would have held a certain opinion or expressed various feelings.

Joseph was clearly angry when he wrote his first letter to the Saints from the jail. He was disturbed by the men he considered traitors—the men who witnessed against him in the court of inquiry in Richmond, Missouri. To read that letter is to feel his resentment. What I tried to trace, as best I could, was the emotional and spiritual process he experienced that brought him to the point that he could express some of the most lofty, inspired concepts spoken by any prophet in any era. I may have invented the spoken words of his conversations, but I don't think I've misinterpreted his growth and deepened spirituality.

In the end, I think it is worth taking on the inherent dangers of fictionalizing a real experience. Most of us know some things about the jail experience—including the myths—but we normally read the inspiring sections 121–123 in the Doctrine and Covenants without understanding the context in which they were received. What I hope this book adds is more sense of who Joseph was and how his own humanity, along with his spirituality, entered into his process of self-discovery and his increased understanding of eternal truths. The story of Joseph's time in jail and the prophetic words contained in the Doctrine and Covenants are among the treasures found in our Church's history. The Lord tells Joseph in Doctrine and Covenants 122:7, "Know thou, my son, that all these things shall give thee experience, and shall be for thy good," but if we comprehend what happened in the jail more fully, Joseph's experiences can bring *good* to all of us.

PROLOGUE

Caleb Baldwin stumbled as a guard shoved him from behind and ordered, "Get to the back with them others."

Caleb caught his balance, then twisted around and stared at the guard. "Don't push me," he said defiantly. But he didn't wait for a response; he crowded in among his brothers from Far West and Adam-Ondi-Ahman. They made room for him, but no one spoke. They all looked disheveled from the several nights they had slept on the floor, and downcast, surely from the treatment they had received. Caleb knew they were feeling what he was: defeated and fearful, whether they admitted it or not. The guards kept vowing that all of them would be convicted and put to death. "Don't even hope for anything else," one guard had told Caleb. But he had looked the man in the eye and said, "The Lord won't let that happen."

It was what he wanted to believe. And yet, his mouth was dry, his hands shaky. The raw hatred of these guards was unnerving.

Several Church leaders were ushered in a few minutes later: Joseph and Hyrum Smith, Sidney Rigdon, Parley Pratt, Lyman Wight, Amasa Lyman, George Robinson. Caleb had learned that these seven had been kept in a nearby log house, chained together. He wondered whether Joseph was shaken by all the rough handling. But the prophet looked resolute. He nodded to the other prisoners—a sign of confidence, Caleb thought—but said nothing.

The room smelled of unwashed men, but there was also the scent of newly cut logs in the windowless little Richmond courthouse, recently built, still unfinished. The lantern light left the room dim, and the wood stove had not yet blunted the cold of the November night. Two guards raised a long wooden pole from the floor and used it to force the prisoners farther back. There were more than fifty defendants, with new ones brought in each day. Now, with the pole forcing them back, they had to crush together so close that there was no room to move.

Several guards with rifles stood around the room. Caleb noticed how jovial they were now that the hearing was finally going to start. One man laughed and called out to his partners, "Now's the chance to shoot your Mormon. I've shot mine." All the guards laughed.

But Judge Austin King walked into the courtroom and the guards stood straighter, became quiet. King was a thin, stiff man, dressed in a suit of black clothes and a puffy silk necktie. He took a sweeping look around at the crowd of prisoners and stopped directly in front of Caleb, who took the chance to speak the words he had hoped to tell the man at some point. "Sir," he said, and King lowered his head to listen. "Grant me a *fair* trial and I'll be satisfied with the result."

Caleb had wanted to explain what he meant by that, but King stepped closer and said, "Tell me your name." Caleb recognized in the man's voice that he was a Southerner.

"Caleb Baldwin."

"Mr. Baldwin, this is not a trial. This is a court of inquiry. What will be decided here is whether enough evidence exists to hold you over for a trial. What you must recognize, however, is that Governor

Boggs has already ordered that all of you leave Missouri or face extermination. This hearing won't change that."

"But sir, what will happen to my family if I'm not there to help them? I have nine children, seven of them girls. Who's going to take care of them if they're plundered and driven out across the prairie?"

"The best hope for you, Baldwin, is to renounce your religion, forsake Joseph Smith . . ." He hesitated and glanced at Joseph. ". . . and witness against him. There is no law that can protect you and the rest of the Mormons who have rebelled against the government of our state."

His eyes moved away from Caleb as though to assess whether others had heard and understood, but Caleb raised his voice and called his attention back. "I will never renounce my religion or turn against my prophet."

Judge King ignored Caleb's words. He surveyed the bunched-up men before him. "If anyone wants to witness against this so-called prophet who has led you into this dreadful situation, please speak up. This is your chance to save yourselves."

The room was silent. Caleb wasn't surprised. A number of leaders had decided to break with the Church, and rumor had it that some were in town ready to take the stand as witnesses against the defendants, but the men who had been held in this little courthouse for several days had all expressed their loyalty to the Church and faith in Joseph Smith.

The jury—a group of men dressed better than Caleb had come to expect from settlers living in western Missouri—was brought in at that point and given seats near the judge. The doors then opened again and far too many spectators tried to push their way into the space between the defendants and the jury box. These were mostly men, and some of them looked as though they had come directly from their farms—in most cases, after an apparent stop at a local public house. They remained standing, and now the room was crowded far beyond comfort. Some of the crowd looked back at the accused and tossed out slurs, which elicited laughter from the others. The thrust of the abuse invariably included a vow that the defendants would all be shot—as they should be. Caleb tried to ignore all that, not look at the men shouting at him, but one thing was certain to him: he would never receive a fair hearing in this courtroom.

King opened the hearing by calling for order, and then, in a measured, formal style, stated again that he was conducting a court of inquiry, not a trial, and explained that if a trial became necessary, the "Mormons" would have their chance for a defense. He then called on the prosecution to bring forward its first witness. When Thomas Birch, the lead attorney for the prosecution, announced the name Samson Avard, Caleb heard a distinct gasp from his fellow Saints. Samson Avard had been the leader of the "Danites"—a band of secret soldiers who had, in Caleb's mind, gone to extremes in their defense of the Saints. It seemed impossible that the man would now separate himself from his own actions and accuse his brothers.

Avard strode into the room and turned toward the judge. He avoided eye contact with the prisoners. He took his oath and answered a few peremptory questions, and then he spoke in what seemed a prepared, even rehearsed account of his experiences with Joseph Smith and the Church. He spoke for hours, taking few questions, and reported the vicious actions of the Mormon militias. Repeatedly, he claimed that Joseph Smith was a dictator whose one purpose in life was to conquer western Missouri and build a kingdom of his own, over which he would appoint himself the ruler.

Caleb listened with growing anger as Avard said that Joseph—but he called him "Joe Smith"—wanted to extend his control of all things spiritual and temporal not only in Missouri but across the entire world. He referred to the scripture in Daniel 2 that described a stone that would be cut out without hands and would roll forth and fill the whole earth, destroying all other kingdoms. Joseph, he said, would never be satisfied until he conquered all governments, invoked his insane doctrines, and dominated the world.

Judge King interrupted and asked Avard to recite again the scripture in the book of Daniel, and then he turned to his clerk and said, "Write that down; it is a strong point for treason."

Alexander Doniphan, the defense lawyer representing the Saints, stood and objected, but King overruled him. Doniphan sat down, but as he did, he muttered, loud enough for everyone to hear, "Judge, you had better make the Bible treason." King ignored the remark.

Caleb wanted to shout out that Avard was lying. He knew, however, that would only make things worse. The fact was, Avard had *directed* the vigilante actions that some of the Saints had taken, and now he was leaving out his own involvement.

Joseph was standing a little ahead of Caleb and off to his left. Caleb could see his profile. He watched as Joseph flinched from time to time, but he remained stolid, didn't reveal his emotions.

The questions continued all day, and Avard described every detail of the defensive actions the Saints had taken, portraying them as acts of rebellion. Caleb was well aware that some of what Avard said was true. He and other Church members had fought back in ways that Caleb was now not proud of. But Avard had a way of twisting and exaggerating that even turned his truths into distortions. Never once did he mention the attacks of the Missourians that had triggered the conflicts. And always, "Doctor" Avard, as he called himself, spoke in the same confident, articulate style, pacing a little, holding his head up, as though he were a high-minded observer of all the events he described, morally superior to the renegade Mormons.

Late in the day Judge King asked Joseph Smith whether he would like to question Avard. "Yes, sir, I do have one question," Joseph said, and then he asked, "Doctor, you said that you had unshaken confidence in me as a prophet of God." Caleb remembered that this was how Avard, at the beginning of his testimony, had described his attitude toward Joseph before he had supposedly recognized him to be a "false prophet." Avard turned around and looked steadily at Joseph, still holding his head high. But then he nodded his assent. "What gave you that confidence?" Joseph asked. "Was it because I taught you to lie, steal, and murder as you have testified, or because you actually believed me a prophet?"

Avard's eyes left Joseph's. He didn't answer. He only turned away. But the judge didn't require him to give an answer.

As it would turn out, Avard continued his testimony throughout the second day of the hearing. At the end of the day, a guard—one less hostile than most—told Caleb that Avard was testifying because he had been caught leaving the state. He'd told Thomas Birch, the prosecutor, that he would be willing to testify against Joseph if he could be pardoned for any of his own actions. The guard said, "I heard him tell one of your men that he ought to swear hard against the leaders of your church if he wanted to save his own neck."

That didn't surprise Caleb. He had long since lost trust in Samson Avard.

◆

The hearing continued for seventeen days, and the tenor of things didn't change. Caleb put in long days standing in the back of the courtroom, pressed against his brethren, taking abuse from the crowd that showed up each day, and then sleeping on the same floor each night with only a blanket for a bed. After Avard's testimony, several other "brothers in the gospel" took the stand and denounced Joseph or described warlike actions of the Saints: George Hinkle, John Corrill, William Phelps, Reed Peck, and John Clemenson.

Caleb's frustration kept mounting; only one side of the story was being told, and that side was distorted. When he had a chance one evening to speak with Alexandar Doniphan, he asked, "What about all the attacks on us? Why doesn't anyone talk about that?"

But Doniphan, in his dignified style, said, "Remember what Judge King told you. This is a hearing. We'll have our chance to offer a defense at the trial. We are bringing in some defense witnesses to exonerate some individuals, but I can tell you now, all our arguments will avail us nothing—not even if a cohort of angels were to come and swear we were innocent."

So Caleb tried his best merely to survive the continuing days of testimony. The time was taken up with witnesses against each defendant, and the only defense was from a few loyal Latter-day Saints. Finally, when the verdict was announced, Caleb was surprised that of the sixty-four defendants, twenty-eight were released for lack of evidence. The other thirty-six were ordered to stand trial, most of them accused of "arson, burglary, larceny, and robbery," for which they were allowed to post bail. But five men involved in the Battle at Crooked River were accused of murder and remanded without bail. They would remain in jail in Richmond. Probable cause for treason, also not a bailable offense, was found against another six, who would be confined in the Clay County jail in Liberty, Missouri. Those men were Joseph Smith, Hyrum Smith, Sidney Rigdon, Lyman Wight, Alexander McRae . . . and Caleb Baldwin.

When Caleb heard his name, his breath escaped him. Treason? He was a veteran of the War of 1812, a loyal American all his life. How could anyone think him a traitor?

But then he heard worse news: he would not be tried until March 6, 1839. That meant three more months in jail. And what would happen to his family during all that time?

As guards led the defendants from the courthouse, Caleb was held until the end and then grouped with the other "traitors." Joseph put his arm around Caleb's shoulders.

"I'm sorry, Brother Caleb," he said. "You don't deserve this."

"We didn't rebel against the government," Caleb said. "How could they say that about us?"

Joseph stopped and looked into Caleb's face. "Put the blame on Samson Avard. That's where it belongs. He's a coward and a liar." And then in a low voice, he added, "He denounced me and, truly, the Church itself. You heard him—the vile things he said about us. But on Judgment Day, I will be a witness against him."

Caleb felt the resolve in Joseph's words, and he liked to think that Avard would answer for his distortions, but Caleb had actually been looking for solace at that moment, maybe a prophetic promise that all would be well. "What's going to happen to us now?" he asked.

"We're going to be tested," Joseph answered. "We'll have to stay strong—stronger than we've ever been."

CHAPTER 1

Each time the wagon jostled, a chain jerked Caleb Baldwin's handcuffs and rubbed against his wrists. This was the second day of travel from Richmond, and the six prisoners, all chained to the wagon, had grown weary and subdued. It was December 1, cold, and now that the tiresome trip was nearing its end, Caleb had begun to wonder what else he and his friends would have to suffer. An entire winter in jail was almost too much for his mind to accept.

The rough-lumber wagon box was open to the weather, with only the high sides to keep out the wind. Caleb couldn't stop shaking. He longed to reach an end to the journey and get inside. As the wagon and the entourage of mounted guards entered the little town of Liberty, a new annoyance began. Local citizens had come out to have a look at the prisoners, and many of them called out insults.

But one man muttered, "They just look like normal folks."

Caleb glanced at Joseph Smith, who shook his head and said, "It makes you wonder what he expected." But no one laughed. They had grown used to being gawked at.

The wagon finally stopped. Sheriff Samuel Hadley dismounted and said, "This here's it, men. I'm unlocking you and taking you inside one at a time. I'll start with McRae here." Hadley was not a bad fellow: a big man, but soft spoken, with a Kentucky twang to his speech. He was no friend to the Saints, but he was business-like, not insulting.

Alexander McRae was the youngest of the prisoners at thirty-one, and the tallest, well over six feet. When the sheriff released him from his handcuffs, Alexander rubbed his wrists and then pushed his red hair away from his eyes. He hopped from the back of the wagon with the ease of an athlete. He had been an army officer before joining the Church and had kept himself fit.

As the sheriff led Alexander away, Caleb looked at the jail: a building that appeared to have been tossed together without care, the stone masonry haphazard. The gray of the sandstone and the heavy, reinforced oak door at the top of a flight of wooden stairs looked forbidding—dreary in the late-afternoon light.

When Hadley returned, he released Caleb and said, "Jump down, Baldwin." But Caleb's knees were aching and he was stiff from sitting so long. He was forty-seven, the oldest of the men. He was not as agile as Alexander even though he had been a military man himself. He stood, stretched his back, then stepped to the back of the wagon, and crouched to ease his drop to the ground.

A large crowd—mostly men—had gathered near the jail to watch the prisoners make their entry. Caleb heard mumbling—a kind of growl—but one voice elevated above the others. "Where's Prophet Joe? We wanna see if he can make these here walls fall down."

The laughter from the crowd sounded more like grumbling than merriment. Caleb didn't look at anyone even when one man hissed at him, "Don't expect to live in there too long. We'll soon drag y'all out and cut your throats."

Sheriff Hadley pointed a finger at the man. "That's enough!"

he ordered. He gripped Caleb by the elbow and led him upstairs to a door that stood about a man's height above the ground. Caleb stepped into what he realized was the upper room of the jail. Alexander was standing inside next to a much shorter man, who said curtly, "I'm Sam Tillery. I'm the deputy jailer. Stand right over here till the others are all inside." His voice sounded neither hostile nor friendly, but Caleb saw hardness in his tight jaw.

At least the room was warm. There was a stove in one corner. But the building was only four or five paces square, and there was a small table and chairs, no beds. Caleb couldn't think how six men could live—and sleep—in such a place.

Hadley soon led in Sidney Rigdon, who looked exhausted and pale. He had been sick in Richmond and the trip to Liberty had been very hard on him.

Hyrum Smith, in a suit of clothes that had become soiled and shabby, stepped in next and received the same cold welcome from Tillery. Hyrum looked around and seemed to assess the conditions. He said nothing, but his look was cheerless, resigned.

Lyman Wight soon followed. He was in his early forties and had been a successful missionary, a powerful preacher, but he looked rough now, his hair straggly and his face unshaved. Still, he walked across the room like a rooster, his head up, his chest high.

Caleb heard a new roar outside. Someone shouted, "Hey, Joe, what've you got to say now? I don't see no angels looking down on you."

Hadley had left the doors open wide enough that Caleb could see Joseph when he stepped to the landing at the top of the stairs. But instead of walking inside, he turned and looked toward the crowd. He stood erect and gazed down at the men, who were still shouting at him. Then he raised his floppy-brimmed hat, made a little bow, and said, rather formally, "Good afternoon, gentlemen."

The greeting caused a burst of laughter, then curses, but when Joseph walked inside, he looked pleased with the little stir he had generated.

Captain Bogart of the Ray County Militia—and leader of the Missouri forces in the battle at Crooked River—stepped into the room behind Joseph. He had traveled with Sheriff Hadley from Richmond. As Hadley shut the door and the big hinges rasped dryly, Tillery said, "Those aren't *gentlemen,* Joe. They'd kill you in a minute if we let them have the chance."

Joseph nodded, still looking content. But he replied, courteously, "I don't mind if you call me Joseph, Mr. Tillery, but I prefer not to be called Joe."

"I guess I'll call you whatever I want," Tillery said, but not with force, as though he didn't know how to respond to Joseph's politeness.

"All right, men," the sheriff said. "This is not where you're going to be staying. Your place is down below, in the lower room of the jail."

"We call it the dungeon," Tillery added. He lifted a trapdoor, then retrieved a ladder that was leaning against a wall and lowered it through the opening. Caleb saw nothing but dark below.

"Just a minute," Bogart said. "Mr. Smith wants me to take a letter to his wife, and I told him I would do it. Let him write something, and then I'll be on my way." Caleb thought it strange for Bogart to be so helpful, but he had heard Joseph chat with the man a few times on the way to Liberty. The prophet's manner had been relaxed and natural and Bogart had become increasingly friendly. It was something Caleb had seen before, people tempering their animosity as they got to know Joseph.

"There's nothing to write with," Tillery said, but Sheriff Hadley told him to hurry down to the guard station outside and bring back what Joseph would need.

After Tillery shut the door behind him, the men stood silent for a time. Caleb was wondering about sleeping in that lower room. Lyman Wight must have had the same thing on his mind. "What's this about a *dungeon*? What kind of place are you putting us into?" he asked.

"We have straw down there that you can bunch up into beds," Hadley said. "Or split logs, cut flat, to use as cots. Other men have been held down there and they've managed all right."

Lyman seemed ready to respond when the door creaked open again and Tillery stepped in with a sheet of paper, a dip pen, and a glass ink well. Caleb had noticed before that Joseph liked to recite what he had to say and let someone else act as his scribe, but this time he wrote the note himself. He only wrote a few lines, and then he blew on the ink and waited a few seconds before folding it. He wrote Emma's name and "Far West, Missouri" on the outside fold, then stood up and handed the letter to Bogart.

"Thank you for your kindness, Captain," he said.

Bogart nodded and then told Joseph, "It may be a few days before I can deliver this."

"That's fine," Joseph said. "I appreciate your willingness to take it."

Bogart lived south of Far West, so the delivery would be several miles out of his way. Caleb was amazed that such a staunch enemy would make the effort.

"All right, it's time for you fellas to climb down this ladder," Tillery said. He caught sight of Sidney clinging to Hyrum to keep himself upright and added, "A couple of you better help Rigdon. He don't look like he can manage the climb by himself."

"I'll go down first," Alexander said. "You men help Sidney get started and then I can get hold of him and lower him the rest of the way."

But that was not an easy task; Sidney had put on weight these last few years. Hyrum and Lyman held Sidney under his arms as he started down the ladder. Sidney grunted with the effort and then seemed to lose strength and begin to sink, but Alexander got hold of him and he didn't fall.

Hyrum and Lyman followed Sidney and then Joseph said, "After you, Brother Caleb. I'm surely in no hurry."

Caleb wasn't eager to go down either. As he descended into the dark, the stink of the room struck him first. He recognized the stench of rotting straw and mildew, but worse was an outhouse odor. When he stepped off the ladder he looked around. Two slits of light from narrow horizontal openings at the top of the walls allowed him to make out a floor covered in straw, but little else.

Once all the men had climbed down, Tillery followed. He was carrying a candle that cast flickering light into the darkness, illuminating a few blankets piled in the middle of the room and wooden "honey buckets" in two of the corners. The idea of six men using those buckets, and nothing more, was disgusting enough, but Caleb also wondered whether he would have a chance to clean up at some point—at least wash himself with soap and a basin of water.

"This place ain't fit for hogs," Lyman Wight told Tillery. "How do you expect us to live down here?"

Tillery walked toward Lyman, holding the candle toward Lyman's face. "I say it *is* fit for hogs. I also say that's what you men are. You're murderers and traitors, and you're the lowest kind of so-called humans that ever come to this state."

Lyman stepped toward Tillery, got so close that the candle was only inches from his chest. Caleb had often seen Lyman when his eyes were cool and resolved, but he also recognized the look he was seeing now: the rage in his eyes. Lyman's voice was fierce when he said, "There's six of us down here, Tillery, and only one of you. Maybe we'll start murdering right now, and we'll leave you in this pit to rot while we go on our way."

"You could do that, Wight. No doubt about it. But the minute you step out of this jail my guards will be on you, and if they don't kill you, the men in this town will mount up and chase you down. You won't get a mile from here before you'll be scattered over the ground with buzzards ripping at your flesh."

"And what if God's on our side, not yours? Maybe your local boys will be no match for that."

"It's exactly that kind of talk that's got you where you are right now. Keep trying it and see where you end up."

"Let's end this kind of talk," Joseph said from out of the dark across the room. "We aren't going to murder anyone, and we aren't afraid to stand trial. We know we haven't committed any crimes."

"What will that matter?" Lyman roared back at Joseph. "Do you think these people care one bit about justice? They just want to kill us—and they'll start with you."

Tillery laughed. "We do want y'all to die. But you'll get your day in court first. And that day will come after you put in a long winter down here in this nice pigsty."

Lyman continued to stare, his eyes clear in the candlelight, but he didn't make a move toward Tillery.

Joseph calmly said, "Mr. Tillery, I assure you that we'll co-operate with you. I'm wondering, though, whether we have enough blankets. We're all cold from the ride we've taken today in the back of that wagon, and this room is freezing. We'd appreciate it if you could bring us some heavy quilts."

Tillery turned, the candle swinging, the flame casting shadows in a pivoting circle. "There's covers for you right there," he said, and he stretched his arm to cast light toward the stack of blankets. "You can build a fire if you want, but the smoke don't vent out of here too good." These last words caused him to chuckle.

"I see the blankets," Joseph said. Caleb knew Joseph was controlling himself and being careful to sound reasonable, but he was also becoming angry, and Caleb had learned that Joseph had a breaking point. "It appears that we might have one for each of us, but that won't do. Our friend Sidney is not well, and he'll need more warmth than that."

It was only then that Caleb recognized that Sidney, in the dark, had slumped onto the straw on the floor. Tillery turned so the yellow light fell on Sidney, who was on his side, his knees pulled up, his body shaking.

"You *must* bring us more blankets," Joseph said with restrained force. "Either that or let us sleep in the upper room, where you have a stove."

"You're all gonna sleep down here. That's what the sheriff told me. And there'll be no climbing up that ladder. I'll pull it up when I leave and I'll lock the trapdoor. You're forgetting that you're prisoners and you've committed more crimes than I can name off. The way you been stealing and killing and burning houses, y'all are lucky we've let you live this long." He turned back toward Joseph and stared into his face. "So don't talk to me about *more* blankets."

"Mr. Tillery, we *are* prisoners. We accept that. But we are also—"

"Hogs! I told you that's what you are, and that's how I'll treat you."

Joseph took two strides toward Tillery, stood the way Lyman had, his face gleaming in the candlelight. "*You will not* speak to us that way again," he said, his voice still restrained, but powerful.

"I'll speak to you any way I want. And you won't—"

"*Silence!*"

The room did fall silent.

"You will respect us, Mr. Tillery, or I promise you . . ." He paused and edged forward, then said, one commanding word at a time, ". . . you will feel the wrath of God!"

He finally raised his voice, shouted into Tillery's face, "Buzzards will pick *your* bones, sir, not ours, and when you stand before a holy tribunal, you will be cursed for all eternity."

Tillery took a single step backward, then slowly moved toward the ladder. He didn't say another word.

"Leave the candle," Joseph said.

Tillery handed the candle to Hyrum. He then climbed the ladder, but before he disappeared into the upper room, he said, "I can maybe get another blanket or two."

He stepped off the ladder, hoisted it up, then closed the trapdoor.

The men stood in the candlelight for a time, no one moving. Alexander finally asked, "How can we live down here, Brother Joseph?"

"I don't know." The ire was gone from Joseph's voice now. He stood in the dark, the candlelight across one side of his face. Caleb was certain that reality was setting in on him, as it was with all the others. But Joseph spoke with resolve when he said, "We'll have to manage. Maybe our lawyers can persuade the sheriff to improve our conditions. Doniphan plans to file a writ of habeas corpus to get our trial date moved up, but the truth is, he doesn't hold out much hope for that to happen."

"What difference does it make what our *conditions* is?" Lyman asked. "You heard what he said. One way or the other they're gonna kill us. We'll get no fairness from these people."

Joseph took his time before he said, "The people have heard nothing but lies about us, Lyman. So it's not surprising that they want to take our lives. But it's not a man like Tillery I hold in contempt. It's our own members—men we considered brothers in the gospel—who offered up barefaced lies for evidence." Caleb heard Joseph draw in air, and then his voice took on authority again as he said, "I promise you, brethren, God will afflict them with agonizing pain and sorrow."

Caleb accepted the promise, but he heard a hostility in Joseph's voice that he found disturbing. Certainly, Caleb understood; he had felt his own rage when Avard had presented himself as a decent man who had escaped Joseph's tyranny. But was this the time for such animosity? The men had been thrust into a dark hole, a dungeon, and right now Caleb needed Joseph—*the prophet*—to say something that would help him survive.

It was Lyman who said, "That's all fine and good, Joseph. The Lord may punish them in the next life, but right now they're warm and safe somewhere, and we're stuck in here."

That was exactly the problem. The damp cold was already penetrating Caleb's body, and he could only imagine how far the temperature might fall during the night. And yet, his own safety wasn't his biggest worry; he kept thinking of his wife, Nancy, and his nine children. They were in Far West trying to get by without him, and he wasn't sure they had food enough to last the winter. Stories had come to Richmond about so-called militia men burning the Saints' homes, destroying crops, shooting animals—and doing terrible things to women. He didn't want to imagine what men of that sort might do to his daughters.

Hyrum spoke softly. "Brethren," he said, "we have to trust in the Lord, no matter what's happened so far. We can't lose our faith that God is with us."

"Yes, Hyrum, that's right," Joseph said, his voice now subdued. "I told you before—when we were in Richmond—that the Lord had spoken to me, reassured me that in the end, all would be well with us."

Caleb liked hearing that, but his thoughts kept catching on the words "in the end." He wanted Joseph to tell them that they would be lifted from this place *soon*.

Quiet set in again. As the candle slowly burned down, the men silently stacked up straw for beds and arranged the split logs in rows that allowed as much spacing as possible. Alexander was so tall his head nearly touched the ceiling, but the bigger problem was that the blankets were all too short for him.

Hyrum sorted out the few blankets and found they could give Sidney two, while the rest of them would have to settle for one tattered quilt each, clearly not thick enough to hold out the cold.

Sidney seemed only half aware of what was happening to him. He kept mumbling about being cold, but he also rambled on about various subjects—something about his shoulder aching, and sometimes calling for his wife to help him. Caleb tried to tuck the blankets tight around him, but Sidney thrashed about and the blankets slipped off.

Lyman told Sidney, "Stop your moaning. We're all cold. Quit acting like you're the only one who's suffering."

"Lyman, we're brothers," Joseph said. "Sidney's sick, and he can't help what he says. We can't turn on each other."

Lyman didn't answer, and Caleb knew that he was mostly just venting his own frustration. Caleb had known him for years, from the beginning of his membership in the Church, and the man had always been quick to speak, slower to consider. But now Lyman was down on his knees trying to create a bed, bunching up a pile of straw, stirring up the smell from the rotten layers below.

"I think we need to pray together," Hyrum said.

Joseph agreed, and he called the men together. They knelt around Sidney. "Hyrum, you offer the prayer, will you?" Joseph said.

And so they bowed their heads and Hyrum prayed for Sidney, for more blankets, for justice to be done.

Caleb tried to find faith in Hyrum's words. He returned to the spot he had chosen for his own bed. Actual night was an hour or two away, but Caleb wrapped himself in his blanket and lay in the straw. He wondered whether he would ever be warm again.

It was maybe half an hour later that Caleb heard footsteps upstairs and saw light as the trapdoor opened. A voice spoke from above, gruff and familiar. Tillery.

"Here's a few more blankets."

The blankets dropped near Caleb's feet and the trapdoor closed. The dungeon felt darker than ever. But Tillery's change of heart seemed a partial answer to Hyrum's prayer, so Caleb offered a prayer of gratefulness.

Still, he couldn't fight back the feeling that he couldn't endure an entire winter in this dark pit.

CHAPTER 2

Caleb and the others filled the room, with only narrow passages between each bed. Joseph had chosen a spot to sleep along the south wall of the dungeon and Alexander had stretched his length along the north end. The other four were lined up next to one another at right angles to Joseph and Alexander, with Caleb close to Sidney.

Tillery had brought only three additional blankets. Hyrum told Caleb to give one more to Sidney and suggested that Lyman and Caleb take the other two. Caleb hesitated to keep one for himself, but Hyrum laughed.

"You're the three oldest." In truth, Hyrum was about the same age as Sidney, but he added, "I think my frock coat is heavier than yours—and I have more padding on my bones, even after losing some these last few weeks."

Caleb accepted the generosity, but first he crawled to Sidney with one of the blankets. Caleb loved Sidney for the good friend he had long been, and he pitied him for his increasing frailties.

The two of them had known each other for years. Caleb had become part of the Campbellite religious movement, and he had moved to Warrensville, not far from Kirtland, partly to join the congregation led by Sidney. Caleb had been living there in 1830 when Parley Pratt and Oliver Cowdery had visited the area and converted most of the members of Sidney's congregation. On the very first night he heard Parley preach, Caleb had submitted himself for baptism. Soon after, Sidney had also joined the Church. Many leaders were strong speakers, but Caleb considered Sidney the most eloquent. He could weave together theological concepts to create masterful sermons. But recently, he had changed. The beating Sidney had taken from a mob in Kirtland, and even more, his confinement in Richmond, had broken him. He had been physically sick but also overwhelmed by the primitive living conditions and by the infuriating unfairness of his imprisonment.

Caleb tucked the blanket around Sidney—who was now asleep—as tightly as he could and crawled back to pull his own extra quilt around himself. He felt a little warmer after a few minutes, but he feared that if he slept now, he would be awake before morning when the cold would surely be worse. So he remained sitting up and he tried to think of some reason to hope, something that would sustain him.

The candle soon guttered out, so the only light was a thin yellowish strip angling from the narrow opening at the top of the west wall. Caleb watched Joseph, who was only a dim figure propped against the wall in a dark part of the room. He was sitting with his knees raised, his arms on his knees, and his forehead on his arms in resignation. Caleb knew Joseph was called of God; he had no doubt about that. But he was also a man—an injured man. He had always wanted to lead, to preach, to lift his people, but he must be wondering how he could do that now.

After a time, Lyman asked, "Are they not going to feed us?"

"They *must* give us something," Hyrum said.

But Caleb had no idea what the jailers "must" do. It was hard to stay calm with Lyman's resentment amplifying Caleb's fear.

Another half hour or so passed before footsteps sounded in the upper room and the trapdoor lifted. A stream of light fell onto the straw next to Caleb's leg. He looked up, saw the silhouette of a man's head in the opening. Tillery's voice echoed through the room.

"I got some supper for y'all," he said. "The sheriff says you can climb up the ladder and eat it up here."

Caleb crawled to Sidney, knelt next to him, and shook him awake to explain what was happening. Sidney pushed Caleb away until Hyrum said, "You will need to climb the ladder, Brother Sidney. You can sit by the stove and warm yourself."

Sidney stirred when he heard the words, and then Hyrum and Caleb helped him to his feet.

"I'll climb up first," Alexander said. "You two help him get started, and then I'll lift him."

Working together, they helped Sidney to the upper level, and Alexander walked him to the stove, where Sidney curled up on the floor and lay very close to the heat. Caleb, by then, was smelling meat, and he realized how hungry he was. In a big iron pot on the table was what appeared to be a bean soup with a ham bone sticking above the rim. A single plate of cornbread was laid out beside it. It wasn't much food for six men who had gone all day without eating.

"Is that all we're getting?" Lyman asked.

Tillery pointed his finger at Lyman. "I think you better say, 'Thanks for this here good food.' If you can't say that, I'll take it back to people who want it."

Lyman didn't offer thanks, but he stopped his complaints.

Joseph walked closer and looked the food over, and then said, "Thank you, Mr. Tillery. The soup smells good."

Tillery nodded. "Dig in and eat so I can carry that pot back."

Four chairs had been arranged on the four sides of the table. Joseph looked around at the other men. "Sit down, brethren," he said. "Eat something, and then we'll see what we can do for Sidney."

Caleb sensed that Joseph was working now to control his discouragement and show his best self to the other prisoners—and to Tillery.

"What about you, Brother Joseph?" Caleb asked.

"I don't mind standing up to eat. It feels good to be up here where I can move around a little. Go ahead, Caleb, sit down and fill your bowl."

Caleb sat, and Lyman took another chair. Hyrum and Alexander joined them. Caleb ladled out the soup into tin bowls and made the portions equal.

Caleb soon realized there wasn't much meat or many beans in the watery soup, but what there was tasted wonderful. The corn bread was rough, the corn not well ground, and cutting it six ways didn't offer enough to be filling. Still, Caleb felt some strength return. He also liked being upstairs, where there were slightly bigger window openings and somewhat better light. The men ate and afterwards Hyrum took a bowl to Sidney, helped him sit up, and spooned the soup into his mouth. The other men collected around the stove, which was not very hot but felt glorious compared to the cold in the lower room.

Sidney revived with the food and the warmth. "Thank you, Brother Hyrum," he said, his voice grainy. "Can we stay here by the stove now?"

Tillery was the one who answered. "Not long. Finish eating and then you'll have to go back down for the night." But his harsh tone was gone.

Caleb went back to the table and pulled the ham bone from

the pot. He used his spoon to scrape off as much meat as he could into the bowls of each of the men. They took their time eating, surely stalling to stay upstairs as long as they could. Eventually Tillery said, "All right. It's time to head back down." But he didn't press for an immediate response, and all the men gathered around the stove and stayed until Tillery repeated his order. When he did, they helped Sidney through the trapdoor in the same way they had before, and then they all followed.

The dungeon was not the shock to the senses it had been before, but the cold struck harder. Caleb and Hyrum helped Sidney back to his bed and wrapped him in his blankets, but by then Lyman was exploding again.

"That wasn't enough food to fill us," he barked. "Is this what we have to face all winter? This cold, this blackness, never enough food? And Tillery always telling us we're hogs?"

"We have to show him what we really are," Joseph said. "Most of the people don't know our side of the story."

"They know more than they admit, Joseph. I was in Jackson County from the time we first come to this state. So was Caleb. Those people hated us before they ever knew us. They beat Caleb within an inch of his life, and they chased me across a prairie like they was hunting a wild animal. I say there ain't no justice to be had in this state. And our learned lawyers, smooth talkers or not, are Missourians too. After all is said and done, they can't—or won't—do a thing."

"Brother Lyman, you go too far sometimes," Joseph said. "Alexander Doniphan saved our lives after Hinkle betrayed us. If anyone makes my blood boil, it's Hinkle for lying to us, then turning us over to the enemy. That, and Avard prancing around in front of us, turning truth upside down—placing the blame for everything that happened on us."

Caleb understood all that. But something had been bothering him for weeks, and he felt a need to say it. "Brother Joseph, I know how you feel. But not everything those men said was false. We did empty those stores in Gallatin and we did carry off goods. I feel ashamed of some of the things we did—or at least that *I* did."

"We were in a war by then, Caleb," Joseph said, "and our enemies were destroying our crops. We were procuring provisions we needed for our storehouse—to help our people through the winter. After all the attacks on us, we had a right to fight back."

"I understand that. I'm only saying, most of what Avard described—even though he took none of the blame on himself—actually did happen."

Lyman was shouting again. "What did you expect us to do, Caleb? Gallatin was the headquarters for the mobs that were trying to drive us out of Daviess County. It was time to stand up to them."

"I know why we fought back," Caleb said. "I'm only saying, we can't claim that *everything* Samson Avard said was a lie."

Caleb expected Lyman to come back on the attack, but he didn't. He only said, "A half-truth *is* a lie, Caleb."

No one spoke for a time, and Caleb wondered what his friends were thinking of him. He hadn't meant to take the side of the people who had attacked the Saints—the ones who had outright murdered men and boys at Haun's Mill. But he had had a few weeks to think about what he had done in Gallatin, and he wasn't proud of himself. He and some others had ordered a family out of their house and out of the county, and he had felt justified at the time. But an image had stayed with him. A little boy, maybe six or so, had stepped out of his house, looked at Caleb and the others, then buried himself in his mother's skirt and cried.

"Will they hurt us?" he kept asking his mother. So many

Mormon children had faced the same fear. Caleb had not considered what it would mean to turn the tables and force a family—children—from their home. He and his company of Saints had let the father carry out the things he wanted to save, and then they had torched the house while the family watched. He still felt regret for doing that.

Joseph had returned to his end of the room. His calm voice seemed to emanate from the dark itself. "Caleb," Joseph said, "there's something you may not have thought about. The people who wanted to drive us out knew that the payments for our homesteads were coming due, and they saw a chance to take over our farms without paying us anything for them. They may not have liked our religion, but mostly they wanted the county for themselves and they were willing to kill to get it."

"I only said—"

"I know what you said. But Lyman makes a good point. What right did the people of Jackson County have to say we couldn't live there? And after that, what right did anyone have to demand we leave Clay County and then Caldwell and Daviess Counties? No one should be able to do that in the United States of America. What did you expect us to do? Ask them politely not to attack us anymore?"

"I'm not saying any of that, Brother Joseph," Caleb said. "I'm only feeling my own regrets."

But from the other dark end of the room, Alexander spoke, sounding careful but a little upset. "It's not as simple as you're making it, Joseph. I've heard our people brag that the Lord *intended* for us to take over these western counties. That angered the people here. And once we decided it was time to take a stand, we didn't have to make threats the way we did."

"What threats?"

Alexander lowered his voice. "Sidney stood up on the Fourth of July and said we were ready to fight a war—a war of *extermination.* That was Sidney's word—'extermination'—and Boggs got report of it. He tossed the word straight back at us. Sidney threw down a challenge to the local people, and he didn't have to do that."

Caleb had assumed that Sidney was asleep, not listening—and Alexander had surely assumed that too—but Sidney stirred now. He didn't sit up, but his voice came from the floor.

"I spoke nothing but the truth," he said. "You heard Joseph. It was time to stand and fight. Joseph heard every word I said that day, and he agreed with me."

"Yes, he did," Alexander said. He hesitated a moment and then added, "Joseph, you sat on the stand that day, and you waved your hat in the air and shouted hallelujah. I suppose I did too. But then you printed Sidney's talk and circulated it. What did you expect the old citizens around here to do? Read those words and not react?"

"I expected to put them on notice that we would not give way to mobocracy. I didn't want war. I merely wanted them to know that they couldn't scare us into retreat."

"I don't doubt your motives, Joseph, but we challenged these folks to a fight, and they were happy to oblige us. And the trouble is, it was a war that we had no chance of winning."

"We expected the Lord to fight with us," Sidney said.

"Yes," Lyman said. "Joseph, you talked of angels fighting with us. I thought there was no way that we could be defeated."

Joseph didn't respond for a time, and when he did, he spoke softly, "I did say some things of that sort. And I believed what I said. I thought we were intended to remain here and see Zion restored. But I see now that we weren't worthy to have the Lord with us." He waited a moment, then added, "I did what I thought was right. You say that printing that speech was a mistake, but it seemed necessary at the time, and I don't know that I was wrong."

"We went too far, Joseph," Alexander said. "And it's not just Sidney's speech I'm talking about. I'm a military man, and I wanted to fight as much as anyone. But burning Gallatin was more than a mistake. It was the excuse Boggs needed to unleash the mobs that were only too ready to come after us."

"But Boggs made it sound like we were on the march, killing and burning. He never mentioned all the attacks on our people."

"I'm well aware of that," Alexander said. "But we fell into the trap of behaving too much like our enemies."

Lyman assumed an exaggerated tone of graciousness. "You're right, Alexander," he said. "We should have thanked those fine people for being such good friends, and maybe—"

"Let's not talk that way, Lyman," Joseph said.

"Not before I say what I think," Lyman said. "You promised us a victory. But so far as I know, no angels showed up at our battles, and the mobs came out on top over and over again. Now we're stuck in this stinking jail and the good Lord doesn't seem to be worried about it."

The words were stunning—blasphemous in Caleb's mind. They filled the dark and left everyone silent. Caleb had wanted to express his own concerns, but he hadn't expected this confrontation with Joseph. It couldn't be easy to make decisions for the Church—as Joseph was called to do—and then hear others second-guess him.

"Lyman," Joseph said, "I did say that the Lord was with us, and I still believe that." A full minute must have passed before Joseph completed his thought. "Brethren, we can't give up on God. I promise you, he knows where we are and what we're suffering. We'll need him to get through this. I may have promised too much. Maybe it was me speaking—not the Lord. And maybe I'm being chastised for that now. But we'll overcome these people—even with Hinkle and Avard on their side. That much I can promise you."

"We do trust God," Hyrum said. "And we need to trust each other. I know we're all feeling beleaguered right now, but we can't let a spirit of anger prevail."

"I haven't given up on the Lord," Lyman said. "I just don't understand why things turned out this way."

"I suspect that's why we're here," Joseph said. "To find out."

Lyman blew out a big breath and sounded frustrated as he said, "I don't even know what that means, Joseph."

"We need to look into our hearts, Lyman. I'm not the man I would like to be. I have growing to do. It's one thing to be called, and it's another to be sufficient for that calling. I need to discover what more I need to do—how I need to change."

"It's what we all need to do," Hyrum said. "Every man needs to keep seeking—"

"It's more than that, Hyrum," Joseph said. Caleb heard resignation in his voice as he said, "My spirit feels wounded. I can't seem to put off the natural man in me right now. And the Lord isn't speaking to me. I try to call on him and I get no answer. I've begun to fear that he has withdrawn my calling. I need to find his voice again or I'm not likely to be allowed to live much longer."

Caleb took a breath. "Brother Joseph, I'm sorry I brought all this up. I know you're carrying a heavier burden than any of us. I didn't mean to add to that."

"It's all right, Brother Caleb. You and Alexander have said things I need to consider as I go forward. And yes, I am burdened. No question. But I accepted my call, and now I have to rise to it."

Caleb felt Joseph's anguish and wished he could say something to relieve it. But Caleb needed Joseph to be more than a burdened man; he needed the prophet he knew so well. The dark of this dungeon would be too much for him if Joseph couldn't bring in any light.

CHAPTER 3

Emma Smith was worried.

Most of the men jailed in Richmond had been exonerated or released on bail and they had now returned to Far West. Some of them had visited her and let her know that Joseph and Hyrum and four others were being transferred to a jail in Liberty, Missouri, and Emma had assumed that Joseph would get a letter to her as soon as he could find someone to carry it. But days had passed and she had heard nothing.

Emma tried to control her fear and worry, but far too many men had vowed to kill Joseph. Would Missouri militia soldiers—the men who had warred with the Saints—now deliver him safely to another jail? She wanted a messenger who could tell her that Joseph was still alive, but another day was stretching on with no word, and she gradually felt not only frightened but desperately lonely.

For weeks she had sequestered herself and her children in her house. The renegade attacks on Far West had slowed, but incidents continued to happen, and that made her reticent about walking outside or letting Julia and Joey go out to play. As often as she could, she hurried over to see Mary, her sister-in-law, who had given birth three weeks earlier and was struggling to recover. But that was the only respite from tedium that Emma had taken.

Emma finally couldn't stand to fret any longer. She wrapped up Alexander, who was only five months old, and she asked Julia to take Frederick by the hand. At the door, she stopped and told young Joseph, "Stay close to me. We'll walk directly to Mary's house—and walk fast. I don't want you straying away from me."

Joey, as Emma usually called him, always loved to make this visit. His cousin John—born to Uncle Hyrum's first wife, Jerusha—was six, Joey's same age, and he was Joey's only chance these days to play with a friend. But Emma knew that Joey was frightened to be outside. As he walked by her side, he kept looking about cautiously. He had been alarmed far too many times by raiders who galloped through the town, shouting and firing their weapons.

Emma saw no one suspicious, and she found a brief pleasure in the brisk, bright day. When she reached the house, she knocked softly, then opened the door.

"Mary, it's Emma," she said, and she stepped inside. Mary sat in the bed across the room, covered in quilts and holding her sleeping baby.

Not wanting to allow a draft, Emma stepped in quickly, ushered her children inside, and shut the door.

"How are you feeling, my dear?" she asked.

"I'm getting stronger," Mary said, but she didn't look strong. She was pale and her skin was stretched tight over her cheekbones. Mary seemed to recognize Emma's doubt and added, "I've been up twice today. Mercy helped me."

Mercy Thompson was Mary's sister. She also lived close by and had spent much of her time looking after Mary both before and since the birth.

"That's good to hear. Did you walk around a little?"

Mary's eyes drifted away from Emma's. "Not really. I just made it there and then back in bed." She pointed to a chamber pot.

33

"Well, that's all right. I'm glad you could do that much."

"Mercy wants me to eat more, and I know I need to, but I'm still not hungry, and almost anything I eat distresses my stomach."

"I know. It's hard. But you're alert now, and your eyes have light in them again."

Mary had married Hyrum about a year earlier, after Hyrum's first wife had died. Mary and her brother and sister, Joseph and Mercy Fielding, had emigrated from England to Canada, then joined the Church and moved to Kirtland. Mary was well educated, had been a teacher and a governess. She was a resolute, confident young woman, but physically, rather delicate. The birth of her son had come at a bad time, just when she was experiencing raw anxiety over her husband's arrest. It had been a difficult birth and afterward she had only survived with the help of her sister, her sister-in-law, and her other Far West sisters in the gospel.

Emma set Alexander next to Mary so she could take off her coat. By then Joey was saying, "Where's Johnny?"

Mary smiled at Joey and said, "I'm sorry. Sister Thompson took the children home with her." She looked toward Emma. "Mercy told me to rest for a while. But the baby fell asleep in my arms, and I've liked holding him against me and hearing his sweet little breaths. I sleep too much anyway; I need to stay awake longer each day."

"Mama," Joey said, "can we go to Sister Thompson's so I can play with Johnny?"

"No, dear. Not today." Emma wanted to stay with Mary a short time and then return to her own house. She still hoped that someone would show up to let her know about Joseph.

"I can run to Johnny's house alone," Joey said. "I looked every way and I didn't see any of those men."

"Don't beg, Joey. You know what our rules are."

"I *hate* our rules."

Emma decided not to rehash the issue with Joey. When soldiers rode into town and bellowed their threats, he was reluctant to step away from her side, but when all was quiet, he became bored, even cranky. He often quarreled with Julia, who tended to be too bossy with him even though she was only a year older.

"Did you hear the men last night?" Mary asked.

"Of course we did."

"I heard 'em," Joey said. "They said they want to kill 'Old Joe.'"

"But they won't, Joey," Mary said in her tender English accent. "The Lord will look after your father, and he will look after Hyrum and the others. I pray a thousand times a day for them, and I know God hears my prayers."

"That's right," Emma said. "I keep telling Joey not to worry."

But Joey had lost interest in the conversation. Johnny had a tiny wagon with a pair of carved draft horses attached—a favorite toy for Joey to play with. Frederick joined Joey, the two kneeling on the floor as Joey made the wagon travel about and made clopping noises to imitate the sound of horse's hooves. Julia took Alexander from Emma, then sat on the floor near the fire, away from her little brothers. She was like a little mother to Alex, who adored Julia.

Emma took a seat on a wooden chair near the bed, and Mary whispered to her, "Oh, Emma, did you hear the vicious things those soldiers were shouting?"

"It's all the same thing, over and over. I try not to pay attention."

"But they stopped outside my house and yelled about Hyrum—the things they would do to him. They said they would use knives on him to do . . . filthy things."

"They say that about Joseph, too, but I feel sure that Joseph and Hyrum are in Liberty by now, in the jail, where men like that can't reach them."

"You don't know that. The jailers might give murderers access to the jail."

Emma knew that might be true, but Mary's eyes were wide open now, tense with anxiety, and Emma didn't want to say anything that would affect her nerves.

"Why do they hate us so much, Emma?" Mary asked, still whispering. "What possible reason do they have to kill our husbands?"

"What they really want is for us to leave Missouri, and they think threats will scare us away."

"We do have to leave, don't we?"

Emma didn't know. She was still clinging to the belief that somehow God would soften the hearts of the people and open a way to establish peace. Joseph had once been certain that was possible, and Emma had trusted in his faith. But now she didn't know. Joseph was always hopeful, always ready to make friends, and sometimes he didn't recognize the enemies around him.

"What we must not do is let hatred seep into our own hearts," Emma said. "When we hate, our enemies have defeated us. They've turned us away from God."

"I suppose. But there are times when I justify what I feel as righteous indignation. How can I listen to the cruel vows those men make and not feel that they belong in hell?"

The truth was, Emma often had to fight her own anger. She caught herself wishing that some harm—retribution—would come to the men who plagued her life, always shouting outside her house, using language that surely offended God. She had no doubt that the world would be a better place if God would strike down such men, humble them, force them to kneel and beg the Saints for forgiveness. But that was up to him, not her.

"I'm sorry, Emma, but I do hate George Hinkle and the soldiers who dragged Hyrum away from me. I'm not even trying not to."

"But with time, you—"

"No. I'm not up to it, and I don't know that I ever will be. After our men gave up their weapons, and the militia men acted like wild animals, Hyrum was still here, and I hoped they wouldn't come for him. But then they showed up, shouting and pounding on our door, and Hinkle was with them. I know he led them to our house. Hyrum told the men that we were all sick and I was about to give birth, so he needed to stay with me. But they cursed him and carried him away, *Brother* Hinkle watching the whole thing. And the next day, when they brought him back for his cloak and hat, they wouldn't let him step through our door, wouldn't let him say a word to me or to his children. One of the men—the one the others called 'Sergeant'—growled at me that Hyrum's doom was sealed, that I would never see him again."

"I know, Mary. It was the same for me. Joey tried to hang on to Joseph, and he kept asking, 'Will they kill you, Father?' One of the soldiers used the side of his sword to push him aside, and shouted, 'Go back, or I'll run you through.'" Emma lowered her voice even further and said, "That frightened Joey so much that he's been worried ever since. He wakes up in the night and calls for me. He keeps remembering what the man with the sword said to him—the same thing that sergeant said to your family: 'You'll never see your father again.' He asks me about that every day."

"I'm sorry, Emma, but I don't understand such wickedness. How could a man say something like that to a little child? Do you really think the Lord expects me to forgive something like that?"

"Yes. No doubt, he does." She took a breath. "But that doesn't mean I've done it yet. Still, there's one thing I know. Many of those men go home to their families, sow their crops, go about life about the same as we do. They've been told that we've come to conquer them and take their farms away—and they think they're fighting a war against evil invaders. They talk each other into a frenzy, and then they think that threatening women and children is fully justified. It's the only way I can start to forgive them—by trying to understand the way they think."

Mary was silent for a time. Her baby's head was against her chest, just under her chin, but she lifted him away to look at his face. Emma saw her love, but also understood her anxiety for the little one.

"I understand what you're saying," Mary finally said, "but I honestly believe they're in Satan's grip."

"Maybe so."

After the men of Far West had been called to the town square and forced to give up their weapons, the militia had visited terror upon the Saints for several days. Many homes, especially on farms outside the town, had been pulled down, the logs carried off for firewood in the militia camps. The affected families had fled into town, where they had to double up with other families in houses that were already fully occupied. But worse, Mormon men who were caught outside trying to harvest their crops had been beaten, and their fields of corn and wheat had been trampled. People had also told Emma, in whispered tones, about women who had been accosted and used for the soldiers' pleasure.

"But Emma, I don't hate most of the time. What I do is worry. I want Hyrum to be safe, and I fear for this lovely little spirit." She looked at her little son, tears pinching from the corners of her eyes.

"I want to take him to the jail to receive a blessing from his father. Hyrum needs to see him, and my little son needs a name."

"As soon as you can travel," Emma said, "we'll visit Hyrum—if the jailers will let us in—and your baby can receive that blessing."

"Yes. That gives me something to strive for every day."

There was a commotion from the corner of the room; Joey and Freddie had begun to contend for control of the toy. Joey grabbed his brother's hand rather roughly, pushed it away, and pulled the wagon to himself. At the same time, Alexander had begun to fuss. He would need to be nursed soon.

Emma said, "I think we should leave now and let you rest. I'm afraid I've only upset you, and that's not good for you. If you like, I can take the baby home with me for an hour or two."

"No. I just want to hold him a little longer, and then I'll put him down—and maybe I should sleep a little. I still get very tired."

Emma bundled up her children again and was getting ready to leave when a knock came at the door. Emma flinched. But the knock had sounded gentle, so she took a chance and opened the door a crack. It was Eunice McRae. She was a tall, pretty young woman, but she looked beleaguered today.

"Sister Emma, when I didn't find you at home," Eunice said, "I assumed you must be here. May I speak with you for a minute—you and Mary?"

Eunice stepped inside with her little son, another boy named John. When John saw the toy on the floor, he knelt by it, and Joey and Frederick joined him. Eunice was also carrying her own little Joseph, who was slightly older than Emma's baby. But she didn't put Joseph down, and she didn't take off her cloak. Her breath came in little surges, tears glimmering in her eyes.

"What is it, dearest?" Emma asked.

Eunice had to take a long breath before she answered. "I've

waited for my husband to come home, and he hasn't. But just now I got word that he's been sent to Liberty with your husbands, and he's accused of *treason*."

Emma worried when she saw Joey look up. She doubted he understood the word, but he had certainly heard Eunice's emotion and fear. Emma desperately wanted more information—especially if Eunice knew whether Joseph had made it to the prison—but she also needed to reassure Joey—and Eunice.

"Eunice, it's a false charge, and it won't hold up. Don't trouble yourself too much. The Lord will protect all our husbands. I'm sure of it."

"I wish I felt the same. We've prayed so long, and . . ." Her voice failed her and she began to sob.

Emma embraced Eunice with Eunice's baby between them. She whispered, "I'm glad you came to us. We have to sustain each other. We'll survive this trial, and we'll do it together."

"Will you pray with me?" Eunice asked. "I'm not confident in my own prayers anymore."

Emma had always considered Eunice beautiful, but today she looked drastically older than her twenty years. Her face was white in spite of her just coming in from the cold, and a new thinness was in her cheeks and jaw.

"Yes," Emma said, "let's all pray together—each in turn. And let's ask for help for all of the Saints, not just for our families."

"So many women are suffering," Mary said. "All of the sisters we love so much."

"And our children," Emma said.

Emma gathered her children, and so did Eunice, and they knelt around Mary's bed. Emma prayed first, and she asked the Lord to protect the Saints, to strengthen them in this dire hour. And she asked, "Please, Lord, wilt thou bless our children, and help us as mothers to protect them? And please, we ask, guide us to know how we can support one another—and all our sisters."

When Mary said her prayer, she sounded stronger than she had in recent days, and Eunice's voice was steady now. She was clearly comforted. After she closed, Eunice looked across the bed at Emma, then toward Mary, and said, "This is what I needed from you."

"We're sisters," Emma said. "We have to lift each other every way we can."

———◆———

It was the following day when Emma heard another knock, this time at her own door. She hesitated, listened for any noise outside, heard nothing, and finally opened the door just slightly. She didn't know the man outside, but he didn't look threatening. He took off his hat and said, "Mrs. Smith, I've brought a letter from your husband."

She was too eager to read the letter to worry about the identity of the man. She opened the door wider and invited him in. But before he handed the letter to her, he said, "My name is Samuel Bogart. *Captain* Bogart. I'm sure you recognize me by that title."

Emma took a step back. She suddenly feared why he had come. Was it to gloat about Joseph's fate—or his death—or did he mean some harm to her and her children? The letter suddenly seemed a ruse to get inside her house.

"I'm sorry to startle you," Bogart said. "Your husband asked me to bring you this letter and I promised to do it. I'm a man of my word."

Emma stared at him. "You killed our men at Crooked River," she said, "and now you stand at my door and say something like that? Give me the letter and leave my house."

"I'm only too happy to do so, ma'am, but don't forget that Mormons shot down some of our men. And don't forget who started that skirmish." All politeness had left his voice.

"How can you say such a thing?" Emma asked. "You kidnapped two of our men, and our people were only there to gain their release."

"They shot first."

"That's what you claim, but it's not the truth. And you killed David Patten, an apostle of God. You'll answer for that on judgment day."

Bogart stood stiff. He was a stout man, stern, and clearly angry, but he was fighting for control. "I'll not argue with a woman," he finally said. "The courts will settle this matter, and it's Joe and the others who will face trial, not me or my men."

Emma was on the edge of igniting, but she thought of Joey. He didn't need to hear any more of this. "Just give me the letter. Is Joseph in jail in Liberty now?"

"Yes. I helped to escort him there."

"And I'm sure that brought you great pleasure."

"No, ma'am, I wouldn't say that." Bogart's face had lost its hardness.

She waited, wondered what he meant.

"The two of us talked along the way. He's not quite the man I thought he was. I do think he's to blame for most of the trouble between our peoples—he said too much about wanting to have our land and build his own kingdom on it. But I thought he was crazy and fanatic, and I think now he's just misguided. He was friendly and forthright with me, and I liked that."

"But you hope he's convicted by your courts."

"What I hope is that all of you will leave our state. That would be good enough for me."

"I'm sure we'll do that. But it isn't fair. We have as much right to live here as you do."

"What you don't seem to understand is . . ." But he stopped. "Never mind. Here's the letter."

Emma suddenly felt that she had been too harsh. It was what she and Mary had talked about: forgiving enemies, being like Christ.

"Thank you, sir," she said. "I've been waiting to hear from him, so I appreciate your keeping your promise. I do wish that we all could have gotten to know each other better. Maybe none of this needed to happen."

He nodded twice, set his hat back on his head, and walked out.

Emma hurried to open the letter, which was painfully short. Joseph only said that he had been committed to the jail in Liberty and that he and the other men with him were "all in good spirits." He added at the end: "Remain where you are at present."

Emma took a breath of relief. At least she knew Joseph was alive and was claiming to be all right, but she had to wonder: Was he only trying to reassure her?

Joey was standing next to her by then. "Is the letter from Papa?"

"Yes," she said. "He's fine. He says he's in good spirits, and we have to be in good spirits too."

"Will they keep him in the jail for a long time?"

"We don't know. But no matter what people say, we know that your papa is a good man, and Heavenly Father knows it too. I believe Papa will come home to us. We have to pray and we have to—"

"We do pray, and he doesn't come home."

"But he will."

Julia, who'd been listening from across the room, spoke up. "Did he say anything else? Is the jail a decent place?"

"He didn't say much. I'm sure he'll write again soon. But now we know he's safe and well."

Her children seemed reassured, which was a good thing. But Emma couldn't fight away her worries, and she didn't want Julia and Joey to sense her concern. It did help to remind herself that God would surely not abandon Joseph, or the Saints. But she had expressed this kind of faith before, and terrible times had followed. There were still people who wanted to kill Joseph. Would God protect him from all his enemies?

CHAPTER 4

To Caleb, each night in jail seemed endless, and the days were tedious. The only relief came three times a day, when the prisoners were allowed to climb the ladder, eat their meals at the table, and take comfort in a few minutes by the stove. But the food was scanty and often dirty. Tillery usually delivered a small ration of meat and a larger ration of johnnycakes in a basket that had apparently acted as a roost for chickens, and he brought a coffee pot that only contained cold, leftover dregs. One day when Lyman complained again that six men required more food, Tillery ruffled.

"I've heard enough from you," he told Lyman. "You ain't here as men of honor. I ought to shoot every one of you and save the expense of keeping you fed."

Joseph did the last thing Caleb expected. He laughed.

Tillery abruptly turned to look at him, clearly taken back.

"Don't shoot us, Sam," Joseph said. "Just think of the mess you'd have to clean up. And then you'd have to haul us all out of here. Alexander would be your biggest job. It would take ten strong men just to carry him to a wagon, and that many more to dig a hole long enough to bury him in."

To Caleb's even greater surprise, Tillery smiled. "That *would be* a chore, but he's thin. You're the one who ain't no lightweight. We might have to hoist you out with a derrick." He laughed then, but he sounded almost apologetic as he added, "You have to understand, all I got to feed you with is what I can hold back from my own family."

"I'm sure it's not your fault, Sam," Joseph said. "I'll have Mr. Doniphan, our lawyer, talk to Sheriff Hadley. Maybe we can work something out so the whole burden's not on your shoulders."

"No. Don't say nothing to Sheriff Hadley—that just gets me in trouble. I'll do what I can to bring a little more. Maybe the sheriff can find a few more supplies to help me out. But it's better if I talk to him so he don't dig his heels in against a lawyer telling him what to do."

"I'd appreciate your doing that," Joseph said. "We *are* growing boys, you know."

Tillery smiled again. "I ain't making no promises, but I'll try."

The following day the food ration was somewhat enlarged—but not tastier or cleaner.

Still, food was not the most important issue for Caleb even though he was hungry most of the time. What disturbed him was that Joseph, even though he seemed himself at times—as he had when he'd joked with Sam Tillery—always returned to the dungeon after meals, walked into the dark, and became silent. He seemed little more than a shadow against the wall, and when he was enticed by the others to converse, he usually said no more than was necessary. If he was looking inside himself—as he had said he needed to do—that was probably for the best. But Caleb longed for the jovial man, the strong leader, that he had come to know, and he longed to hear words from Joseph that would lift him through these trying days.

The realities of being confined night and day were oppressive. It seemed impossible to Caleb to live in his present condition for long, so he fussed with the straw he slept on, adjusted his blankets, stuffed straw into the window openings to stop the flow of cold air—anything to find a bit of comfort. The men had tried building a fire in the dungeon one night, but the smoke, as Tillery had warned them, wouldn't vent, and it soon sent them into fits of coughing. There seemed no escape from the circumstances that had been forced upon them.

What made things worse was that Caleb had too much time to think. He was constantly preoccupied with worry about his family. Nancy, his wife, was resourceful, even stubborn, and he knew she wouldn't give way to despair. But he hated to think of the trials he had brought upon her. She had been the pretty daughter of a judge, a prominent citizen of Cleveland, Ohio, and had grown up in a beautiful home—not like the log cabins Caleb had built for her in Missouri. She had a good education, liked to read, and had been raised in a home with music, nice furniture, and fancy dinnerware. Caleb knew she must miss those things, but she never said so, and she never made him feel guilty for the life he had given her.

Now, however, with only two of their children married, Nancy had six daughters and a young son to care for. The older girls were good at looking after their little sisters and they were hard workers, but what if his children didn't have enough to eat? Or what if the rabble decided to tear down their log house? It reassured him to know that Nancy would take on whatever troubles came, and Clark, their married son, would do all he could to help, but Caleb needed to be there. Locked up in jail, however, there was no way for him to be the husband and father he wanted to be.

Caleb knew that all his brethren in the jail had the same worries, and Joseph had more. Piled on top of his concerns for his family was his responsibility to lead the entire Church. In all the dark hours, day and night, Caleb knew Joseph must be asking himself why such tragedy had been visited upon his people—and what he could now do to lead the members while hidden away in this dungeon.

With all of the anxiety and thoughts of survival the men were dealing with, it didn't surprise Caleb that the men spent much of their time in silence. But Caleb longed for perspective, for the connection to the Spirit that he had long known.

Caleb found himself reflecting more than he ever had in his life. He prayed almost constantly. He wore himself out—and feared he wore out God too—pleading over and over that a release from the jail would soon come and that his family would be kept safe in the meantime. He wondered, was it possible God was chastening him? He knew he had grown since joining the Church, but had he grown enough? He doubted that he was very much like Christ, but he truly wanted to be.

He had begun to realize that it would take more spiritual strength than he had ever found in himself to meet the demands he was now facing. No one could give him that, not even Joseph. He had to hear God's voice himself. He had to do more than complain to Father about his conditions; he had to change himself and not just the dirty straw he was lying in. Caleb wished for Joseph to say more, to encourage him and the others, to pronounce a revelation that would ease their worries. At the same time, he understood that Joseph had vast issues to consider and a deeper need to receive guidance. If Caleb was considering the state of his own spirit, surely Joseph was trying to penetrate the immense realms of the heavens, to understand his place—and the place of the Church—in history, in all eternity.

In spite of Caleb's worries, he also fought against the stupor that filled his head. He was feeling that dullness one afternoon when the trapdoor pulled open with a sudden jar. Tillery shouted through the opening, "You can come up. You've got visitors."

Caleb felt a burst of relief. It was a chance to climb into the upper room sooner than he had expected. But who had come to the jail? Only their lawyers had been allowed to enter so far, and they had never been called "visitors."

The men took their usual approach, Alexander going first, and then helping Sidney from the top. But Sidney gasped as his head and shoulders reached the upper room.

"Oh, Phebe," he said, "you've come."

Caleb hurried up the ladder and saw Phebe, along with Emma Smith, standing in the upper room. Young Joseph III stood next to Emma, and Wickliffe, Sidney's son, was leaning against his mother. Caleb knew that "Joey" was six or so, and Wickliffe was a little older. Caleb bent over the opening in the floor and called down, "Brother Joseph, Emma is here!"

Joseph quickly appeared at the top of the ladder, smiling with a joy that had been missing for weeks. He hurried up and grasped Emma and Joey. "I can't tell you what happiness this brings me," he told them, sounding like himself. "But you feel so cold. Are you frozen clear through?"

"It's been a hard journey," Emma said. "This room is the first warmth we've felt in two days."

"Come to the stove."

The Rigdons were already gathered there, but they made room for Emma and Joey to draw close. Phebe was a tall woman, not handsome, but striking with her dark hair and her fair, thin face. She had always seemed rather severe to Caleb, but she looked happy now, and their frail little son was clinging to Sidney.

Caleb watched Sidney, saw life returning to him, but Caleb was troubled by what Sidney kept saying. "I don't belong here, Phebe.

I've done nothing. I wasn't there when the other men fought their battles and burned down houses."

Emma soon turned to the other men in the room, greeted each one. Caleb had been hanging back, but Emma said, "Oh, Brother Caleb, Nancy asked me to send her love. I'll tell her that you look fine." She stepped to him, shook his hand, looked him over, and laughed. "But I won't admit the whole truth. You actually look a little worse for wear. All of you do."

"We're holding up," Caleb said. He smiled. "It's just hard to brush our clothes or shave ourselves." He glanced around and realized that he had gotten used to the ragged look of the men. Their beards had grown and their hair was long. Bits of straw were clinging to their worn-out frock coats and vests. It must have been especially shocking for Emma to see Joseph. He was normally one to shave often, but now his sparse beard was stubbly, his skin gray.

"We don't get any sunlight in here—especially down there," Caleb told Emma. He pointed to the opening in the floor. "Now and then, they do take us out to let us wash, but that's the only fresh air we ever breathe."

"It's all right," Emma said. "You're alive and you're doing your best. You need to know, everyone in Far West is praying for you every day."

These words touched Caleb beyond their content. Emma was a refined woman, more than almost anyone living in this rough western land, and her voice had a gracious quality, grounded in kindness. She took hold of Caleb's hand again, and he felt the smoothness against his own roughened skin.

"I talked to Nancy on the day before we departed," she said. "She told me to tell you that she is doing all right. The children are helping her, and your married son . . . I can't think of his name."

"Clark."

"Yes, Clark. He's making sure that she and your children have enough food. Your cow was . . . lost . . . I'm afraid, but—"

"Lost?"

"Well . . . yes. I wasn't planning to tell you this, but some of the militia soldiers have tried to make life miserable for us. One of them shot your cow and merely left it on the ground. Clark was able to butcher it and provide some meat, but there's no milk now, no cheese."

Caleb suddenly felt the rage he had been trying to subdue. How could anyone shoot a cow just for the sake of cruelty?

"Maybe I shouldn't have told you that, Brother Caleb," Emma said. "The important thing is, Nancy is as proficient as anyone I know at getting the most out of what she has. And she's always looking out for people who have even less. Your children are doing quite well too—Clark and James and all your lovely daughters— and they send their love."

About then Sam Tillery opened the creaking door and carried in more food than usual.

"I thought you might like to share a meal," he said, and he sounded courteous. Maybe he had been impressed by the quality of the women visitors. "I'll bring up some more chairs." He set down a big pot of stew, and his son, who had come in with him, placed a large plate of cornbread on the table. Caleb could only think that Tillery had brought his family's entire meal, and that it was he who would have to scrounge for something else to eat.

Joseph offered seats to the two women, and in a minute or so, Tillery and his son returned with two more chairs. It was not easy to get six chairs around the little table, but they managed, and Alexander and Lyman took their meals to separate corners, where they sat on the floor. Caleb felt honored to be offered a seat next to Emma. Joseph sat across from her.

Hyrum ladled out stew for everyone, and as he did, Joseph said, "Tell me about our children."

Emma reported that there was considerable turmoil in Far West, but the children were managing to live with their new circumstances. "Julia is frightened, I know, but she doesn't show it. She's like a mother to the boys." She glanced at Joey, who was sitting on the floor with Wickliffe, close to the stove.

"Julia thinks she can tell me what to do," Joey said. "I don't do it, though. I do what I like." But he was smiling.

Joseph turned and looked at him. "You have to do your best right now, Joey. And you need to help your mother and sister in every way you can."

"The truth is," Emma said, "he *is* a big help to me. And he's been very brave. He and Julia do quarrel some, but they love each other. I have no doubt of that."

"I have some doubt," Joey said. But this time he laughed.

"Julia has a special place in my heart," Caleb said. "Nancy and I and the Murdocks were all living together on the day she was born—the day her mother died."

Emma nodded. "That was such a sadness for Brother Murdock—but we'll always feel blessed that he thought of us."

Caleb remembered that day very well. Emma had given birth to twins, both of whom had died, and on the same day Sister Murdock birthed twins of her own—and *she* died. John Murdock was left with five children, including the newborns, and he knew he couldn't find someone to nurse them and do everything else necessary for two infants. He offered the babies to Joseph and Emma. As it turned out, one of those twins, a boy named Joseph, died before his first birthday, but Julia had grown to be strong, and a great help to Emma.

As everyone ate, conversations began. Sidney was speaking

more than he had since entering the jail in response to Phebe's reports of home. Lyman and Alexander also asked for details about conditions in Far West, and about their own families. Caleb liked the sound of voices, the warmth and light in the upstairs room, even the compassion in the voices of Emma and Phebe. Above all, he liked to see Joseph enlivened.

Still, it was hard for Caleb not to be envious. In his house filled with daughters he had grown accustomed to laughter and chatter—and almost constant affection. He thought of Eunice, the oldest of his children still at home. She had always been the most serious one in the family and had turned to Caleb with her questions about life, the gospel, her worries. He thought of a day when she had been milking their cow, and he had meant to walk by with nothing more than a greeting. But she had stopped him and asked his opinion about something. He couldn't think what it was now. But she had looked up from her bucket, her pretty blue eyes intense with concern, and he had seen in those eyes that she trusted he would give her wise advice. He wished he could see her face again, be with her at least long enough to talk a little, to know that she wasn't too upset by all that was happening to the Saints right now. He wanted to tell her how much he loved her—tell all his family that. He knew he hadn't said those words often enough.

When Joseph and Emma began to talk in whispered voices, Caleb didn't mean to eavesdrop, but he was close enough that he could hear what they said.

"Joseph, are you really well?" Emma asked. "I've never seen you look so weary."

"Yes. I'm well enough—at least as well as a man can be in a place like this. But what about you and the children? Are you holding up all right?"

"We miss you terribly, Joseph. But don't worry about us. We

haven't gone hungry, and we try not to become too downcast. Julia is a little wonder. She's cheerful no matter what comes, and she helps me keep Joey under control. He needs to run and play, but I simply can't let him go outside. Who knows what our enemies might do to him if they recognize whose son he is." She hesitated, and then said, "Joseph, the soldiers always claim that they are going to kill you, and Joey hears those things. He wants to be a little boy, and play, but he's very scared."

Caleb saw Joseph look down at the table, clearly feeling the uneasiness in Emma's voice. "I'm so sorry," he finally said. "You need me there with you. And there's nothing . . ." Joseph's voice trailed off and he ducked his head. But he looked up after a few seconds and asked, "What about the other little boys?"

"Freddie is hale and happy. He has no idea what troubles there are in the world. And little Alexander has had a cold this winter, but he's doing fine now. He's too young to understand that you're gone, but I know he'll love to see you when you return. You could always make him smile."

"I'm just relieved to know that you're all staying healthy." He reached for Emma's hand, and in a sorrowful voice said, "Your life has been too hard, Emma. And so much of it has been my fault, the way I've moved you about and asked so much of you. My trials have been easy compared to yours. You've experienced enough pain to break most people."

Caleb understood what Joseph was saying. Before Emma had lost the twins in Kirtland, another set of newborn twins had died—all before little Joseph Murdock had succumbed to his illness. Five of Emma's first six babies had died as infants, and Emma had faced far too many other trials. Joseph had been dragged into court multiple times, and even though he had always been acquitted, Emma surely lived every day with the fear of what enemies might do to him.

Caleb could only think that he had been feeling sorry for himself. Joseph and Emma had survived much more than he and Nancy had had to suffer.

"We *have* met with difficulties," Emma was saying, "but we always come out all right."

"Still, I worry that I've asked too much of you. Here in this jail, with time to think, I find myself wondering whether you'll always love me—whether I've given you the life you deserve. There are times when I wish we could have a farm somewhere, and a simple life—just work and raise the children and have time in the evening to sit and watch the fireflies. We've never had enough time to ourselves."

"You didn't ask for this life, Joseph. You were called to it by God. And that means that I was, too. I never regret that I married you, and I never doubt your calling."

Caleb tried not to look at Joseph. He didn't want him to know that he was listening. But he glanced and saw tears in Joseph's eyes. "Please, tell Julia that Papa hasn't committed any crimes. And tell her the Lord will release me from this place, maybe soon, and I'll come home to her and the boys."

"I will. She'll want to hear that."

"And Emma, if something happens and it doesn't go that way. If they do try us and . . . convict us . . . or if someone shoots us down, always tell the children that you know I was called of God."

"Don't speak of such things. You'll be released. The Lord still has work for you to do."

Joseph nodded, but Caleb saw the solemn look in his eyes. He thought he understood better now what Joseph had been contemplating during his times of silence.

"Will you always love me, Emma?"

"You know I will, Joseph. Never doubt that."

Joseph's gentle whispers seemed to be generated from the prophet's deepest self. He had been asked to do things no one else was required to do, and which ran against his longing for a quiet life. Joseph had always been outgoing, could even seem arrogant at times, but here with Emma, Caleb was reminded of a child: questioning himself, uneasy about what lay ahead, and above all, needing to be loved by the person in the world who knew him best.

Joseph called Joey to him then, and he pulled the boy on his lap and held him close. It was nice to see Joseph, a father, another part of being a man and a prophet.

Caleb kept watching Joseph, took pleasure in father and son clasping one another. More than anything, Caleb wanted to hold his children the same way. He thought of little Elizabeth Elmina, only a year old, so lovely and innocent, and yet surrounded by gloom and hatred. He longed to hold her in his arms, to protect her from such ugliness. But she was far from here.

Quietly, Caleb bent forward and lowered his head.

CHAPTER 5

The prisoners and their guests remained in the upper room of the jail long after they had eaten their supper, but eventually the sound of turning locks signaled that Sam Tillery was entering through the consecutive doors. He shut the inner door behind him and waited a moment, but once everyone was looking at him, he asked, "Ladies, are you about finished with your visit?"

Caleb was surprised by the gentle tone of his voice.

"Might they stay overnight with us?" Joseph asked. "They plan to start their return trip tomorrow, but they have nowhere to stay tonight."

"Well, sure. They can stay the night, but they'll have to climb down that ladder, the same as you men do."

"Why can't they sleep up here where there's some warmth?" Lyman had fed the fire a couple of times, and the upper room felt like a heavenly place to Caleb, with some light shining through the window and the pleasant smell of firewood in the air.

"I'm just doing what the sheriff tells me to do. He wants no one upstairs at night. That's been the way of things no matter who's been jailed here."

"I understand," Joseph said. "But I don't see what harm it could cause for the women and the boys—"

"It's all right, Joseph," Emma said. "We can climb ladders the same as anyone else, and I'd rather be with you."

"Yes," Phebe said, "I want to look after Sidney. I'd stay with him every night if my children didn't need me at home."

Emma and Phebe were dressed nicely in dark wool dresses, and they had worn heavy cloaks. Caleb hated the thought of them soiling their clothing in the dungeon, but he liked that they wanted to be with their husbands. If Nancy were here, he wouldn't want her to suffer below, but he couldn't deny it would be nice to have her nearby.

Tillery stood with his arms crossed over his chest. After a time he said, rather awkwardly, "I don't mean to say things that might embarrass you nice ladies, but down there, there's nothing but chamber pots—really just buckets. Before you go down to the . . . lower room . . . you could make a visit outside to the outhouse around the corner, and maybe I could let the men go out too, one at a time, so long as I walk out with each prisoner. That should make everyone more comfortable."

"That would be more than kind of you," Joseph said.

Caleb was glad for the offer. He was thrilled to step outside, no matter how cold it was, and he had wondered about the need for privacy in the dungeon.

"All right then," Tillery said. "You folks visit up here for a while yet, and then I'll come back. Unless any of you want to take that walk outside right now."

Caleb was more than ready, so he said, "I would appreciate going now." That set off more responses—and the parade began.

Tillery let everyone stay upstairs longer than Caleb had expected, but a few hours later, after the sun had gone down, the men helped the women and little boys, and everyone descended into the dungeon. Tillery allowed them to take two candles, both considerably taller than he usually provided, and that held back some of the dark below. But the cold was there, as always, and it seemed worse than ever after spending time in the upper room.

"Oh, my," Emma said when she stepped from the ladder. "I had no idea."

She didn't explain, but she didn't need to—everyone knew what she was reacting to. The stench, the dampness, the dark, the close confinement. Phebe soon followed, and then she and Hyrum helped Sidney to the pile of straw he used for a bed. He grunted as he settled down, but Caleb knew he was holding back, not letting Phebe hear the misery he normally expressed to the men.

"Are there no other blankets?" Phebe asked. In her dark clothing she was hard to see, except that candlelight was gleaming off her pallid face and her wet, glistening eyes.

"He has more than the rest of us," Lyman said. "We about freeze every night."

"We'll bring you more blankets," Emma said. "We didn't know what you've been suffering."

But Hyrum was quick to say, "From what I hear, you folks in Far West are no better off than we are. Don't take blankets off your own beds. We're getting by."

"We have firewood," Emma said. She sat down close to Joseph and pulled Joey between them, her dark hair gleaming in the amber light cast by the candles. "We may crowd two or three families into one cabin, but no one's living in freezing houses. We can make sure you get more blankets."

"Yes, please," Sidney said. "I can't get warm. I shake until I feel like I'm coming apart." But Sidney's voice sounded steadier than usual. Phebe had cuddled next to him with Wickliffe between them.

No one spoke for a time, and the desolation of the place seemed to settle in. Joey had begun to whimper. "It's too cold down here," he whispered.

"I know," Joseph said, and then Caleb watched as Joseph pulled the boy onto his lap and wrapped his arms around him. Joey tucked his head under Joseph's chin, and the blanket covered the rest of him. "Is that better?" Joseph asked.

"Can't I go up by the stove and sleep up there?"

Joseph only said, "I'm sorry. I wish you could."

In the quiet that followed, Hyrum asked, "Sister Emma, can you tell me a little more about Mary and my children? Are they truly getting by all right?"

Caleb knew that Hyrum had six living children. One night recently, as the prisoners had talked about their families, Hyrum had related a painful experience: He had held his second little girl, two years old, as she had quietly died in his arms. Most pressing on him now, though, was his fear for his newly born son.

That dismal night, after hearing Hyrum's concerns, each man had admitted his fears for his own family. They wondered whether their wives and children would be forced out of their homes and exposed to the harsh winter weather. Caleb had especially thought of his little daughters Ellen and Elmina, and his grandson Julius, not yet a year old. So often it was the little ones who succumbed when exposed to the cold and wind on the open plains. He had never forgotten the grief he had felt years ago as he held his own son in his arms as the tiny infant had taken his last labored breath.

"Your family is getting by all right, Hyrum," Emma said. "The same as all of us. Your baby seems strong. He's growing fast."

"But what about Mary? When can she come to visit me?"

"I don't know. Mary will be fine, I'm sure, but she's weak right now, and she's been sick. She wouldn't be able to manage the cold just yet. More than anything, I hope you're out of this place before long and you can come home to her, so she won't have to make the trip at all."

"But I hear something in your voice. I think maybe she's worse than you're telling me."

"No. She's been slow to recover from her confinement, but she's a strong woman. I see her every day. So does Mercy. And others are also looking out for her. You're blessed to have dear Lovina. She takes care of the younger children."

"She ought not to have so much to worry about. She's too young for that."

Caleb guessed Lovina was only eleven or twelve, but he had also watched her at Church meetings looking after her brothers and her two young sisters. It seemed to him a good thing for a girl that age to learn family responsibilities. And yet, Caleb worried about all the added burden each family in Far West was now suffering. Nancy was forty now, not old, but she had paid a price in bearing ten children, picking up and moving many times, and working hard to care for their home. She tended to the animals, milked their cow, made butter and cheese, weaved and sewed and mended. Their children had become good helpers, but overseeing them, teaching them, sorting out their disagreements, Caleb knew, had also taken its toll on her. And all the while, Nancy had insisted that her children learn to read and write, learn arithmetic and history and geography even when schools were not available, so she had taken it upon herself to teach them. Her great regret, she had often told Caleb, was that she had no piano. She wished that her daughters could learn to play, as she had done. Caleb had thought many times in the last few days that when he was acquitted and released, he would move his children one last time, settle in a good place, and obtain a piano before the girls were all grown and gone.

Now Lyman spoke up. "Have you talked to Harriet? Do you know how she's faring?"

He and Harriet also had a new baby, born just before the men had entered the jail. Caleb knew the family well. The Baldwins and the Wights had moved to Jackson County together and shared some of the same early hardships. Orange, Lyman's oldest child, was a bold boy with a manner like his father's. He was fourteen or fifteen now, and he had two sisters and three brothers.

"I spoke with her," Emma said. "Orange is acting like a man, chopping wood, doing chores."

"But we left Diahman and hurried off to Far West with not much more than the clothes on our backs," Lyman said. "The Daviess County mobs chased us the whole way, and they ran off our stock. I don't know how Harriet can get through the winter."

"People are sharing what they have," Emma said. "Harriet told me your family has had enough to eat. Orange works with other boys and they glean what wheat and corn they can from the trampled crops. Some folks still have their cows and chickens, so they share their milk and eggs."

"The mean men keep coming back," Wickliffe said. "They yell at us and call us names. I saw some of them use a rope and pull a house down."

"Are they still doing that?" Joseph asked.

"Not so much as they did at first," Phebe said.

"They still yell at us," Wickliffe said, his little voice rising from the blankets and the dark. "And they say bad words. My friend Jesse saw a soldier hit a Mormon man over the head with his gun barrel. He had blood running all over his face, and the soldiers laughed about it."

"Let's not talk about that," Phebe said. "Don't worry your father about such things."

"If we don't leave, they'll kill us," Wickliffe said. "That's what they say to us. And they say they're going to kill Joe Smith. They shout that, over and over."

"Wickliffe, that's enough," Phebe said. "We'll be all right. Some of those men like to sound important, but the Lord will protect us. That's all you need to think about."

Silence returned. The men had heard most of these things, had received letters and talked to visitors during their time in Richmond, but hearing the fear in young Wickliffe's thin little voice made everything real to Caleb.

Joey was whimpering again. "Will they shoot you, Papa?"

"No, son. Don't even think about that," Joseph said. "The Lord will protect me—all of us—until our work is finished."

"The mean men don't know about things like that," Joey said.

"You mustn't listen to them." But then, in a tender voice, Joseph said, "I want to give you a blessing, son. Would you like that?"

Caleb could barely hear Joey as he whispered, "Yes." But in a moment, still holding the boy, Joseph raised one hand from the blanket and placed it on the boy's head.

"Joseph Smith the Third, I take you in my arms to give you a blessing." He paused, then spoke gently. "I bless you with comfort, but also with courage."

Caleb loved the feeling that filled the room as Joseph went on to speak of the hardships he knew Joey and his brothers and sister were facing, and he advised Joey to be a strength to them and a help to his mother. And then, in a slightly stronger voice, he advised him that if he would be true to the gospel, righteous and firm, he would someday help to gather Zion, build the kingdom of God on Earth, and be a leader to the people.

After the blessing, Sidney raised himself up enough to give Wickliffe a similar blessing. Caleb wished he could do the same for his own children, but he was touched by the spirit of love that filled the small, dark room.

When Sidney was finished, Emma said, "We'll be all right. I feel certain about that. So let's not talk about troubles. Let's sing some hymns together."

"Yes. That's just what we need to do," Joseph said. "You choose the hymns and then lead us."

"I'm happy to do that," Emma said. She paused to consider and then said, "Let's start with this one." Her strong, clear voice filled the room with the first line of a hymn. "Glorious things of thee are spoken, Zion, city of our God."

Caleb certainly understood her choice. Joseph often said that Zion would yet be redeemed, and it was what everyone in the Church hoped for—to return to Jackson County. Caleb couldn't remember all the verses, but Emma knew them and pulled the others to sing with her. He loved being reminded of the words to the tenth and final verse:

> *Fading are all worldly treasures,*
> *With their boasted pomp and show!*
> *Heav'nly joys and lasting pleasures,*
> *None but Zion's children know.*

It was what Caleb tried to tell himself each night in this miserable place. Maybe Zion was lost for the moment, but God would not let the mobs win the ultimate victory. Sometimes, he knew, the members had been a little too enamored with the pleasures of the world. He wanted to teach his own family, when he finally got out of this place, that the lasting pleasures were the ones that mattered.

Emma began another hymn, and they all sang together:

We're not ashamed to own our Lord,
And worship him on earth;
We love to learn his holy word,
And know what souls are worth.

They followed with "Now we'll sing with one accord," and "Awake, O ye people! the Savior is coming." The music reverberated in the tight room, with everyone joining in. Lyman had a scratchy voice, but Sidney's rich voice, though weakened, took on some of its old power. The close walls and ceiling seemed to forgive any notes that weren't quite pure.

Caleb felt himself filled to the brim with joy. It was the best he had felt since he had been taken away from his home in Far West.

Eventually, Emma led everyone in a hymn Caleb dearly loved:

As children of Zion
Good tidings for us:
The tokens already appear;
Fear not and be just,
For the kingdom is ours,
And the hour of redemption is near.

Everyone seemed to sense that the hymn was a benediction, a closing of their little worship service, but Caleb wanted just a fragment of a sermon to go along with it. "Brother Joseph," he said. "Is the hour near? Will Christ soon remove us from all this suffering?"

Joseph took his time in answering, but finally said, "Not quite, Brother Caleb. I don't believe the time is too far off, but I fear we must yet suffer hardships. All the prophecies speak of difficult times as the end draws near."

It was not what Caleb wanted to hear, but Joseph's words felt prophetic.

"The Lord is sifting us," Joseph added. "The weak are losing their nerve. They're turning from us and giving up on the idea of Zion. We've witnessed Satan grabbing up some of our stalwarts, turning them into vile, bitter enemies. I fear there will be more of that as our afflictions drag on. We will have to find our own strength, swallow our pride, and accept what the Lord has in store for us."

Caleb didn't want to spend another day, another hour, in this dark jail, but he told himself that he was not going to falter.

"Lord, help me to be strong to the end," he whispered, and he thought that the others were saying similar prayers.

CHAPTER 6

Caleb slept for a time that night and then awakened, cold and aching. He was aware that others had talked most of the night and slept very little. Emma and Phebe had asked Tillery to come to the jail early to open the trapdoor so they could get underway. They both got up in the dark, and when the door opened from above, Joseph picked up Joey and carried him to the ladder.

"Son, go ahead and climb up," he said. "I'll follow you."

Caleb watched Joey, who was clearly groggy. He managed, with help from his father, to climb the ladder, and then Joseph clambered up himself and reached down to help Emma. As she stepped off the ladder, Caleb heard her say, "Oh, the warmth feels so good."

Alexander helped Wickliffe and Phebe ascend the ladder, and Caleb decided to climb up too to say goodbye to the visitors. He also admitted to himself that at least half his motivation was to steal a few minutes by the stove. By the time he reached the ladder, however, Sidney grabbed his arm.

"Help me, Caleb. I want to go up."

So Caleb turned to help Sidney, but he managed to make the climb with little help. Caleb could tell that Sidney had regained much of his strength. The visit of his wife and son had lifted him considerably.

Caleb followed Sidney, as did Lyman and Hyrum. It was a rustic group that assembled in the candlelight above, everyone rumpled and coated with fragments of straw, including Emma and Phebe. It pained him to see two such elegant women looking almost as shabby as the men. It struck Caleb that the Saints were being degraded to a level he had never thought possible.

Though Caleb had felt his faith the night before—powerfully—a sense of abandonment returned to him now. He and the men would be stuck here, and these women would have to return to the despoiled place Far West had become. An abysmal thought sometimes crossed his mind lately—one he pushed away as quickly as he could. In moments like this, however, when utter defeat seemed possible, he had to fight against the thought that he and all the Church members were as misguided as the Missourians claimed they were. When that impression came to his mind, it seemed entirely possible that God had nothing to do with anything in his life, that a whole society had invented a lie and a prophet.

It was this ultimate doubt about the very existence of God and prophecy that frightened Caleb more than anything. To combat the impulse, he tried to think of miracles he had seen, of the joy he had felt in the ineffable realms of the Spirit that had sometimes visited their meetings. Those things were undeniable. But intruding on those memories was the picture he saw around him now: the humiliating conditions he was living in and the disappointment of pleading for help every day and receiving no answer to his prayers.

To Caleb's surprise, Sam Tillery had brought a large plate of sliced ham, a generous supply of johnnycakes, and even two pots of coffee that sat now on the table in the little room. Something in this act of kindness felt like respect, and it helped him push his misgivings from his mind. Caleb had thought that Tillery would merely show up and open the jail for the sisters to leave, not feed them first. He knew that Tillery—and surely his wife—had had to rouse themselves very early to get such a breakfast ready, and the only explanation he could think of was that the women had touched him in some way. Maybe Tillery was sensing who the Saints actually were—that they had families, wives and children, and that they were not, as he had been told, beasts.

Everyone ate in relative silence, perhaps because they were tired, but more likely because it was painful to end the visit and face a cheerless day. When Emma prepared herself to leave, Joseph took her in his arms and held her. He whispered words to her that Caleb couldn't hear, but he saw Emma whisper back, tears on her face. Across the room, Sidney and Phebe were bidding their own tearful goodbyes.

After that, Joseph knelt and wrapped his arms around Joey.

"Be strong," Caleb heard Joseph say, and then to Emma, "Don't let the little ones forget me. Tell them I love them, and don't let them think I'm a bad man—no matter what they hear people say about me."

Emma touched Joseph's face as he stood up. "They will never think ill of you. I promise you that."

Then the women and their sons were gone, the heavy hinges grating against the frame as the door closed.

"Sam's left us up here," Lyman said. "I wonder how soon he'll be back."

"Soon, no doubt," Alexander said, "and then he'll herd us back to the dungeon."

Hyrum stepped to the stove, reached for a stick of firewood from a stack by the wall, then opened the lid and shoved it in. "Let's warm ourselves as much as we can before he does come back," he said.

But Tillery didn't return, and the men lay upon the floor, as close to the stove as they could all fit. Caleb preferred to extend his feet close to the fire, since his worn boots left his feet cold almost all the time. He found comfort lying on the wooden floor, no matter how hard it was. He slept that way, lying on his back, for what must have been two or three hours. When he finally awoke, it was because Joseph, next to him, had stirred, and soon the others began to come to life. The window opening on the east side of the building let in a bit of light.

The men were surprised when Tillery showed up at midday with a sparse but adequate supply of food, and more so when he stayed in the room and chatted with the men rather comfortably. He even said, when he left, "I'll leave you in this room for now. But you'll have to go back down after supper."

And that became the pattern. The men stayed in the upper room all day, almost every day, and visitors often showed up: family members, Church leaders, friends. The guests often brought food and they always brought the best wishes of the members. It was not as though the jail became pleasant. The nights remained an ordeal, the meals meager, but the extra food from Church members helped considerably, and the bitter nights now represented a waiting time until the men could climb upstairs, warm themselves, and reclaim the sleep that escaped them at night.

Caleb felt the tender mercy of this comfort, and he scolded himself for thinking that God had abandoned him. Or at least he told himself that when he sat by the stove. It was at night that he still felt forsaken, and it was then that he had to fight against his uncertainties.

One cold December day Joseph told Alexander, "Brother Markham brought some writing paper yesterday. I want to send a letter to the Saints. Will you act as my scribe?"

"Of course."

Joseph and Alexander sat down at the table across from one another, Alexander with his dip pen ready and an inkwell set near the paper. Caleb was sitting on the floor, leaning against the wall next to the stove. He could see past Alexander to the solemn look on Joseph's face. But Joseph didn't begin immediately. He concentrated, seemed to search inside himself, then began with a greeting: "To the Church of the Latter-day Saints in Caldwell County and the saints scattered abroad, and are persecuted and made desolate, and are afflicted in divers manners for Christ's sake and the gospel's, and whose perils are greatly augmented by the wickedness and corruption of false brethren."

Caleb was surprised that Joseph's thoughts had returned to those "false brethren," but they had clearly hurt Joseph more than any of the other adversaries. And it was also the Church and the members that Joseph hated to see disparaged by such witnesses.

He continued, "May grace, mercy, and peace be and abide with you, and notwithstanding all your sufferings, we assure you that you have our prayers and fervent desires for your welfare both day and night. We believe that, that God who sees us in this solitary place will hear our prayers and reward you openly. Know assuredly, dear brethren, that it is for the testimony of Jesus that we are in bonds and in prison."

Still, those "dissenters," as he called them, were in the forefront of his mind: "But we say unto you that we consider our condition better (notwithstanding our suffering), than those who have persecuted us and smitten us and borne false witness against us, and we most assuredly believe that those who bear false witness against us do seem to have a great triumph over us for the present."

Joseph went on to compare them to Haman in the book of Esther, who had sought the death of Mordecai, and he explained the connection he saw.

"I say unto you that those who have thus vilely treated us like Haman shall be hanged upon their own gallows, or in other words shall fall into their own gin and trap and ditch which they have prepared for us and shall go backward and stumble and fall, and their names shall be blotted out, and God shall reward them according to all their abominations."

Caleb felt uncomfortable. The reasoning seemed fair enough, but Joseph sounded severe. He inveighed against the unjust treatment by Missouri officials and the false claims that had led to his and others' confinement, but he reserved his deepest resentment for the turncoats who had testified against him: George Hinkle, John Corrill, Reed Peck, William Phelps, and especially Sampson Avard. He also named others who had become dissenters in recent years: William McLellin, John and David Whitmer, Oliver Cowdery, Martin Harris. He denounced Thomas Marsh and Orson Hyde as men whose hearts had become full of corruption.

Caleb found himself wanting to say, *Joseph, don't send this letter. It's not what the members need to hear right now.* But how could he say such a thing to the prophet?

Only at the end of the long, sometimes-rambling letter did Joseph take a different tone: "And the very God of peace shall be with you and make a way for your escape from the adversary of your souls; we commend you to God and the word of his grace, which is able to make us wise unto salvation. Amen."

Joseph took a breath or two when he finished, then asked to see the sheets Alexander had used to record the letter. Alexander handed him the pen with the sheets. As Joseph read, Caleb watched him make little corrections, scratch out a few words, and change them. Finally, he looked around the room at the men, his gaze falling on Hyrum as though he sensed that his brother had something to say.

"What do you think, brethren?" Joseph asked. "Is there anything you would add or change? I'm going to ask Alexander to recopy it, so now is the time to make your suggestions."

The question had been directed to everyone, but now he was looking back at Hyrum.

Hyrum sounded hesitant when he said, "Joseph, I don't disagree with anything you said. But it's a stern letter. It might not encourage our people who are suffering so much right now."

"I understand what you're telling me, Hyrum. But the members need to know that they have been wronged by men they have loved. Sometimes we have to speak truth, no matter how offensive. I want our people to know that we're not in jail for anything we've done but for the things these wicked traitors have lied about."

"But you sound angry, Joseph. You sound—"

"I am angry, Hyrum. And I hope you are too. Why shouldn't we be? The Lord doesn't expect us to accept such behavior without indignation. Christ turned over the tables of the money changers. He didn't say, 'I truly hope you men alter your ways.' He told them they were disgracing the temple."

"That's exactly right," Lyman said. "You spoke nothing but the truth. As for me, I curse those deserters. I pray that the Lord will strike them down and send them to hell."

Lyman's words were clearly stronger than Joseph liked. He stared down at the table. After a time, he said, "Caleb, I know what you think. You told me Avard wasn't lying. And Alexander, you agreed with him."

"No, Joseph," Caleb said. The truth was his own resentment against Avard and the other witnesses was nearly as strong as Joseph's. "Avard didn't explain the motives we had for our military actions—and he didn't admit to the atrocities against us that prompted those actions. He was wrong to do what he did." He hesitated, then added. "But Joseph, your letter *does* sound angry, and that's not the spirit I expect from you."

Joseph studied Caleb, considered his words, but he didn't respond.

Hyrum said, "I'm not saying that we have no reason to be angry. But I think it's time to move past that and give the members hope and encouragement, not more reasons to be aggrieved."

Joseph didn't speak for at least a minute. Caleb felt his own breath hold. He didn't want to criticize the prophet. He hadn't meant to do that.

"You're right," Joseph finally said. "My letter does sound angry. But I'm going to let it stand as it is. I've declared my opinion of the dissidents, and I don't think it was wrong to do that."

"I say you have no reason to take anything back," Lyman said. "We was fighting a war, and it wasn't one we started. You can't fight a war by telling a mob, 'We plead with you to treat us better.' We tried that for a long time, and then we took the matter into our own hands. As far as I'm concerned, we had no other choice."

"That's true, Lyman," Joseph said, "but you get as aggravated as I do."

Hyrum put his hand on Joseph's shoulder and waited for his brother to look at him. When he did, Hyrum said, "I'll never challenge your inspiration, Joseph. You know that. All I'm saying is that you, as our prophet, need to offer the rest of us hope for better days. You need to call for the best in us, and I didn't hear much of that in your letter."

Joseph was nodding now. "I don't deny it, Hyrum. And I'll write other letters, better letters, when I'm ready. You're right that we need to let loose of all those feelings and move beyond them. But I'm still enraged. Call it righteous indignation or *unrighteous*, I don't know which it is. I only know that these men have cut me to the bone. They walked among us as fellow Saints—and I loved them as brothers—and yet they stood before Judge King and denounced me for a scoundrel. I hear their words constantly run through all my thoughts." He paused, as though to test his own conviction, but then said, "I need to send this letter."

Caleb thought he understood. He had felt much the same as he had listened to Avard, Hinkle, and Corrill speak carefully crafted accusations against Joseph—and against himself. But Caleb did agree with Hyrum. He wanted the prophet to lead him—and all the members—to a higher state. Caleb knew Joseph, knew his kindheartedness. The members needed that Joseph, that prophet, to help them through such trying, dangerous times.

CHAPTER 7

On December 20, after breakfast, the prisoners were once again allowed to remain in the upper room of the jail. They were scattered about on chairs or on the floor, some of them asleep. Caleb was still sitting at the breakfast table, taking his time with a bowl of disgusting mush that Tillery had provided that morning. It was filled with grit, and it was all he could do to get it down. Still, he knew he would be hungry all day if he didn't eat as much of the stuff as he could.

When Caleb heard a dog bark outside, he thought little of it. There always seemed to be locals milling about outside the jail, and when they shouted insults at the men inside, the raised voices usually set off dogs barking in a kind of rhythmic accompaniment. But when this dog barked, Joseph stood up and walked to the window. Then, in less than a minute, the outer door of the jail creaked open and the big key turned in the lock of the inner door. Tillery opened the door just enough to slip in. He smiled at Joseph, but before he could say anything, a huge dog forced its head through the opening.

"Major!" Joseph shouted.

The dog pushed its way through the door then took one bound, leaped, and slammed its paws against Joseph's shoulders.

A lesser man would have been knocked to the ground, but Joseph was not only sturdy but strong. He held his own with the dog and then joyfully wrestled with him and rubbed his ears.

"My old friend," he said, "I've longed to see you."

Major still barked in intervals, as though he understood what Joseph was saying to him, and as if to answer, he washed Joseph's face and stubbly beard with his big pink tongue.

Caleb had known Major for years, and frankly, had always feared him. Major was friendly more than hostile but overpowering all the same. He was a fawn-colored English Mastiff and must have weighed two hundred pounds. Back in Far West, he had once knocked Caleb off his feet and onto his backside.

Joseph was soon looking to the door, as were all the men. A smiling Emma stepped in and seemed to take delight in Joseph's affectionate embrace of their dog. She waited patiently until Joseph finally broke away and came to her.

"Oh, thank you, Emma," he was saying. "I asked you to bring Old Major, but I didn't think you would manage it."

"It's your birthday present. I wanted to step in first and tell you I had something for you, but I couldn't hold him back."

"You couldn't have done anything better than to bring Major for a visit."

But Joseph had spoken too soon. Little Joey, who had been standing behind Emma, slipped around her now and Joseph caught him up in his arms.

"What a joy! What a joy!" Joseph said. "I hoped you'd come before Christmas, but I wasn't sure you could stand the trip again so soon."

"Tell the truth," Emma said. "It's Major you love the most."

"No, no. It isn't so. But I do love that big fellow." He turned and the dog jumped against him once again.

"I'd rather have that giant here with you than eating up all the food in my house," Emma said. "Mr. Tillery just promised me that Major can stay—at least for a time—and he will bring in extra food for him."

That was astounding for Caleb to hear, but not as astounding as what he saw next.

Nancy stepped through the door.

Caleb stood and stared for a moment, unbelieving, but then he hurried to his wife and grabbed her in his arms.

Behind her, in the space between the two doors, stood both his sons: Clark, who was twenty-one, and James, who was twelve. Caleb couldn't speak, couldn't imagine that he would ever again feel such elation. He grabbed James by the hand and pulled him into the room and then he wrapped one arm around him and used the other to beckon Clark closer.

"Oh, boys, you look healthy," he finally managed to say. "I've worried that you would starve this winter."

"We're fine," Clark said. But then he stepped back and looked at Caleb. "You're the one who isn't eating enough. I can see that."

Caleb hadn't seen a mirror in weeks. He had no idea how he looked. But he felt his clothes hanging loosely on him, and the bristles on his face had turned into a bushy beard. He had also begun to push his hair back as it continually fell in strands around his face.

"I'm not so bad off as I probably look," he said. "We're getting by. They let us stay up here in this warm room much of the time now. And we do the best we can at night."

"We brought you more blankets," James said.

"Hurrah for you!" Hyrum called from across the room. "That's the best news you could have brought us."

For a time, everyone talked at once as the men asked questions about their families and Emma and Nancy reported on them as best they could. But Caleb wanted to hear about his own children, so he got a chair for Nancy, set it in a corner, then sat on the floor and waved for his boys to join him. Alexander hurried over with another chair and told Caleb, "Here. Sit by Nancy. You needn't sit on the floor."

Caleb thanked Alexander but watched him as he slipped away to the corner by the front doors and sat on the floor by himself. He was a kindly man, and surely happy that Caleb could have some of his family about him, but it must have been difficult not to have visitors of his own.

Caleb looked back at Nancy. She was seven years younger than Caleb and beautiful, with dark eyes and a tender smile that had touched something inside him the first time he had met her. He felt his love for her surge again now, but the feeling was blended with pain. What he saw in her expression concerned him. She looked tired, even toughened, in spite of her attempt to be cheerful. Caleb knew she was carrying too many burdens.

"Tell me the truth," he said, "do you have enough to eat? Are all the girls staying warm?"

"Clark brings firewood to us, and I chop it," James said. "We keep a fire going all the time."

James was rather slight, but Caleb liked that he was taking pride in helping Nancy and his sisters. This was something new, and promising, that his boy had begun to respond to such needs.

"What about you and that pretty wife of yours?" Caleb asked Clark. "Are you two doing all right?"

"Yes, we're fine." They had been married for only a few months. Ann was a happy and hopeful young woman, and Caleb felt certain that she would always be a good wife to Clark.

"No sickness at all?" Caleb asked.

Clark clearly understood what his father was asking. He smiled. "No, not yet. I guess that will come in time."

Nancy was smiling, but James looked confused. "Naw. I doubt it. She's strong as anyone, and healthy too."

"Good. That's good to hear," Caleb said, and he and Clark shared another knowing smile. Caleb's oldest daughter, Maria, was married and had two children, but he was ready to welcome more from Clark and Ann.

Caleb asked about each of his daughters, and Nancy assured him that all were doing well, including their little Elmina, who had passed her first birthday and was walking now. Caleb could only think how much he would like to see her, take her on his lap and make her laugh.

◆

Tillery brought in extra food—including meat for the dog— for both meals that day, and he was pleasant with everyone. He seemed to have taken a liking to Major, taking his turn scratching behind the big mastiff's ears. Even though the noise in the room was excessive at times, Caleb found it a good noise and a wonderful change.

When evening came, however, Tillery told everyone, "Sorry about this, but I'll have to ask y'all to go down into that . . . lower jail. I'll bring the blankets in that Mrs. Smith and Mrs. Baldwin brought. That'll make things a little better for everyone."

Clark offered to help him carry the blankets, so Tillery took him along, and when they returned, he offered, as he had before, to take everyone to the outhouse. After that, he opened the trapdoor, and the entire group descended into the dark. Joseph had intended for Major to stay by the stove upstairs, but before Tillery could shut the door, the dog stuck his nose into the opening and whined. So Joseph climbed the ladder, pulled the bulky dog onto his shoulders, carried him down, and released him below.

Emma handed the blankets around, and then set up a better bed for Joey than the time before. Joseph, Emma, and Joey welcomed Major among them, and they all nestled together.

Once everyone was arranged and covered in quilts, Emma said, "We need to sing Christmas songs this time. I tried to work things out to be here as close to Christmas—and to Joseph's birthday—as possible. I left enough time for us to get back to our other children before Christmas Day, but we plan to stay two nights this time, so we'll have tomorrow with you as well. Still, let's start our Christmas celebration tonight."

Caleb didn't want his girls to be without their mother and brothers on Christmas Day, either. Still, the thought of Christmas only reminded him that he wouldn't be with his family. That feeling only grew when Emma began to sing, "Joy to the world! The Lord will come!"

Caleb especially liked the second verse:

> *Rejoice! rejoice! When Jesus reigns,*
> *And Saints their song employ:*
> *While fields, and floods, rocks, hills, and plains,*
> *Repeat the sounding joy.*

Major liked joining in with his own version of singing, but Joseph playfully clamped his hands around his jaws and the dog seemed to accept the censorship as a kind of game. Next, they sang, "Hark! The Herald Angels Sing," and then "While Shepherds Watched Their Flocks." These were hymns Caleb had sung in church as a boy in Nobletown, New York.

"We don't think of this next one as a Christmas song," Emma said, "but in my mind it is. And it's one of my favorite hymns."

She began to sing, and Caleb recognized the tune. The words touched him:

> *From the regions of glory an angel descended,*
> *And told the strange news how the babe was attended:*
> *Go, shepherds, and visit this heavenly stranger;*
> *Beneath that bright star, there's your Lord in a manger!*
>
> *Hallelujah to the Lamb,*
> *Whom our souls may rely on;*
> *We shall see him on earth,*
> *When he brings again Zion.*

Emma began the second verse, but Joseph spoke up emphatically, his voice tight with a tension Caleb thought he understood. "Let's stop right there."

"What's wrong, Joseph?" Emma asked.

"Let's not sing that."

"Whyever not?"

"William Phelps wrote it."

"I know that. It's a beautiful hymn. Listen to the—"

"Emma, you should have heard what he said about me during the hearings."

"We can love the sentiments and the poetry, all the same. You can be that big, can't you, Joseph?"

The reprimand silenced Joseph.

Everyone waited. Seconds passed and then minutes. But finally Joseph said, "Give me some time, Emma. I'm angry with the men who turned against us, but I'm angrier with myself. I've been searching for the Lord in this revolting place, and I can't seem to find him here."

He hesitated, and as though he knew what Emma would say next, added, "I understand. I have to be the kind of vessel the Lord can fill. And I'm simply not that vessel right now. But I'm *trying* to open my heart."

"I know," Emma said. "We all know who you are, and we love you. But we need you to guide us, not harbor feelings that keep you from doing that."

Joseph nodded, considered for a time. "Yes," he said. "Thank you, Emma. Let's sing the rest of Brother William's hymn."

So Emma began and everyone followed as they sang the second verse:

> *Glad tidings I bring unto you and each nation;*
> *Glad tidings of joy, now behold your salvation:*
> *Arise all ye pilgrims and lift up your voices,*
> *And shout—The Redeemer! while heaven rejoices.*

Caleb felt better after singing those words, but he worried about Joseph. Emma had said that the members needed him to guide them—Caleb had said almost the same words to him—and Joseph had admitted they were both right. But Caleb knew something else. No man, not even Joseph, could live up to the demands placed upon him every minute of every day. Maybe he needed this time away from the demands of daily leadership. But he needed to lift himself soon. Caleb, the Church, the members—and the Lord—needed him.

CHAPTER 8

After two nights in the jail and two more days of travel, Emma was weary when she arrived in Far West. Poor Joey had tried to be strong and brave, but the cold had sapped his strength; he was so tired he struggled to speak, but as Clark Baldwin halted the horses near the front door of their house, Joey asked almost inaudibly, "Can we build a fire?"

"Yes," Emma said, "of course."

Clark jumped down from the wagon and then reached up to take Joey, who was still wrapped in a quilt, into his arms and walk him to the house. Clark had already dropped off his mother and brother, and Emma knew he was eager to get home to his wife and to his own fire.

She hurried ahead to open the door but found it slightly ajar. She stepped inside, but what she saw stopped her. Everything in the house was disturbed, furniture turned over and pots and pans strewn about the floor. Emma didn't know whether it was an act of malice or whether thievery was also involved.

"Oh, Sister Emma," Clark said. "What's happened?"

Emma had begun to cry.

Joey, squirming in Clark's arms, looked about. "Who did it?" he asked. "Those men?"

Emma realized that she had to be careful. Joey was frightened enough without seeing her go to pieces. She took a breath, waited a moment, then asked Clark, "Would you go ahead and build the fire? I'll begin to set things right as soon as I can. I don't want to bring the little boys into this. I may need to leave them with Mercy one more night."

"Yes, of course," Clark said. He set Joey down close to the fire-place. There was a pile of kindling nearby. He stacked it inside the fireplace and then said, "I'll bring some firewood in, and I'll see if I can get fire from one of the neighbors."

After Clark left, Emma walked into the bedroom. She saw immediately that the bedding was gone—not just tossed off the bed but carried away. She knew that she would have to look about to see what else had been stolen, and she found a decorative wooden box cast on the floor. When she opened it, she discovered that her jewelry was gone. It was nothing expensive, but she was stung to discover that a valued brooch and necklace, passed down to her from her grandmother, had been taken. Someone had pried open a chest and stolen her cloth, along with some lovely buttons she had kept for years. When she looked into the wardrobe, she saw that most of Joseph's clothing had been stolen.

Emma sat on the ropes of her bed, not sure what she would do for bedding now, but even more, deadened by this intrusion, hurt not so much by the loss as by the cruelty of people who would take advantage of her leaving town to visit her husband. Thieves had pocketed things that couldn't possibly mean as much to them as they did to her. Tears had begun to slide down her cheeks again, but she swallowed and told herself not to give way. She had told Joseph she was strong, that she was holding up against all the troubles, and now she had to prove it.

"I don't need any of those things," she said out loud.

She heard Clark come back through the door, so she walked out to see him kneeling by the fireplace with a burning stick of wood and some wood shavings to get the kindling started. Without looking at her, Clark asked, "Is anything missing from your house?"

"They took a few items from my bedroom." She glanced at Joey, aware how frightened he was. "But it doesn't matter. Those are just things. My husband is still alive and the Saints aren't defeated. We'll carry on."

But all that was for Joey, and maybe for Clark. It wasn't what Emma was feeling. And she wasn't entirely sure that the Saints were as strong as they needed to be. All these defeats were disheartening, and too many of the members were falling away—more than Joseph knew about. Lots of people were generous, willing to share; others were grasping at what food they could find and turning away from leaders who encouraged a spirit of oneness. She had also heard from some of the leaders that maybe it wasn't good for the members to gather in one place anymore, and that gathering in great numbers was what had led to problems with local citizens. But she could only think that if the Saints gave up on gathering, Zion really was lost, and Joseph's vision—the Lord's purposes—would also be lost.

The fire was gradually taking hold.

Emma was also taking hold. "Clark, thank you," she said. "Now go to Ann. I'll straighten things up as much as I can and then I'll see what bedding I can find, at least for the night."

"They took your bedding?"

"Yes." But she didn't want to talk about that. She wanted to start working, doing something.

"I'll see what I can do," Clark said. "We'll find bedding for you. Are your blankets all gone?"

"All that were here in the house are gone—except the ones we used coming back in the wagon."

"People will want to help you. I'd like to stop at home long enough to let Ann know that I'm back, but then I'll gather what you need." He hesitated. "If I can."

The words struck Emma hard. She knew how destitute people were. It had been no easy matter to find blankets and quilts to take to the prisoners, and she didn't want anyone to go without necessities for her sake. She had never liked to be dependent on others. And yet . . . her children all needed something to wrap up in for the night.

Clark promised again, and then he left.

Emma stood for a time, looked around the room. The truth was, she doubted she had the energy to take on all the work ahead of her. She wondered how many more tests she would have to face before the Lord decided she had proved herself.

Joey stared up at her, surely waiting to see what she would do.

"We'll be all right," she told him as she knelt to pick up the shards of a broken dish.

Joey set aside the quilt around him and said, "I'll help."

"Yes. That's good of you, son. You know where everything goes. Just put things right, as much as you can."

But he looked baffled, seemingly overwhelmed by all the mess and confusion.

"Just start with anything that needs picking up. That's all we can do for now."

So Joey knelt and picked up a poker by the fireplace, then leaned it against the stones. The crane and heavy pot had not been disturbed. Emma was thankful for that. At least she could cook something warm for supper.

Only half an hour or so passed before Mercy opened the door and came in.

"Clark told us what happened," she said. "Oh, Emma, I'm sorry. We tried to watch the house. I was here this morning, and nothing was amiss. I should have come back and—"

"No, Mercy, it wasn't your fault. Let's not fret. Let's just get things in order. Are my babies all right?"

"Yes. They're lovely. I'll keep them with me awhile yet. I'm going out to look for bedclothes now. I know people will want to help you." But a sob broke from her. "Oh, Emma, I think this *was* my fault. William McLellin was in town today. He was bragging and shouting at people, telling them what terrible men Joseph and Hyrum are. When he saw me, he swore that he would kill Hyrum if the state didn't hang him."

"What blame does that put on you, Mercy?"

"I'd stepped outside to throw out some dishwater, but Freddie had wondered what I was doing, and he ran to the door. When William saw him, he asked me, "Is that Joseph's boy?" I told him yes, that I was looking after him, and I said, 'While Emma is . . .' And then I stopped. But he guessed my meaning and said, 'Has Emma gone to see Joseph again?' I didn't say yes, but he must have known where you would go. So then he said, 'I hope she says goodbye. I doubt she'll ever see Old Joe again.' And he grinned like that made him happy."

"He said that?"

"Yes. But Emma, he must have known your house was empty. He must be the one who broke in here. He, and maybe some others."

"That doesn't mean you're to blame, Mercy. If he did it, it's the hatred that's in him that's at fault. It's hard to believe that a man who sat with Joseph in the highest councils of the Church would take on the ways of the mob and call him 'Old Joe.'"

"He called him worse things than that."

Emma glanced at Joey. "I don't doubt it," she said. "But we won't let such men set us back. If you'll keep my children a little longer, I'll get things in order here."

"Yes. And we'll find what you need. What else was taken besides the bedding?"

"Nothing I need tonight," Emma said. She was starting to feel some strength. She wasn't going to let such pitiful men break her resolve.

◆

Emma did make a good start on straightening things up, and Joey helped as much as he could. Mercy came back with supper to share and she—and others—brought more bedding than Emma actually needed, so Emma told the sisters to share with others in greater need than herself. That night, she brought her children into bed with her. And the house was warm.

The following day, when she still had much to do, she heard a voice outside.

"Emma Smith, have you come home?"

She recognized the voice of William McLellin. Emma didn't answer, but when a knock came—with a vow to kill "Joe"—she stepped to the door and opened it a little. She wanted to tell him what she thought of him.

"What do you want?" she asked. "Didn't you get everything yesterday? What a degraded, despicable human being you've let yourself become."

McLellin broke into a boisterous laugh. "I don't know what you mean, my beloved sister. Are you accusing me of something?"

"Leave me alone. I never want to see your face again."

"How do you like my new vest? I look quite a dandy, don't you think? Almost as fine as the Prophet Joe, the Moses of our own day, the voice of warning crying in the wilderness."

"You disgust me. You've been drinking. Is that what makes you so brave?"

"I might have taken a little grog this morning. Do you condemn me for it?"

"I condemn you for being a coward and for breaking into my house. We loved you once, William, and I think you loved us. How can you do this to us?"

Emma's words seemed to bite at him and he stepped forward menacingly. Emma tried to shut the door, but he slammed his hand against it and pushed back. She held her own, but she couldn't shut the door.

"Because I could, Emma. That's why I did it. Your great husband is nothing now, and he can't lift a finger to stop me."

"He told me about you—what you did in Richmond."

"What? What did he say?"

"You came to the jail and asked to beat him." Emma watched William, expected him to deny it, but he didn't. "He said you wouldn't fight him—not unless you could use a club to batter him."

"I only . . . it was not like that."

"You know it was. Joseph was willing to take you on, even to let you use a club, but the jailer said no to that."

"That's how Joseph tells it, and he's a liar. A damned braggart and a liar."

"So how was it? What part wasn't true?"

"He's twice the size of me. I wasn't asking for anything that wasn't . . ." But he seemed to sense how foolish he sounded.

"You *are* a coward, William. You had such great possibilities, but your jealousy destroyed you. Now look at what you've become. You're *pitiful*—a thief and a liar."

William was swaying a little, probably from the alcohol, but it seemed to Emma as though she had struck him a blow. In his shocked silence, she shoved hard against the door and was able to shut and bar it. He swore then, oaths and curses directed against her and against Joseph, but she had the distinct feeling that William was not so irate as he pretended. She hoped that he was ashamed of himself. But she wasn't sorry that she had shown him for the weakling he was.

◆

People, mostly sisters, came to Emma's door all that day. Some had brought more blankets—which she didn't take—and others had brought food. All of them had words of condolence. Emma was too busy to spend the day hearing endearments that only implied that she was disheartened more than she was. She had been glad to look William in the eye, let him know what she thought of him, and then watch him teeter in response.

It was midafternoon when Emma heard gruff shouting outside again. She thought for a moment that McLellin had returned, but it was a different voice.

"I've come to pay a visit. I'll even preach a sermon if you like," the man bellowed.

Emma decided not to respond. She turned to Joey, who had been nervous all day. He had been sitting on the floor with Freddie, trying to entertain him, but now he was looking up at her. "Don't say anything," he told her.

Julia had been washing kitchen items that had been scattered on the floor, but now she turned to Emma. "Yes, Mama, don't listen to him. It doesn't matter what he says."

Emma went about her business. But the voice continued.

"Some of us is going to ride down to Liberty and pay a visit to Old Joe. Got anything you want us to tell him before we hang him from a tree?"

She took a step toward the door and Joey said, "No, Mama. He'll hurt you."

But that only fired her anger. "He *can't* hurt me, Joey. He's too much of a coward for that." She opened the door.

A big man in a dilapidated brown hat and a rough buckskin coat was sitting atop a horse. He grinned at her through gapped and broken teeth. "My friend William told me you was back. He said you insulted him, and that's something I won't stand for. He's about the only Mormon I know who tells the truth about all of what you folks has done to our county. We ain't going to put up with it no more. It's time you get out."

"I suppose you've come here to scare me and my little children," Emma said. "It takes a brave man to come to a woman's home and insult her. I hope you're pleased with yourself."

"I don't care about scaring women and children. I'm just telling you to get out of our state, and do it soon, or we'll come back and burn your house. We ain't putting up no more with you murdering our people and stealing our property. Anything we took from you is what you owed us."

"Get away from my house."

"No, ma'am, I don't think I will. I'm thinking I'll move my

wife and children into this place. It's right nice the way you got it all fixed up. And you won't need it anyhow once we kill Joe."

Emma knew she had made a mistake to come to the door. Behind her, Julia insisted, "Don't talk to him, Mama. Come back in the house."

But Emma wasn't going to let the brute win. She found herself saying, "You make me sick. You're the lowest of human beings—if you are indeed human. But you don't scare me. I've met other cowards like you before. If I had a gun to point at you, you would turn tail and run."

The man reached with his right hand—the one away from Emma—and he pulled his rifle from its holster. He slowly brought it across his body until it was pointing at her.

"You talk like you're a man, Mrs. Smith. You think you can call me names and get away with it. But it don't work that way. Tell me you're sorry right now or I'll shoot you right here in front of that kid back there."

Joey must have come to the door too, but Emma didn't look back. "My, my, you are a brave man."

He pulled the hammer back on the rifle. "Tell me you're sorry for the things you just said. Either that or I'll pull this trigger."

"You do that. Show what a brave man you are. Shoot me right now. I won't flinch." Emma could see rage in the tightness of his face. It crossed her mind that she had made him angry enough that he really might shoot her. But she didn't apologize, didn't look away. "Go ahead. Pull the trigger. I'm waiting."

But now she could see that he couldn't do it. His eyes drifted away from hers. "This ain't over," he said. "I won't shoot a woman. But I'll kill your husband. That's a promise."

He turned his horse and then flipped the reins. The horse trotted away.

It was only when the man was gone that Emma realized she was not so brave as she wanted to be. She was shaking and not sure she hadn't taken too great a chance.

Behind her, Joey was crying. Julia had her arm around his shoulders, but she was staring at Emma. "Why did you say that, Mama?" she asked. "I thought he was going to shoot you."

Emma worried that she had frightened her children more than she should have, but she told them, "Don't let a man like that scare you. He didn't have the nerve to pull the trigger."

"He said he's going to kill Papa," Joey said, and now he was crying harder.

Emma stepped to him, took him in her arms, and then pulled Julia close as well. "I'm sorry," she said. "You're right. I shouldn't have said those things."

As she held her children, she couldn't stop thinking of the man's threats. There were a lot of men vowing they would kill Joseph, and it would only take one of them to prove his "manhood" by doing it.

CHAPTER 9

Christmas in the jail was a day like any other. Church members had visited and brought extra food, even cakes and pies, so the men did have a feast of sorts. But Caleb thought of his children all day, and he assumed the other men, who remained mostly quiet, were preoccupied with similar thoughts.

Joseph especially seemed distant. He spent much of the day in the upper room with his dog sleeping next to him. Caleb assumed that he was contemplating, but if he was learning anything, he didn't speak of it, and Caleb saw little indication that the prophet was finding solace in his silence. At times like this, he seemed to Caleb like an injured man trying to recover from an accident or illness and only partially aware of all that was going on around him.

And yet, in the following days there were times when he tried to be himself. One morning in January, the men were still eating their breakfast when they heard a racket outside. It only took a moment to realize that it was the usual thing: a pack of boys shouting insults.

"You Mormons is a pack of thieves," they yelled. "You'll all die and go to the devil. And that's just what you've got coming to you."

Caleb wondered what the boys had heard about the Saints, and who had taught them all the nonsense they hurled at the prisoners.

They surely knew nothing of the Church and its teachings. But they were more persistent than usual that morning. It was warmer than it had been lately, and maybe they were enjoying their time outside.

"Hey, Joe, come out of that jail! We want to kill you," one big voice kept hollering. "I'll fight you and bust your skull."

Joseph was sitting at the table across from Caleb. He looked up and smiled with a bit of mischief in his eyes, perhaps finding the taunt silly. When he had finished his breakfast, he walked to the window—a small, barred opening that only a tall man could see through. He looked down on the boys and called out, "Here I am—the man you hate so much. It's very nice to see you boys. How are you feeling today?"

The abuse suddenly became wilder.

"Come out and fight me," that stronger voice was yelling. "I'll send you to hell."

Joseph shouted back, "I'd like to fight you, young man. That would be good sport. But Mr. Tillery won't let me out."

The boys seemed joyous to receive a response. "I'll talk to Tillery," the boy yelled. "I'll get you turned out."

"I'm not so sure I'm brave enough to come out there," Joseph called. "I fear you could best me. But what about this?" He turned and called, "Major, here, boy. Here, boy."

Major loped over from his spot behind the stove and jumped up to put his paws against Joseph's chest.

"What about this, my friend? Would you like to fight my little dog? I'll send him out right now." He slapped Major on his big shoulder and said, "Ho, boy. Ho, boy."

Major let out a loud howl and then barked excitedly, his deep tones leaving no doubt how big he was.

"He's ready to come out now. Just wait while I get the jailer to open the door." Joseph watched for a moment and then broke into a big laugh. "They're scattering like a flock of chickens with a fox after them."

Major shuffled about excitedly and continued to bark.

"Too bad, boy," Joseph said, still laughing. "They don't want to fight you. I don't know why."

Caleb laughed harder than he had in two months. And all the other men laughed too, even Sidney.

Joseph looked at Alexander and said, "I know. I know. I've gone too far again. I've proclaimed war when I shouldn't."

"Quite all right," Alexander said. "I think we should get Major to fight all our battles for us. We might keep these Missouri rascals on the run."

Joseph petted Major, talking softly to him to calm him. But then he looked around the room and his countenance grew serious again. "I'm sorry, my friends."

"Sorry for what?" Hyrum asked.

"I haven't said much lately. I know you wonder what I'm thinking."

No one spoke. Caleb was moved by Joseph's concern, his admission, but he didn't want to admit that he was troubled by the detachment he had been feeling from Joseph these last few weeks. He had said so little to the other men, other than when visitors were there, and that had never been Joseph's way before now.

"I've been busy all my life," Joseph said, "and the Lord has always prodded me, let me know what I needed to do. But now I feel unneeded. Forgotten. Maybe you feel the same way."

"It's different for you," Alexander said. "We hate these days too, but not so much is expected of us."

Joseph nodded, but then he said, "Still, we've all been called. And this jail has stolen away our chance to serve." He looked down for a time, patted Major's head. "I feel lonely. I miss my family. I miss the members of the Church. But I do need this time. I still have much to think about, much to learn about myself, and much to reconcile with what's happened to us and to the Church." He hesitated for a moment and then added, "I wish I could say we'll leave this place soon, but I don't know that. I fear that I need more time—and that becomes a burden to all of you."

No one answered. But Caleb was relieved to know the prophet was using his time, not just withdrawing into himself out of discouragement or self-pity. Caleb often wondered now what would happen to the Church, whether Zion was lost, and where the Saints would end up if they were forced from Missouri. He had waited for Joseph to offer answers, but when the men posed such questions, Joseph had not been forthcoming—as though he didn't know himself.

◆

The days after that were mostly dark and heavy. Caleb tried to fight against the bleakness by reading from his scriptures and by pacing about to stimulate his body and not allow his leg muscles to lose strength. Church leaders, family members, lawyers for the defense, all came to visit or discuss various issues, and always, they tried to bring reassurance. One hope was that the lawyers might bring a writ of habeas corpus before a Clay County judge. The writ would probably not speed up the date of their trial, but would give them a chance of obtaining release on bail so that the men could return to their families as they awaited their day in court. Alexander Doniphan and other lawyers reported, however, nothing but delays and inaction in response to their entreaties. They expressed no optimism for anything to happen soon.

On January 16, Joseph dictated a letter to Brigham Young and Heber C. Kimball. Caleb was relieved to hear the somewhat more cheerful tone of Joseph's letter. But he was confused when Joseph said to the members, "It is not wisdom for you to go out of Caldwell with your families yet for a little season, until we are out of prison, after which time you may act your pleasure."

That suggested that Joseph thought the men might be allowed to leave the jail soon, but Caleb wondered why it wouldn't be better for the members to accept the reality that they had to leave Missouri. That seemed the only way to avoid the attacks that would surely occur if they didn't at least show preparations for an exodus.

Joseph did add direction to the apostles, words that allowed for a departure, if necessary: "Though you take your families out of the state, yet it will be necessary for you to return and leave as before designed on the 26th of April."

Caleb knew about the revelation that Joseph had received the previous April. He had called the Twelve to depart on missions "over the great waters," and to leave one year from that day. While in Richmond, some of the guards who harassed the Mormon prisoners had known of this revelation—had probably learned about it from the dissidents who had turned against the Church—and had taunted Joseph about this mission call, claiming it was one prophecy that would never be carried out. Surely Joseph wanted to prove his detractors wrong, but Caleb also knew that Joseph wouldn't put the apostles in danger merely out of pride. The Lord had spoken, and Joseph meant to follow his command.

The prophet continued his letter and directed changes to the leadership of the Church: "We nominate George A. Smith and Lyman Sherman to take the place of Orson Hyde and Thomas B.

Marsh," he said. He also instructed that Brigham Young serve as the President of the Twelve.

These words heartened Caleb. It was obvious that in Joseph's quiet hours, he was thinking about the future, trusting that the Church would go forward. And yet, another thought crossed Caleb's mind: Joseph might be strengthening the Quorum of the Twelve to prepare his apostles to lead the Church after he was gone.

◆

A few days later, after returning to the lower room in the evening, Caleb began to feel sick. He often noticed uneasiness in his bowels after eating the food that Tillery or one of the other jailers brought, but this was something more, and it came on fast after he had discerned the first discomfort. He thought that he might have to vomit, but as he was asking himself whether he would actually need to do that, Sidney rolled out of his bedding and began to crawl toward the bucket in the corner that was closest to where Alexander slept. He didn't make it to the corner, however, and with a moan and then a gasp, he hunched his back and retched. Caleb heard the puke gush into the straw.

The acrid smell struck Caleb within seconds, and that was more than he could stand. He got up and hurried to the other bucket, the one closer to Joseph. He made it there, and vomited, but then the nausea returned in surges, time and again. It wasn't long before Hyrum tried to reach the same bucket and his shoulder pushed against Caleb's. He missed his target and accidentally nudged Caleb aside so that when Caleb vomited again, he missed the bucket on the other side.

"What's happening?" Alexander asked. "What's made you all so sick?"

But he was the only one who needed to ask. Joseph and Lyman didn't seem quite so pressed to get to the buckets, but Joseph had crawled near to Caleb and Hyrum, and when Caleb realized Joseph was there, he moved out of the way. At the other end of the room, mostly hidden in shadows, Lyman was heaving noisily.

Caleb started to return to his bed, but the smell by then was so overpowering that he turned back. Before he could get to the bucket, however, he gagged. He hunched, waited, but nothing came up. He decided there was nothing more in him, so he turned again and crawled to his side of the room. He didn't want to foul his own bedding, but he lay down, curled himself up, and hoped that the nausea would soon leave him. At both ends of the dungeon, men were still retching, and the stink was overpowering.

The next hour was as horrible as anything Caleb had ever experienced. His insides cramped, his muscles ached, his head seemed to swell. The vomiting was over, but pain was gripping his middle, folding him into a ball. All through the room he could hear moans and sometimes new vomiting. Old Major seemed to understand the danger to Joseph and made a moaning sound himself.

At some point Alexander, who was still not sick, walked to the slice of a window on the west side of the room and shouted for help. "Tillery, are you there? Is someone there? We're sick down here." He repeated the call over and over, but no one answered.

"They've poisoned us," Lyman said. "They've put something in our food. They won't come. They'll wait for us to die."

"I ate the same food," Alexander said. But then he added, "I didn't drink any coffee, and all of you did. Something must have been in the coffee."

"They've always wanted to kill us," Lyman gasped. "This is the easiest way for them to do it."

"Tillery wouldn't kill us," Alexander said.

"Don't believe that. And there are others up there who could put something in our food—or in our coffee, if that's where it was."

Caleb was also quite certain that he had been poisoned. It didn't seem possible that he could stay alive much longer. But he was too sick to care very much.

Alexander continued to shout through the window until finally the trapdoor opened above. Light from a candle filtered into the dark room. A voice above said, "What's going on? What's that smell?"

"We're sick," Alexander said. "We need help. Let us climb the ladder and get out of here."

"I can't do that."

"Tillery allows us to come up there."

"He's the one who told me not to open this door all night—no matter what you said."

Major was barking now, as though to make his own protest.

Alexander began, "You can't leave us down here in all this . . ." But he stopped, as though he knew he wouldn't win the argument. "Can you at least get me a pail of water and some soap?"

The man didn't answer.

"There can't be anything wrong with that."

Joseph had gotten up and Caleb glimpsed him standing at the foot of the ladder. "Young man, you surely must feel sympathy for men who are deathly ill. You can tell by the smell that we've been vomiting. Will you—"

"I can't let you come up. If you start climbing, I'll shut this door."

"That's all right," Joseph said. "Could you get us water and soap? Plenty of it?"

"I guess I can do that," the man said, and then he shut the door.

He did return after a time, and he brought a pail of water that he then replenished three times. Caleb lay on his bed as Alexander moved around the room, washing up as best he could. At one point, he passed the honey buckets up to the young man, who let out a stream of profanity in his disgust. The smell gradually dissipated, replaced in part by the strong odor of lye soap, but none of that changed how Caleb felt. He told the Lord that he was ready to accept his will, even if death was coming, but he asked, above all, that his family might be looked after.

◆

As it turned out, the men did survive the night and the following few days, but it took that long for them to recover. They all felt certain that they had been poisoned and that whatever the poison had been, it had not been quite strong enough to kill them—either that, or the Lord had guarded them from the worst of it by helping them throw up the poison before it took full effect.

Caleb wanted to believe the Lord had been with them, and that's why they were still alive, but he felt broken. It had taken the full three days before he had been able to hold down food, and the loss of nourishment had stolen his strength. However disheartened he had been by the sameness of his life, this new test had cast him down as never before.

Caleb had hoped that he was growing spiritually, using his time in jail to good purpose, but now he only felt numb and debilitated. What bothered him almost as much was to see the loss of energy in all of the men, as though talking, or even thinking, was too much to expect of each other. He had feared hopelessness before, but without putting his thoughts into words, a new awareness had taken over: he really was abandoned. All his prayers had been ignored. He knew he ought to be grateful to be alive, and he did try to trust in that thought, but what he felt more powerfully was that the Lord had not yet finished his chastening, and he wasn't sure he could pass whatever tests might lie ahead.

◆

Caleb's despair continued another day. When the men were permitted to climb to the upper room the morning after that— four men helping to get Sidney up the ladder—everyone ate what they could and said very little. But after a jailer had cleared the pots and metal plates, Joseph stood up from the table and said, "There's something I need to say this morning."

Caleb heard the change in Joseph's voice. He spoke softly, but with a confidence Caleb hadn't heard for quite some time.

"I thought I was dying a few nights ago, the same as you. I accepted death and felt certain that's what the Lord intended. I concluded that the Lord needed to remove me and put someone else in my place."

Caleb watched Joseph breathe deep and then straighten. All the men were looking toward him, even Sidney, who was curled up by the stove.

"When I made it through the first night, and then the second, and started to think that I would live, I turned to God as never before. God has not spoken to me here in this place, and I've felt alone, but I've now begun to commune with the Lord again. I can feel him with me."

Caleb drew in a long breath and felt his chest—and maybe his soul—take life again.

"I don't have all the answers I want," Joseph said. "And I don't know how long we must stay here, but I do know the Lord hasn't given up on me. Power is flowing back to me, and I want to share my new strength with you. Please, let me bless each one of you."

Caleb looked around to see that Hyrum was shedding tears, and all the men looked changed, enlivened.

So Joseph knelt first by Sidney and asked the others to join with him in placing their hands on his head. He blessed Sidney that he would recover and eventually return to his family.

Joseph had the others come to a chair that he turned away from the table, and he called Hyrum first, and then Alexander, Lyman, and finally Caleb to take a seat, again with the others joining the circle. He blessed Caleb, invoking the power of the priesthood, that he would see many days of life yet, and that he would see his children grow and produce a mighty progeny. He promised Caleb that he would learn much from this test of his faith. He would in future days, Joseph said, use what he was learning to bless his family and the Church.

By the time Joseph and the others said, "Amen," Caleb felt his chest fill up, as though his spirit was pressing to expand itself.

CHAPTER 10

Emma was frighteningly cold. She was making the two-day trip to Liberty once again, this time with her sister-in-law Mary and with Mary's sister, Mercy. Mary had received letters from Hyrum, who had told her how deeply he longed for her to visit him. He wanted to have some time with her, and he wanted to meet his little son.

Many of the sisters in Far West had told Mary that it was too soon for her to travel, but she admitted to Emma that she feared that if she didn't make the trip, she might never see Hyrum alive again and their son would not receive a blessing from his father. So Emma asked Don Carlos, brother to Hyrum and Joseph, to carry them in his wagon, and asked Mercy to go along to help Mary. Mercy was also a nursing a baby, so her little Mary Jane had to come along, and Joseph III was also to make the trip again.

But travel had proven more difficult than Emma's previous trips, with snow on the ground and extreme temperatures. The women had bundled themselves and their babies in all the blankets they had been able to gather, and Joey had huddled close to Emma. They had stayed overnight with a family in a warm house, and only that had kept them from turning back. By the time they reached the jail, they felt frozen. Emma was worried about Mary, who looked pale, her face almost blue. Her little son, not yet three months old, had fussed a good deal the first day, but he had gradually become alarmingly silent. When Emma held him for a time, he hardly moved. She really wondered whether the trip had been too much for him. She couldn't imagine anything more terrible than to lose him on his way to be with his father for the first time.

"Heavenly Father," Emma prayed as she held him, "please sustain this tiny soul. Bless him to live and thrive and carry on the work of the kingdom."

But when the wagon stopped at the jail, she noticed little life in him. What made things worse was that a pocket of men gathered near the jail as the women were getting down from the wagon.

The men recognized Emma, and whether they knew who Mary was or not, they started in with their usual insults. One hefty man in a shabby blanket coat called out, "We hear that Old Joe is fixing to break out. Tell him to try it now. We'll finish him off and save you having to come so far again."

Don Carlos jumped down from the front of the wagon. "Say one more word like that and I'll grab your heart right out of your chest," he said, and he walked toward the man.

All the men were grinning. They didn't back away. But Sam Tillery walked around the corner of the jail and said, "That's enough, boys. You talk big, but I'll tell you something. Not one of you could last a full minute fighting Joseph Smith."

The men grumbled, but they dispersed.

Tillery said, "Good afternoon, Mrs. Smith. You look cold. Let's get all of you inside. The men are in the upper room."

So the women took their children while Don Carlos dealt with the horses and wagon. Emma carried Mary's baby and helped Mary up the stairs, but after Tillery opened the door, Emma handed the little one back to her and said, "You walk in first."

Emma also let Mercy go in with her baby and waited a moment with Joey as Hyrum and Mary reunited.

"Mary," she heard Hyrum say, "you've come."

As Emma stepped inside, Hyrum was still embracing Mary with the baby between them.

Mary stepped back and said, "Take him, Hyrum. See what a beautiful boy he is." Then, obviously weak, she sat on one of the chairs by the table.

Hyrum did take the baby and looked carefully at his face. "He *is* beautiful," he said. "But is he all right?"

"He's very cold."

By then Major had vacated the back of the stove and charged toward Joey. He thrust his big head against Joey's middle, and Joey had to catch his balance not to fall. He patted and petted the big dog, then wrapped his arms around his neck.

Joseph greeted Mercy and Mary, then pulled Major back and knelt by Joey and took him in his arms. "You've had a hard trip. I can feel how cold you are." He stood and embraced Emma. "I'm so glad you could come back. We've all been sick. But we're doing better now, and seeing you lifts my spirit even higher." He turned. "And look at Hyrum. This is what he's needed."

Caleb, from across the room, said, "I can feel the cold from your clothing all the way over here. Come to the stove, all of you. You need to thaw." Mary and Mercy moved toward the fire. Hyrum carried his son to the stove too, knelt, and reached out to hold him close. Joseph took Emma's hand and led Emma closer, but she held back. She was cold, but she would warm soon enough. The babies were the ones who needed attention.

In a few minutes Don Carlos knocked on the door and Tillery let him in. Emma could see that Joseph was surprised. He grabbed his brother and held him in his arms.

When Don Carlos stepped back, he said, "I'm happy to see you, Joseph. But I hate to tell you, you're not much to look at."

"We all got sick—poisoned, we're thinking. I hope I don't look so bad as the rest of these pitiful fellows. They're all I have to look at, and they don't look good at all."

Emma did see the difference in Joseph. His face was thinner than it had ever been, his cheeks concave and his eyes deep. Even his voice seemed weaker. But Emma thought he was also more energetic than he had been before.

Don Carlos had brought some blankets with him from the wagon. He wrapped one around Emma, then walked to the other women. The blanket was cold for a minute or so, but it soon began to warm Emma. A surge of strength ran through her, and she noticed the same change in Mary and Mercy. Most encouraging was hearing both babies begin to cry.

"They're hungry," she told the women. "That's good. Sit down in these chairs and nurse them." She moved two chairs closer to the stove and then helped the women arrange their dresses and cover themselves with blankets.

Tillery had waited all this time, but now he said, "I'll bring you some supper as soon as I can, but you ladies can plan to stay in this upper room tonight. I don't want you and your babies to get cold all over again." He stepped to the door, but then he turned back and said, "In fact, all of you can stay up here tonight if you have a mind to. There's little comfort with no beds, but you could bring your blankets up and keep the fire stoked."

"We don't want those stinking blankets from the dungeon up here," Lyman said. "I'll sleep on the hard floor and think I'm floating on a cloud."

Joseph was quick to say, "Thank you, Sam. I, for one, will

bring my blankets up, and it will be nice to sleep in a heated room. It's kind of you to bend your rules a little."

Tillery seemed at a loss for words, as though he feared he had sounded too friendly. He nodded a couple of times, and then, without saying anything more, opened the heavy door and stepped from the room.

———◆———

The next hour was a joy to Emma. The room was crowded, but the men took seats on the floor and let the women use the chairs. Major was still excited. It was all Joseph could do to keep him from overpowering Emma and Joey with his elation—and his tongue.

After Mary nursed her little son, she walked to Hyrum and sat on the floor next to him. He took the baby in one arm and wrapped his other arm around Mary. Emma heard her say, "Oh, Hyrum, you look so tired. Are you sure you're well?"

Hyrum spoke softly. "I'm well enough. But seeing you, seeing our son, all this is almost more joy than I know how to hold inside myself." He looked down for a time, and when he looked up, tears shone on his cheeks. "When I was sick, I was almost certain that I wouldn't live another hour. All I could think was that I needed to see my new son, and I needed, at least once more in my life, to see you."

The room fell silent, everyone clearly moved by Hyrum's emotion. Emma could only think what a tragedy it would have been if the men had died from the poison. What encouraged her was to learn that the men were holding on, not destroyed by their experience. Even more, Joseph seemed more resolute than when she had visited him before Christmas.

Joseph motioned for Joey to come to him. The boy crossed the room and sat on the floor by his father. He tucked his head against Joseph's chest.

"Hyrum, I want you to bless our son," Mary said. "That's the reason we braved the cold to be here. It's what you said you wanted to do in your letter. The poor little fellow needs a name."

Supper arrived soon after that, but later, when all was cleared away, Hyrum said, "I want to perfrom the blessing now, and I would like all you brothers to join with me." He stood up and took the baby from Mary. As the others approached, he looked down at Mary and asked, "Have you thought of a name?"

"Yes. But I want you to find the right name in your own heart—one the Lord gives you."

"What if it's different from the one you have in mind?"

"That's all right. Let's let the Lord choose."

So the men gathered in a circle, their shoulders touching, and all reached to place hands under the baby. Hyrum evoked the power of the priesthood and said that they were encircled around the child to give him a name and a blessing. But then he waited, and Emma knew he was listening for inspiration. "And the name chosen for you is Joseph Fielding Smith."

Emma felt the rightness of the name and the power of the moment: such an innocent little thing receiving a Spirit-inspired gift in the midst of a squalid jail.

"This is a noble name," Hyrum pronounced. "Joseph is the name of uncles on both sides of our family. And the names Fielding and Smith connect the lines of our family heritage. Lord, grant this our son the spirit and nobility to live up to such names. Grant him the power to lead forth in carrying out thy work all the days of his life."

When Hyrum closed the blessing, he looked down at Mary, who nodded.

"Yes, that was the right name," she said. "I've been calling him Joseph from the beginning, at least in my own mind. But thank you for adding Fielding."

———————◆———————

On the following day, Don Carlos got the wagon and horses ready, and Emma helped Mary and Mercy bundle their babies for the return trip. Hyrum held his son one last time and was clearly sorrowful to see Mary leave so soon. But Emma had agreed with the others that the crowded conditions in the jail made a longer stay too difficult.

Joseph held Emma in his arms a very long time. She felt how thin he was now, but she also sensed more gentleness. But then he laughed, with obvious effort, and said, "Let's not make this too difficult. I'm hoping I'll see you before long in Far West. If our writ of habeas corpus is granted, we could be released on bail. Our lawyers think that might happen."

He turned and rubbed Major's ears. "You go home for now, my friend. I'll see you soon."

Joseph walked toward the door and motioned to Major, who bounded out the doors and down the stairs, obviously cheered to be outside, and surely not understanding that Joseph wasn't coming with him.

As the party walked outside and began to settle themselves under blankets in the back of the wagon, Sheriff Hadley appeared. He shook hands with Don Carlos and greeted the women, but he spoke softly to Emma. "I want you to know that Joseph and the others have changed the way Sam Tillery and the guards and I think of your husband, and I'm hearing from Jefferson City that Governor Boggs, more than anything, wants the Mormons to leave the state. Once you do that, I doubt he'll want to hold Joseph and continue to face the criticism he's receiving from newspapers all across the country."

Emma held onto that prospect, that hope, as she traveled back to Far West. But Joseph had admitted to her that the local judge may not grant their writ, and if he didn't, the men would have to wait until at least March for a hearing and then—finally—a trial. Even though he had tried to be optimistic about the writ, he still advised her that she should leave the state as soon as she could. For the sake of their children, Emma thought that was right, but she hoped she could wait for warmer weather, and she hated to think of leaving while Joseph was still in jail.

The return trip home was better for the women and babies, and for Don Carlos too—partly because the temperature had risen a little, and mostly because they were all basking in the reassurance that they had done the right thing in making the visit and allowing little Joseph Fielding Smith to receive his blessing.

◆

Emma had been home for a few days when a knock came at her door. She was used to women coming by, but this was a firm, persistent rap, and she hesitated to respond. When the knock came again, she peeked out and was taken by surprise to see George Hinkle.

She cracked the door open. "What do *you* want?" she asked.

"My house."

"What do you mean?"

"I sold this house to Bishop Partridge when I moved to DeWitt, and he sold it to Joseph, but I've never received payment for it. I'm sorry, Sister Emma, but it's my house. You're going to have to move out."

Emma knew that George and his family had lived in the house at one time, but she had never heard what the financial arrangements had been for the sale. She opened the door a little wider. "So I'm 'Sister Emma,' am I, and in the same breath, you want to take my house from me?"

"I'm not your enemy, Emma. But right is right, and my family needs a place to live."

"So does mine."

"It's time for all of you people to leave, and it would be better for everyone if you start now. I want to move in as soon as possible."

"So it's 'all of you people,' is it? At least you're admitting the truth now. You turned on Joseph and you've rejected the Church."

"Emma, I know what Joseph might have told you, but it's not true. I didn't betray him. The members here in Far West had no choice but to lay down their arms and leave the state. Joseph understood that and he agreed to the conditions that General Lucas put forth."

"He agreed to meet with Lucas. He didn't agree to be arrested and thrown in jail."

"He knew he couldn't just walk away without being held accountable for—"

"I'm not going to argue with you. And I'm not going to listen to you place the blame on Joseph. You saved yourself and gave up our leaders, and then you testified against the very brethren you had served with."

"I didn't testify *against* anyone. I merely answered the questions I was asked, and I answered honestly."

Emma took in some air, tried to stare George down, but he

met her gaze and didn't flinch. Emma saw him as a fallen angel, a defector, and he clearly had convinced himself otherwise, but all that didn't matter. It was the house that she wasn't ready to give up.

"I suppose you haven't been out to your barn yet," Hinkle said. "While you were gone, I secured part of what Joseph owes me by removing your horse, your gig, and the riggings that go with it. But the house is still mine. I'll give you a day or two to move out, but that's all. You don't want to face the sheriff and his men when they come to dump you out in the street."

Emma tried to stare Hinkle down, but he didn't look away. "And they won't want to face me when I tell them to get off my property."

"That won't matter, Emma. You know it won't. You might as well accept that your days here are almost over. Joseph tried to take on the militia forces of these counties and he lost. There's no turning back from that."

"I'm going to close the door now, George. You've cleaned out my barn, but you haven't cleaned *me* out."

Emma closed the door, and for a few minutes she thought of the fight she would put up before she gave in. But it didn't take long for her to realize the Saints had indeed lost, and Hinkle had found a way to save himself. At least for now, she saw no way to resist his demand.

She turned and looked at Joey, who asked, "Will we have to leave our house?"

She hesitated before admitting, "I don't know. But we'll be strong." All the same, she felt tears on her own cheeks.

It was evening when another knock came, but Emma also heard a voice she knew. "Sister Emma, it's Brigham."

Emma opened the door and Brigham Young stepped inside.

He took off his hat and hesitated as though he didn't know what to say. "I heard what Hinkle's doing," he said.

"Can he take my house?"

"He couldn't if law prevailed in this county. And by all rights, he should be thrown in jail for stealing your horse and gig. But we're powerless now, and there's no judge to take our side on matters like this."

"If I had a rifle, I'd defend myself."

Brigham was holding the brim of his hat with both hands. His strong hands seemed ready to tear the hat into pieces. Emma liked Brigham's directness, and she liked his loyalty to Joseph, but she had often felt that his mannerisms—his speech and his abrupt judgments—were unpolished, less refined than she expected of an apostle, especially one now called to lead the Quorum of the Twelve.

Brigham continued to look down for a time, but then he said, "Sister Emma, it's what I wish I could do. Get a gun and defend you. But we've tried that, and it all came to nothing. We're leaving now. And we're not waiting until spring. Too many forces are against us, and I hate to think what some of these men around here will do if they don't see us moving out. Joseph now agrees, it's what we have to do."

Emma knew all this was true, but she was angry, and she wanted Brigham to call a curse down upon Hinkle and the men who were thieving from her, scaring her children, threatening her husband. She hated the idea of merely acceding to such wickedness.

"For right now," Brigham said, "it might be wise to move in with someone else and—"

"I know. I've thought about all that. I'll take the children to George and Lucinda Harris's house. They've told me I can do that. I don't dare stay here and put my children in further danger."

"Good." Again Brigham looked down. But when he looked up, she saw authority in his face. "Sister Emma, I'm sorry. I'd like to grab Hinkle by the neck and throttle him, and I'd like to take on the whole bunch of these cowards who bother you night and day. But we have to leave—at least for now—and I vow that no one will be left behind. The poor will be cared for, and the widows and the women whose husbands are imprisoned will be assisted in every way. Within the next two or three weeks we're going to start our trek—not as a single camp, but in small wagon trains. And each group will be led by someone who can help those who need assistance."

Emma was moved by Brigham's vow and by the concern she heard in his voice.

"We're getting everything organized. Joseph has asked me and Heber Kimball to lead out, and we've accepted that responsibility. But I promise you, the kingdom will roll forth. Our enemies will not prevail against us—not in the end."

Emma liked Brigham's strong words, and she liked his kindness to her, but it was hard for her to accept the idea that running from the enemy was anything but bitter defeat.

CHAPTER 11

As January neared an end, word finally came that the prisoners would appear before a county judge to make their request for release on bail. Caleb felt a surge of excitement just to know that something was finally going to happen. He knew that the judge was probably not brave enough to release them, but maybe the Lord would finally open a door.

So Caleb prayed. He asked for a miracle. And he tried to exercise his faith fully and purely.

It was clear now that the Saints would have to leave Missouri, and if Caleb and the others were released, they would have to stand trial later. Still, their lawyers were speculating that if the men left the state, Missouri officials would be happy to have the matter closed, and not even Joseph would be extradited for trial. Caleb didn't know whether that would turn out to be true, but he did know that he wanted to assist his family in the move, and then, if he were arrested and brought back for trial, at least he could be with his wife and children when they needed him.

Caleb was also glad to have a day away from the jail, even though the weather was still very cold.

Sidney had not recovered from the illness—or poisoning—he had suffered with the others. It was a great chore to lift him to the upper room when he couldn't help himself. But all the men worked together, and then, when the sheriff and his men arrived at the jail, they brought in a cot, and four men carried him through the streets of Liberty to the county courthouse. Sidney moaned at times, but he had little to say, and Caleb wondered whether it wasn't cruel to make him attend the hearing.

Caleb was concerned when he saw the crowd that had gathered in the little courthouse. They were a rough-looking group—mostly frontier farmers who had extra time in winter. They probably enjoyed an excuse to come into town, imbibe some hard liquor, and then get a look at Joseph. The men—and a few women—mumbled their usual abuse as the prisoners were brought in, but Judge Turnham was a stern man and warned them, "You'll keep quiet, all of you, or I'll clear the court. I want this procedure handled properly."

Caleb didn't know what "proper" was in this setting, but the judge, with little preamble, announced that the hearing had been called to address a writ of habeas corpus, and he asked Alexander Doniphan and Peter Burnett to present their case. They both spoke, and they used plenty of legal terms, but their argument came down to something simple: the prisoners had been confined for three months—almost a month in Richmond and over two months in Liberty—and no specific charges had been brought against them. A strange list of offenses had been mentioned in Richmond: "murder, treason, burglary, arson, larceny, theft, and stealing." Aside from the overlapping meaning of some of the words, no judge or attorney had stated whom they had murdered, in what sense they were traitors, or exactly what they had stolen. Caleb knew that the men in his militia company had carried back provisions from the store in Gallatin, but it could be argued that they had appropriated very little compared to all that had been stolen *from* them. It was the treason charge that had resulted in these particular six men being held over after the court of inquiry in Richmond, and that charge made no sense at all to Caleb.

Doniphan, in his formal but respectful style, simply stated that a person held in jail had a right to know, exactly, what crimes he was accused of committing so that a defense could be prepared. His other contention was that the prisoners deserved to be released on bail and not confined as they awaited their trial.

Judge Turnham sat stone-faced—sometimes even appearing to pay little attention. No one bothered to speak against the petition, but Caleb was feeling by then that the decision had been reached before the hearing ever started. Still, Judge Turnham did ask whether the prisoners had anything to say.

Doniphan and Burnett had advised the men not to make their own arguments. It was important to present legal opinions, clearly stated, and not bring up complaints about the treatment the men had received. That sort of accusation might perturb a county judge who was likely to side with the local opinion about the case.

But then Sidney Rigdon, still lying on his cot, sat up and announced, "I have something I wish to say."

"Yes, of course," Judge Turnham said. "And what is your name?"

"President Sidney Rigdon of the First Presidency of The Church of Jesus Christ of Latter-day Saints."

"Go ahead. But don't repeat what your lawyers have said. I understand the arguments they've made."

"I have nothing to say in such legal terminology," Sidney said, his voice sounding pinched, even weak. "I wish to make a personal appeal, based on my own experience."

"This is no time to—"

"Just hear me. That's all I ask."

"Go ahead."

Caleb was amazed when Sidney attempted to rise to his feet. Peter Burnett hurried to him and helped him. Once he was on his feet, however, he spread his legs, took a firm stance, and let go of his helper. He breathed for a time, gathered himself, then said, "Judge Turnham, I am a man of God. I've given my life and my will over to Jesus Christ, and I've tried all the days of my life to follow his teachings and preach his gospel in its purest form. I was a Baptist minister, but I was also a truth seeker, so I listened to many proponents of differing denominations. And then I had the honor of meeting Joseph Smith, the prophet, and I became convinced that he was indeed called of God."

"Mr. Rigdon, I'm sorry, but all that has nothing to do with the writ before us. No one doubts that you accept Mr. Smith and his . . . *claims.*"

"That's only to explain myself a little; it's not the main point I wish to make."

Caleb was surprised to hear Sidney's strong voice emerging.

"My theme is this," Sidney said. "Since I accepted the true, restored Church of Christ, I have been mistreated and abused for eight years and more. In Ohio, I was pulled from my house, beaten, tarred and feathered and dragged across frozen ground as my head pounded the earth with every step. I came close to dying that night and was delirious and fevered for many months. My health has never entirely recovered. I—"

"That's too bad, Mr. Rigdon, but we're here today—"

"I know why we're here, and you must let me finish." Without permission from the judge, he continued, and now he was standing straighter, even gesturing with his arms. "I came to this state and stopped in DeWitt, in Carol County. As it turned out, I walked into the fires of hell. My brothers and sisters had established themselves among the people of that town and hoped to live peaceably, but local citizens would not hear of our making a home there. A cannon was brought in to bombard us. Our cattle were shot and left in the streets, our homes destroyed, and our people beaten, even gunned down. We tried to negotiate a peace, but the people of Missouri had decided we were not welcome even though we had done nothing to any of them. We were surrounded and cut off from food supplies, so when a hog or steer wandered in among us—sent from God, we felt—we did slaughter those animals. And now we're accused of theft, but *everything* was taken from us, our farms destroyed, our herds and flocks run off."

Caleb heard some mumbling from the crowd behind him, but it was less boisterous than he would have expected, and Judge Turnham silenced the noise by striking his gavel and staring firmly at the offenders. What surprised Caleb even more was that the judge allowed Sidney to continue.

"So we complied with demands, gave up our farms and property, and we fled the city. As I was forced to march, posthaste, out of DeWitt, my frail health broke and I suffered for many days after we reached Caldwell County.

"In Far West we sought nothing more than to live among the people of this state, practice our religion, sow crops, raise families, and follow, to the best of our ability, the teachings of our Lord and Savior. Our people had been promised that if they left Carroll Country and moved on to Caldwell County, they would be allowed to live in peace. But the promise was soon broken. The heinous depredations began again. We were insulted and harassed, warned that we must leave or die. Our houses were torn down and burned, our fences destroyed, our cattle killed or stolen. When the state government called out militias, supposedly to defend us, the generals themselves—one of them General Alexander Doniphan, with us here today—informed us that many of their soldiers were on the side of the mobs that wanted to drive us away. And so we finally engaged in the battle, only in our defense. Rumors of mobs coming from the south reached us in Far West, then word came that some of our brothers had been taken captive. A group of our men rode out to release them. They met a mob that pretended to be a militia at the Crooked River and gunshots were fired. Men on both sides died, and now we're accused of attacking a militia, and thus, murder and treason."

Sidney paused to catch his breath, or maybe to let his words take effect. Caleb was amazed that the people in the crowded room were attentive and didn't seem offended. Sidney's sincerity and fluency seemed to have reached them. The Spirit was with Sidney and Caleb felt it, but more amazingly, he could see that the rough characters in the room were feeling it too.

"But Judge Turnham, this was a rabble, as far as we knew," Sidney said. "Nothing about these people would have signified that they were representing the government of the state or nation. Our people were merely—"

"Mr. Rigdon, you're arguing your case. And you will have every right to do that at the time of your trial. Today, the issue is—"

"I know the issue, sir. I also know that I'm a patriot, not a traitor." Sidney's voice thundered through the room, and everyone, even the judge, seemed silenced by the force of it.

"I don't belong in jail. And if I'm kept in jail much longer, I will not survive. I was sick in bed on the day of the conflict at the Crooked River. I was in Far West on the day that a battle ensued in Gallatin, in Daviess County. So I ask you, what is it that I have done? I have committed no treason, no murder, and yet, because of my faith—and for no other reason—I have been imprisoned in your city. I sleep at night in a room so cold that I shake until my bones rattle. In Richmond, I was chained to other men for three weeks and abused verbally and physically, but even worse is what I am forced do now: lie on a floor covered in stinking straw and try to sleep in those conditions night after night while I wait to know what it is I have done to deserve all this. I have tried all my life to be a decent, God-fearing man. I have committed no offense to the people of this state."

Sidney finally wobbled a little. He shuffled his feet to catch his balance. Caleb was certain that he had spent all his strength. Peter Burnett took hold of him again and then whispered something that Caleb couldn't hear.

But Sidney, his voice now edging toward a breakdown of emotion, said, "I am not a young man, Judge, and yet I appear much older than I am. Still, I hope for productive days ahead—days in which I plan to do much good in this world. But if you leave me in that jail, I won't last much longer. In recent days we were poisoned—I'm sure of it. I'm trying to regain my strength, but I see little hope without being allowed to go free. So I appeal to you, let me go home to my wife and family, where I can sleep in a bed and be fed and watched over by those who love me. And then I will stand trial and, no doubt, be exonerated." Finally, Sidney's strength gave way entirely. Burnett held him up as best he could but then let him slump back to the cot.

What Caleb saw around the room astounded him. Every man in the place had clearly been moved by Sidney's passion—especially his final words. Caleb actually saw men with tears in their eyes.

Sidney's ill health was real, not something he was inventing for the sake of effect. And Caleb did fear that if Sidney stayed in jail much longer, he *would* perish. All the same, he knew that Sidney's argument would not help the other accused men. He forgave Sidney for making such a personal argument, but he found himself giving up on his hope that all the men would be released.

Judge Turnham seemed as emotionally stirred as everyone else in the room. After Sidney had curled up on his cot, his breath coming hard, the judge said, "I'm going to release Mr. Rigdon on a bail of one hundred dollars. That may give him time to recover somewhat before a trial. As for you others, considering the serious nature of the crimes you are accused of, I do not find sufficient grounds to grant you release."

"Sir, could we at least ask you to move up the trial date?" Alexander Doniphan asked. "These other men also deserve the opportunity to face their accusers and not languish in jail any longer."

"I have no power over that, Mr. Doniphan. These men were confined here because there's no jail in Daviess County, but the trial will move forward at the discretion of officials there."

"Would it be possible for you to—"

"No, sir."

"I understand." Doniphan looked at the floor for a moment and seemed to accept the judge's edict, but he did say, "Judge Turnham, Mr. Rigdon does not have one hundred dollars. It might take some time to raise a figure like that. And that won't be good for his health. Could you—"

A strong voice from the back of the room broke through. "I got ten dollars right here in my pocket. Mr. Rigdon needs to be let out of our jail. Who else will put something in my hat so we can get the man released?"

Caleb was astounded. He had never imagined such a reaction. But others said they would help, and men moved forward and dropped coins or notes into the hat. Within only a couple of minutes, the big fellow, hat in hand, said, "I still need fifteen dollars. Who else can help us?"

It was Peter Burnett who finished off the fundraising, and then the man passing the hat brought the money forward and dumped it on the table where the clerk of the court sat. "All right then," the judge said. "Mr. Rigdon, you may go free whenever you're ready to travel."

But that was the problem. Sidney had no way to convey himself, and it would take a while to get word to Far West to send a wagon.

Lyman Wight was standing next to Caleb, and he spoke lowly when he said, "It's not just being ready to travel. Not everybody around here heard that speech of his. The minute he walks out of the jail with no guard, there's some who will want to shoot him down."

———————◆———————

Sidney had to be carried again to return to the jail, and after they arrived, he expressed some of the same concerns. But his imminent release seemed to lift more than his spirits; Caleb watched him gain strength with each day. Before his departure could be worked out, however, ten days had passed.

A friend with a wagon eventually brought Phebe to the jail, and Sheriff Hadley escorted her inside. After supper that evening, the men put out all but one of the candles in the room as they had planned. Men had been watching the jail since the time of Sidney's announced release, and for Sidney and his wife to leave safely, the men needed to be avoided.

Sheriff Hadley and Sidney walked out of the jail together and climbed down the stairs. When Hadley came back inside, he said, "I warned those men outside to stay back, and I walked past them and out into the woods. When I got Sidney out into the dark, I shook his hand and wished him well, and he's on his way to meet up with the man who's going to carry him back to Far West." Caleb was relieved to know Sidney had made it that far, but he hoped that none of the locals would go out searching for him.

"What about me?" Phebe asked.

"Just wait a little."

Several minutes passed before a knock came at the outer door and a man stepped in far enough to say, "Phebe, come with me. Hurry."

The five remaining prisoners were silent for quite some time as they listened for shots to be fired or for evidence of mobs outside being riled up. But they heard nothing.

"Well, I guess he got away," Lyman said after a time. "I won't have to listen to him complain no more."

"Sidney *needed* to be released," Joseph said. "More than the rest of us—and the Lord opened the way. Let's not speak ill of him now."

"But he only told how bad off *he* was. He never bothered to—"

"Lyman, let it go."

"All right. I understand." Lyman ducked his head and let the moment pass.

"The Lord touched the hearts of those men in the courtroom," Joseph said. "There's no other explanation for such a miracle. Let's concentrate on that and take joy in it."

"The Lord will do the same for all of us," Hyrum said.

Caleb expected a quick response from the prophet, but Joseph took his time before he said, "God is going to do what is best for each of us—and also for the Church. What we have to do is accept the Lord's will. I've accepted that lesson now."

Caleb liked Joseph's humble acceptance. It had not been easy for Caleb to bring himself to the same place. He had believed that somehow a miracle could happen during the hearing, but he had prayed for all the men, not just Sidney. And yet, he knew that

Joseph was right: he could see now that the Lord's will had been done—and he could trust that the other men were not forgotten.

—◆—

The prisoners didn't hear anything of the Rigdons for a few days. But a visitor from Far West later reported on what had happened.

Sidney had walked into the woods and seen no one at first, but then he had heard a voice behind him. He had spun around and made ready to defend himself. As it turned out, however, the man in the dark was his benefactor. The two slipped through the forested area to the place where a horse and carriage were waiting. Then, at a designated house, they had met Phebe and continued their travel to Far West. They were safe, at least for the present.

CHAPTER 12

After Sidney's release, a dismal quiet returned to the jail. Occasional visitors still came, and that broke the monotony, but as Church members began their migration from the state, fewer were left to make their way to Liberty. Jane Blevens and her daughter, who lived nearby, came to the jail often with cakes and pies, and old friend Porter Rockwell carried messages from Church leaders, but many days were spent alone. The men read their scriptures, but living in dim light and many hours of complete darkness—or of smoke when they built a fire in the dungeon—had affected everyone's sight. Caleb's eyes were not only sore; his vision was often blurred. He found that reading the print in the Book of Mormon his wife had brought him too difficult to sustain more than fifteen or twenty minutes at a time.

Joseph, however, spent many of his daylight hours studying his Bible. He sometimes offered his insights on certain passages, and Caleb could tell that the prophet was trying to deepen his understanding of various principles of the gospel: the priesthood, exaltation, the significance of temple worship. And he continued to mention that he was contemplating his relationship with God. Caleb was encouraged to feel less distance from Joseph: an increased feeling of unspoken brotherhood. But the prophet sat for hours some days, his eyes steady, seeming to envision something beyond the walls around him.

When visitors came, Caleb watched Joseph reappear: the man and prophet Caleb had known in Kirtland and Far West. He would be practical, even cheerful, and he could discuss important decisions about the exodus from Missouri. But after the visits he would return to his contemplation. Caleb didn't mind; he felt that Joseph was deepening himself and seeking direction, and when he did share his thoughts, Caleb could see that his quiet times were well spent.

Sometimes the men looked to Joseph for answers to their own concerns. Alexander asked him one dark afternoon when a steady snowstorm had set in, "What's going to happen to our families?"

Joseph looked back at him, seeming unsure what he was being asked, so Alexander explained: "How many are going to die if they start off across the state and get caught in a storm like this?"

Joseph was sitting at the table with his Bible in front of him. He leaned forward with his elbows on the table and he looked at Alexander. Caleb saw the heaviness in his eyes.

"There are going to be more hard times for us, Alexander," Joseph said. "God is not going to reach down and deliver the Saints. We'll have to exercise faith and prove our convictions."

Alexander had been sitting on the floor, but he stood now, his great height dominating the room, especially as he walked to Joseph and bent toward him far enough that his long red hair fell around his face. "What will it take to prove ourselves, Joseph? What's the Lord waiting for? We pray and pray, and we get no relief."

"That's the question I can't answer." Joseph looked back at Alexander for a time, then glanced around the room at the other men. "I'm sorry, brethren, but I don't know how long we have to wait. But I find myself thinking at times that we have to take our own action and rely on the Lord to help us succeed."

"What do you mean?" Alexander asked.

"It's still only something I'm thinking about. But maybe we have to step forward and assert ourselves, not just sit back and wait." Beyond that, Joseph wouldn't explain.

The words confused Caleb. He had never stopped clinging to the idea that God would soon intercede and release them from the jail. He didn't know what Joseph was suggesting.

Joseph looked around at everyone again, seeming to apologize with his eyes, but he only added, "We need to trust the Lord. It's what Hyrum keeps telling us. But he may inspire us to use our own abilities to accomplish what we've been asking for."

———◆———

One morning, a few days later, Sam Tillery told the men, "There's talk in town that you fellas have to be dealt with . . . if you know what I mean. They have it in their heads that the courts won't do it."

Hyrum said, "Sheriff Hadley told us that the governor wants to get rid of us. He claimed that holding us was becoming an embarrassment—because of what newspapers are publishing. Do you think that's right?"

"That might be the way the people over in Jefferson City are thinking, but around here, folks worry that nothing will happen to you. They've got it in their heads that you killed a thousand people, and all kinds of crazy things. They say they won't be satisfied until you men—especially Joseph—are dead and buried."

Caleb watched Joseph, who appeared to be interested but calm.

"So what are you telling us, Sam? Why do you want us to know about these threats?"

"I'm just saying, that's the talk. I ain't letting them in, or nothing like that, but they might shoot me or some of the other jailers to get in here."

"And what can we do about that?"

"Can't Mr. Doniphan and those other lawyers get you out of here and up to Daviess County in front of a judge? You'll have a better chance that way than to have these Liberty men break in here with their guns."

"But you don't think we have much of a chance either way, do you?"

"I'm not saying that. I don't—"

"Tell us the truth. You think we're set to die, don't you?"

Tillery shifted a little, looked away. "I'm not the one to say, Joseph. Sheriff Hadley says to watch for an attack on the jail, and not to let a mob get in, and that's what I'll do." He hesitated, but then he added, "If I can. But the sooner you're out of here, the better for all of us."

"What will you do if they point a gun at you, Sam?"

Tillery didn't answer. He might have shrugged. But then he stepped to the table and picked up the tin plates he had stacked together. "We'll be in danger," he finally said. "I guess the only thing is to tell your lawyers what I've said. Or find some other way . . . to end your time here."

Tillery left, but as soon as he was gone, Alexander said, "He's trying to tell us to break out, don't you think?"

Caleb had the same impression, and he had begun to think Joseph was contemplating an escape. "Maybe he was saying he wouldn't stop us, if we did," Caleb said.

Joseph and Hyrum were still sitting at the table, as was Caleb. Alexander and Lyman were sitting on the floor close to the stove.

"How would we do it?" Lyman asked. "Tillery talks like he's our friend now, but I still remember what he said to us when we first came in this place. I think he'd shoot us, the same as the others, just so the town wouldn't be after him for letting us get away. And anyhow, how could we ever get out of here?"

"I think I know," Joseph said. "I've observed something lately. The jailer who's brought us supper the last few days doesn't take much care. When he unlocks the door and starts to leave, we could grab him, hold him, and then make a run for it. I don't think he would even try to stop us. Maybe that's what Sam was trying to tell us."

"I don't know, Joseph," Lyman said. "We'd be sitting ducks outside. The men who want to gun us down would have a good excuse."

It was a bright day, February 7, but still very cold outside. Caleb worried about the danger of breaking out of the prison only to face the weather, with snow on the ground and no way to travel fast. But he hated the idea of waiting to be shot down like animals in a cage.

Joseph folded his arms across his chest, leaned back a little. "If we stay here and those same men come in after us, we couldn't protect ourselves."

"If we break out," Hyrum said, "I think the Lord will be with us. He'll help us get away."

"That's what we claimed back in Far West," Lyman said. "We all said the Lord was going to help us fight our battles. Look where that got us."

Alexander suddenly turned toward Lyman. "So what do you prefer?" he grumbled. "Sitting here, waiting to die?"

Hyrum held up his hand before Lyman could answer. Then he looked at Joseph. "Ask the Lord," he said. "If the Lord tells you this is what we should do, then I'm ready."

Joseph nodded. "I will ask. Give me a little time."

Caleb didn't know whether Joseph meant to measure that time in minutes or days, but he decided to move away from the table and leave him to his thoughts. The others did the same, and Joseph sat with his head down, his eyes closed. In only a few minutes, however, he looked up and said, "If we all agree to go tonight, after supper, I'm ready to make the attempt. But we all must go—or no one. And we all must ask the Lord for a testimony that it's the thing to do, so we share the same conviction." He looked around, focusing on each man one at a time. "So pray about it. Receive your own answer. If we're all agreed, we'll go forward with the plan."

Caleb walked to a corner near the door. He didn't kneel. He only wanted to feel alone for a moment. He had just begun to pray, hadn't even formulated his question fully, when he felt the calm he associated with an answer to prayer. He finished his prayer, turned and looked at Joseph, then nodded his assent. He didn't want to say anything out loud until the others had reached their own conclusions.

It was not long, maybe five minutes, before Alexander and Hyrum both said they felt right about going. But Lyman walked over and sat across from Joseph at the table. "Tell me again how we would get out of here?"

"These jailers have gotten used to us. They don't take many precautions. We won't hurt anyone, but we'll wait until the guard, whoever it is tonight, is stepping out. At that point, Alexander can grab and hold him. We'll all rush down the stairs. Then Alexander can push the man back and shut him inside. I honestly don't think the jailers will be eager to chase us down."

"And then what?" Lyman asked. "Do we travel together, or do we scatter in five directions?"

"What do all of you think? What would be best?" Joseph looked around at everyone.

Caleb said, "Five trails are harder to follow than one. We can walk hard and keep going all night to stay warm. Anyone chasing after us might not be willing to keep up the pursuit in the dark and the snow. We don't have horses and they do, but we have surprise on our side. We'll have a head start on any posse that might get organized."

"I'm not saying that our lawyers are going to save our necks," Lyman said. "I doubt they will. But *your* plan looks like suicide to me."

Caleb knew that Lyman had a point, but what better idea did the man have? Sometimes he seemed to oppose the others out of sheer willfulness.

"But it's worth a try," Caleb said. "Especially if we trust in the Lord. We've learned what happens when we rely on the judges in this state."

Lyman took his time. "I don't know," he finally said. "I'm not ready to go tonight. I need some time to think about this and get myself ready. Give me until tomorrow, and if everyone still feels the same, I'll go with you."

That made no sense to Caleb. He had no idea why another day would make any difference, and he was about to say that when Joseph said, "That's fine, Lyman. We all have to have an answer—and feel faith in that answer—or the plan will never work."

Caleb felt uneasy about the decision to wait—and annoyed with Lyman. Still, he was impressed with Joseph's patience.

◆

That evening after supper, the opportunity to make the move was so obvious it was painful for Caleb not to shout to the others, "Let's go." The guard, a man named Harvey, didn't even bother to lock the door while he was waiting for the men to eat. He had a newspaper with him, and he sat down and began to page through it. Caleb wondered whether all this inattention wasn't a way of saying, *Why don't you fellows make a run for it?*

But they didn't, and afterwards Lyman said, "I watched everything and I saw how we could do it. So I'm ready to go tomorrow."

But the next night was entirely different. Harvey brought supper again that evening, but he had a group of visitors with him, men from Far West: Erastus Snow, Cyrus Daniels, and four other brethren. The large group of visitors had prompted Sheriff Hadley to send two more guards with Harvey—maybe so he wouldn't be blamed if the prisoners did break out. The two extra guards had walked in with the other men but then stepped outside the doors. Caleb's first thought was that the large gathering of men who supported the prisoners might be a help in the escape. And they surely had horses to help in their travels.

As the prisoners ate, the purpose of the visit became clear. The brethren had come to explain the plan that had been put in place for the ongoing exodus from the state. Families would travel with whatever means they had, but they would travel in small parties, not in long wagon trains. Anyone without means would be taken care of by those who owned wagons and draft animals.

This was something that Joseph had discussed with Brigham Young and Heber Kimball in recent weeks. It would have been better to wait until spring for travel, but the members needed to get out before they were driven out by force, and families needed

to find a place where they could begin to plant crops and reestab-
lish themselves for the coming growing season. There were men in
Illinois and Iowa Territory who were offering land for sale at reasonable prices, and it seemed better to look into those opportuni-
ties than continue to swim against the stream in Missouri.

As Erastus and the others described the migration, Caleb was
watching Harvey carefully. He had a rifle with him, and the two
guards outside were also carrying weapons.

Caleb had come to the conclusion that the prisoners would
make no move that night, but as Harvey gathered everything up,
Hyrum, who was closest to the door, looked at Joseph and nodded,
and then the other prisoners made little nods of their own. Hyrum
suddenly rushed the door and pulled it wide open. Alexander
grabbed Harvey. Caleb jumped up and charged toward the door,
the others with him. The visitors quickly realized what was happening and rushed for the door as well, Cyrus Daniels making it
outside first.

With the doors open, Caleb could see that Cyrus, a big man,
grabbed the two guards outside before they realized what was
happening, but one of them fought him off and turned back. He
jerked the door out of Hyrum's hands and slammed it shut. That
left everyone but Cyrus and one guard inside, and Harvey had
twisted loose from Alexander and now had his rifle at the ready.

At that moment a gunshot sounded outside. Caleb feared that
Cyrus had been killed.

Harvey demanded that the prisoners move away from the door
and that the visitors file out, one by one. As they did so, Harvey
said, "I never thought you men would try something like that.
We're going to watch you better from now on."

When he told the men to climb down the ladder, they obeyed,
descending into the dungeon without a candle. When Joseph

had reached the bottom, last, the door above them dropped into place—the sound more resounding and final than ever before. Caleb could see nothing—didn't even notice the smells. He felt thrust into a bottomless hole. The blackness was not only in the dungeon but also in his chest.

The prisoners remained standing, didn't move to their places. After a time, Alexander said, "We should have gone last night. We would have had no trouble making it out."

Lyman didn't answer, but finally Joseph did. "We can't say that," he told Alexander. "I believe the Lord was in this. It was still light enough outside that people were out and about. Maybe we would have been caught—or shot down—before we got very far. Let's just trust that this was for the best."

Caleb didn't say it, but it was difficult to believe it could be for the best. How could they all have felt inspired to go, only to be wrong?

Joseph answered the unspoken question: "The Lord knew we needed to make an attempt. But he kept us from getting ourselves killed."

As though in fulfillment of what Joseph had said about people being out and about, the sound of voices began to reach the dungeon. At first, the noise was distant, but before long, there were men standing at the little windows, shouting, howling, threatening.

"You think you can get out of here, do you? We can blow this place up, you know. We got blasting powder to do it with."

"Let's go in after them right now," another man yelled. "Let's horsewhip them until they beg to die."

And there were other threats. One man suggested that they drag the men out, hook up horses to their limbs, and tear their bodies apart.

Caleb said nothing, but he felt the fierceness of the threats.

What was it he had done, he wondered, that could possibly make men want to rip him into pieces? But the image didn't leave his mind: he thought of being torn apart, the blood and pain of it, but even deeper, he felt the raw hatred of the pack of beasts who wanted to devour him.

Alexander said, "Maybe tonight was the wrong night to go, but nothing has changed. These people are going to kill us. And the Lord did tell us to try."

"They won't be satisfied until they destroy us," Lyman said.

"Now you say that!" Alexander barked, and he pointed a finger at Lyman. "If you had been willing to go with us yesterday, we could have—"

"No," Joseph said, his voice powerful. "We have to accept what happened tonight as the will of the Lord. But we still face men outside who can't wait to kill us, and we don't have much chance of being acquitted by a judge. So it's true—nothing has changed. We need to get out of here, but probably not until the dead of night, so we can slip away before that mob out there can come after us. That much we learned by making a try."

"But Joseph," Hyrum said, "the guards will watch us closer than ever. They don't want to be blamed for letting us escape— even if they wish we would."

"I know. But I've been thinking about getting an auger brought in somehow. Maybe two or three of them. We could drill through the logs and cut a section out."

"But you know what Sam told us. There's loose rocks behind the logs, and the rock wall behind that."

"I'm well aware of that," Joseph said. "But if we can get through a log, working during the night, we could pull some of those loose rocks through and then work on the mortar around the stones on the outside wall. If we get a few stones out of the outer wall, we could all crawl through."

"I'm sorry, Joseph," Lyman said, "but I don't think that's possible."

"You might be right, Lyman. But it's something we can do instead of allowing the mob to decide our fate."

Caleb didn't like to disagree with Joseph, but he thought Lyman was probably right. Still, Joseph had a point. The men outside continued to scream their insults, and if they could catch him and the others outside, some of them would surely carry out their threats. Caleb did like the idea of trying to do *something*. He would rather stay awake all night drilling with an auger than give up and return to hopelessness.

CHAPTER 13

The prisoners learned the next day that Cyrus Daniels had not been shot. One of the guards had fired on Daniels and missed. It was only later that a visitor from Far West told them that he had tried to run from the guard but had stepped in a hole and fallen. As he had dropped, a bullet had buzzed over his head. He had then scrambled away, run into the nearby woods, and hidden out until he could make connections with the other visitors to the jail.

In the days that followed, the men heard that steady streams of members from Far West were now making their way across the state to Illinois. Caleb, however, had heard nothing from his own family and he didn't know whether they had set out yet, or whether they had adequate supplies.

A few days after their failed escape and after a soft-spoken discussion with Porter Rockwell, Joseph said, "Porter is going to bring us an auger. If he gets it past the guards, we can try to drill through the logs."

The prisoners had not discussed the plan since Joseph had first mentioned it, and Caleb had thought the idea had been dismissed. But now he told himself that the Lord was behind the strategy—this time—and the miracles he had hoped for would actually come about.

On the following day, the men were sitting in the upper room when the door opened and Porter was allowed to enter. After a guard locked the door behind him, Porter climbed down the ladder with Joseph. When they returned, Joseph whispered, "All right, men, we have a good sharp auger and a sturdy handle for it. Porter brought it in strapped to his leg. I tried a few turns, and it cuts into that hard timber quite well. Porter is going to wait a day or two and try to bring another one. But we'll start our drilling tonight. We'll have to bore holes that overlap and that way cut a square we can pry loose."

The men started that night, but the going became more difficult as the auger sank deeply into the foot-thick log. The men took turns, but Caleb found that twisting the auger took all his strength. He didn't last long before he had to trade off with the next man.

All the men did their share, even though it meant getting little sleep. They usually didn't sleep well in the dungeon anyway, and they knew they could sleep the following morning when they returned to the upper room. When Joseph took a turn late at night, Caleb couldn't see much, but he knew from the sound that Joseph was making faster headway, and he continued drilling much longer than Caleb had.

After Lyman took a turn with the auger, he said, "Joseph, you told us we'd hide the auger under the straw in the daytime, but how are we going to hide these holes we're making?"

"When was the last time any of the guards climbed down that ladder?" he asked. "They don't like the smell down here any more than we do. In candlelight, they may not notice the holes anyway, not back in this corner where we're drilling."

That made sense to Caleb, but on the second night, just when he was starting to feel that progress was going well, Joseph twisted on the auger and Caleb heard a snap. Joseph groaned and then said, "Sorry, brethren, but I twisted too hard. I've broken the handle."

There was a long pause as everyone considered the next step. Hyrum finally said, "When is Porter bringing another auger?"

"I don't know," Joseph said. "Soon. But I told him not to come so often that he raises suspicion."

"Could he bring an extra handle?"

"Maybe. But he can only strap so much to his leg and still walk normally. We may have to wait for the next auger and then be more careful with it."

"Careful won't make a lot of holes," Caleb said.

"What about the firewood upstairs?" Alexander asked. "Could we fashion a new handle by splitting any of those sticks? Lyman still has his penknife. It has a small blade, but we might be able to carve something that would fit."

"We can try that," Hyrum said. "But we can't get caught with shavings on the upper floor. And we'll have to hide the new handle as quickly as we can if we hear a guard turn a key in the door."

"We can hide it in the stack of firewood," Joseph said.

Despite the seriousness of the moment, Caleb couldn't help laughing. He had so long thought of Joseph and Hyrum as lofty men of God. It struck him as comical to hear them plotting such deceptions.

As it turned out, carving a handle with a dull pocketknife was not easy. Lyman did manage to insert the stick they fashioned into the auger, but it didn't last long. Fortunately, the next day Porter returned with another auger and smuggled it inside again. That one lasted another night, but then that handle broke—this time when Alexander used too much muscle on it—and the men were still far from drilling enough holes through the log.

They did their best to carve handles again, but those soon split and the work came to a stop. The attempt seemed pointless now, but Porter did come by again to see how things were going, and Joseph asked him to bring two new handles if he possibly could. Porter came back the same day, which meant he had been in the jail four times in only a few days. That, however, proved an overreach, as one of the guards was suspicious enough to search Porter. He checked his legs and felt the handles strapped to his thighs.

The prisoners first realized that their plan had gone wrong when Sheriff Hadley and Sam Tillery, along with a whole crowd of guards, arrived at the jail with a crowd of local citizens. Sheriff Hadley waited until the door was locked behind him and then said, "Joseph, we've tried to be fair to all you men, but you keep taking advantage of that. We know you have drilling tools in here, and we're going to find them."

"It might be easier if we just show you what we have," Joseph said.

"No. I no longer trust you. We'll do the search and not rely on your word. You claim to be more religious than the rest of us, but you're not ashamed to lie."

Joseph had been sitting at the table, but now he stood. "Sheriff," he said, with authority, "we've been held in this stinking jail all winter—surely a place where you would never spend a single night."

"I didn't sentence you. Judge King did, and—"

"That's not the point. We don't blame you." And then Joseph's voice rose, not just with volume, but with might, as he said, "We've been held here for two months, and to this day, we've had no chance to face our accusers in a court of law. And when we do, what can we expect? Justice? We've seen nothing in this state to indicate that we will ever be treated with fairness. Every day, filthy-tongued men gather outside and curse us. And what do they say?

'If a judge won't put you to death, we will.' So let me ask you, sir, if the situation were reversed, and you were waiting in this jail to die, would you try to find a way to escape?"

Hadley had stood stiff all this time, his jaw set. When Joseph finished, he was silent, and Caleb knew very well that he had no good answer. On the other hand, he was certainly aware that the room was packed with men who wouldn't want their sheriff to sound apologetic. Finally, Hadley said, "You were sent to our jail, and it's our job to hold you. I can't stop men from standing outside and yelling insults. I can only feed you, and—"

"*Feed us?*" Lyman shouted. "You feed your dogs better than you feed us."

Lyman was looking directly at Sam Tillery, who looked away.

"Mr. Wight," the sheriff said, "it's not our job to feed you as though you are hotel guests. We do the best we can. But I'll hear no more of this." He pointed to the opening in the floor. "Men, climb down that ladder with your lanterns. Search everything. Turn the straw over, check every corner, find whatever implements they have down there. Sam and I will search up here."

Joseph laughed softly. "I don't blame you for staying up here, Sheriff. No one wants to climb into that stinking den. But tell the men to look under the straw in the southeast corner. They'll find two augers and two broken handles. And if they look at the logs in that same corner, they'll find the holes that we've been making. I don't know that we could have gotten through the loose rocks and the stone wall, but it seemed worth a try. I hope we haven't damaged your jail too much—or your reputation." He laughed again. "And I do want to say that Sam Tillery has treated us with respect, and we've come to think of him as a friend."

But that didn't go over well with Sheriff Hadley. "That's just the problem, isn't it? And it explains how you got augers into this place. I'm afraid Sam has let us down—not guarded you as closely as he should have."

"I *am* careful," Tillery said, speaking with more energy than Caleb would have expected. "So are my guards. Maybe those augers were handed in through those little windows downstairs."

But with Porter being caught, everyone knew what had happened today, and the excuse was clearly unconvincing. Hadley didn't bother to reply. He did take a cursory look around the upper room, as though he were making a search, but he said nothing more to Joseph.

Thirty minutes or so went by before the men who had gone into the dungeon climbed back out. One of them, a brittle little man of sixty or so—someone Caleb had never seen before this day—spoke for the others. "We found these two augers, right where they said they would be—and two broken handles with them. Nothing else."

"How did you like the smell down there?" Lyman asked, but no one answered.

"All right. We'll have to decide what to do about this," Hadley said. "We can't just let a crime of this kind go by without punishment. You will hear from us soon." He told Tillery to unlock the door, and then everyone filed out. Tillery didn't look at Joseph or the others as he stepped out, shut the door, and locked it from the outside.

"I thought they'd send us downstairs to stay," Alexander said.

"That may be coming," Hyrum said.

———◆———

There was not much more to discuss. No one read and no one talked. Caleb had no doubt that all his brothers were dealing with the same crushing emotions he was. The men had clung to a tiny hope, no matter how remote, and now they probably faced constant darkness again. Caleb feared the cold would get inside him and he would have no escape from it. There seemed no way to survive more months of that.

Caleb walked to the window—the tiny opening in the wall—and he tried to see as much of the outside world as he could, but that didn't help. He still saw nothing but blackness. The terrible question he had posed many times came back again, and he couldn't deny his anger: Where was God?

Lyman had been pacing since Tillery had shut the door, but now he suddenly turned and strode toward Joseph. "So what's your next idea?" he demanded.

Joseph turned and looked at Lyman, clearly surprised by his rage.

Lyman took another step closer to Joseph. "Are you thinking we can all slip through those iron bars you're looking through, then flap our arms and fly away? That might work out just as well as the escapes we've tried so far."

"Lyman, I'm sorry. We did what—"

"I don't want to hear it, Joseph. We're dead men. We might as well face it. One way or another, these people are going to take our lives."

Joseph studied Lyman for a time, then slowly looked around the room at the other men.

Lyman must have seen how deeply he had cut Joseph. "I'm sorry," he said quietly. "I get aggravated. But it's not your fault. I'm just . . ." But he didn't finish his sentence.

Joseph waited for a time before he said, "You're right, Lyman. Escaping this place is not the answer, and I was wrong to decide that it was. I shouldn't have led us into such fruitless attempts."

"Joseph, we all thought it might work," Hyrum said. He walked to Joseph and put his hand on his shoulder. "Don't take the blame on yourself."

"But I am to blame," Joseph said. "I'm the one the Lord needs to chasten. He's let me understand that. I thought I had reached the bottom of my disgrace—that I couldn't descend any deeper—but I can see now that I still have more to learn. I'm sorry you all have to pass through this darkness with me."

"It seems we all have more to learn," Caleb said. "It's not just you."

Joseph didn't answer. But he looked more broken than he had ever been.

Before long, Sam Tillery opened the door, and he brought two guards with him. Following them was a big fellow in a leather apron—a blacksmith—and two assistants. They were carrying a length of chains and several tools of the trade.

Tillery looked at the prisoners. "I've tried to be fair," he said, "and now you've stabbed me in the back. Hadley puts all the blame on me, and if word gets around this town that I was too easy on you, my life might not last another day."

"We're sorry about that," Joseph said, "but you have to understand—"

"I ain't listening to you anymore, Joseph. Hadley told me to take no more chances. We're chaining the five of you together. You can complain all you want about that, but it's what you've brought on yourselves."

Wrath unlike any Caleb had known before coursed through him. He jumped to his feet. He would not, could not, let this happen. He strode toward Tillery and shouted into the man's face, "Tillery, if you put those chains on me, I will kill you, so help me God!"

Tillery cringed, seemed to shrink a little. Caleb expected the man, or his guards, to knock him on his back. He prepared for a fight. The guards could kill him if they chose, but he would not submit to chains.

No one moved. Caleb stood his ground, staring into Tillery's face. He told himself if they came at him with the chains, somehow he would keep his promise. He would strangle Tillery with the last strength in his body as the guards tried to stop him.

Tillery took a deep breath.

And another.

Then he did the last thing Caleb expected. He said, "Let's go." He opened the door and let the blacksmiths and guards out, then he stepped out as well, closing the door behind him and locking it.

Caleb felt so weak he thought he would fall to the floor. No one said a word. After a minute or so, without looking around, he muttered, "I shouldn't have said that."

But Joseph was there by then. He gripped Caleb's shoulders. "No. You did the right thing. I know that you would never take Sam's life. But he needed to feel your righteous anger. There are times when God grants us a power beyond our own. It wasn't your words that made Sam back down. It was the honesty of your indignation."

Caleb was greatly relieved by Joseph's faith in him. But he still wondered what Tillery's—and Sheriff Hadley's—next move would be.

CHAPTER 14

It was February 10, and Emma had been traveling across Missouri for three days. The violent snowstorm she'd traveled in had now let up, but a nasty cold had set in. Stephen Markham was leading a train of a few wagons—mostly rough lumber wagons without springs—and he had assigned Jonathan Holman, a quiet man, to drive Emma's wagon. As she rode, she held little Alexander against her body to keep him warm. She had been forced to leave her belongings behind, but she didn't care about that. The few things that mattered to her had already been stolen.

Alexander was eight months old now and usually liked to be crawling about, but he had stopped squirming and was clinging to Emma. She knew the cold had reached deeply into him, dulling his senses, and she was worried. Over the years, in other forced migrations, she had known of the deaths of many babies, especially when exposed to the kind of bitter winds they were facing now. The trip was a distance of 170 miles or so, and Brother Markham tried to get thirty miles behind the company each day, but that meant continuing the trek on winter afternoons after the sun had already set.

So far, Emma had slept in the wagon under all the blankets she had carried with her—she and her four children, with Major nuzzled between them. But now she wondered whether Alexander could make it through another night.

When Brother Markham slowed his horse next to Emma's wagon and asked how she was doing, Emma said, "My baby isn't doing well. Is there any way to get the children inside tonight?"

Brother Markham seemed to consider before saying, "We could ask at a farmhouse along this road, but we'd be taking a chance. Some people are against us, even this far from Far West. They might tell us to move on—and of course, we can live with that—but you know how vicious others have been."

"I don't think anyone would harm us just for asking."

He nodded, then hesitated again. "I suspect you're right."

"But I think you're cautious about asking for me and not for those in the other wagons."

"Well . . . yes."

"I understand. No one could take in all of us."

Brother Markham nodded, but then said, "It appears little Alexander is suffering more than the children in the other wagons. I think everyone will understand."

"Will they think it's only because I'm Joseph's wife, or that I'm not strong enough—"

"No. People know you better than that. Let's see if we can find a place. I'll explain to everyone."

So the horses trudged on through the crusted snow, hooves cracking the surface with each step and the big wagon rocking and vaulting. There was a bit of moonlight, but it was diffused through a thin layer of clouds, and the night was dark enough that it was hard to see ahead. Brother Holman, driving first in the line of wagons, obviously struggled at times not to stray from the road. Eventually, lantern light from a house appeared, and as the wagon neared, Emma could see smoke rising from a chimney. "Oh, please," she prayed, "open the hearts of these people."

Brother Markham told Jonathan to halt the wagon near a lane that led to the farmhouse, then walked back to the other wagons. Emma was sure he was explaining the situation to all the families. The crunch of his steps in the frozen snow had set off a dog barking, and then two or three more added to the ruckus. Major responded with a yelp of his own.

"Will those dogs bite Brother Markham?" Joey asked. He loved Old Major and kept him close in the wagon, but he had always been nervous around angry dogs.

Little Frederick, who was almost three, awoke, having fallen asleep against his mother's side. "Dogs," he said, as though explaining something to himself. "Dogs bite."

"No, no," Julia told him, and she tucked her arm around him. "Dogs won't bite you."

"They *could* bite," Joey said.

"No. We won't let them."

After a couple of minutes, Brother Markham returned and said, "Everyone understands your situation. I'll go knock on the door. The people may not take you in, but I'm not afraid to ask."

As Brother Markham walked toward the house, the sound of the dogs increased, and Emma hoped that they wouldn't attack him. She couldn't imagine that a house with such angry dogs could be very welcoming. But Stephen didn't return quickly, and she wondered whether that meant he had at least been able to negotiate with the people who lived there. She hoped he wouldn't offer anything to barter, since money and supplies were more than scarce.

She heard footsteps after a time and the dogs barked again, but with less wildness, as Brother Markham stepped to the wagon.

"All right," he said. "Let's get all of you down from the wagon. Bring your blankets. They only have a floor for you to sleep on, but it's warm inside."

"Do they know who we are?"

"Yes. When I told them we'd traveled almost a hundred miles in the cold, they guessed who we had to be, and the man said, 'It's a shame what's been done to you people.' He even said we can bring in the small children from all our wagons and the mothers with their nursing babies. It'll be crowded, but it will give the little ones a respite from the weather. I'll take Major, and he can sleep with my son and me. Hannah can take our younger children inside with you."

So Brother Markham held Alexander while Emma got down from the wagon, and then she and Julia helped the two little boys down. Emma carried the baby to the house, her children beside her. The dogs, it seemed, were out in back somewhere, and they had calmed. Maybe the farmer had put them in his barn.

A round little woman with graying hair and a face reddened from too many such winters greeted Emma and her children. Her husband didn't fuss over the children the way his wife did, but he kept shaking his head and saying, "It ain't right what people done to you folks."

The fire was warm, but the man's words were equally comforting. "You're so kind," Emma told him.

"I wouldn't want you to leave thinking everyone in our state could be so wicked."

"I never have thought that," Emma said. "Many people have been kind to us. It's just that some folks get angry and they do things they normally wouldn't do."

"I think it's so," the woman said, her voice tender but filtered through a brittleness that age and exposure had surely brought upon her. "We have a little dried beef and some potatoes and carrots stored over from last fall. I'll put together some stew and see if we can't bring a little brightness to the eyes of all these children."

Joey's eyes lit up immediately, and that made Emma's own eyes fill with tears. "Oh, that would be so wonderful." By then, more of the women and children were coming through the door. "But can you spare that much food?"

"I believe we can. There's just two of us here now, and we get by all right through the winter months." She smiled, showing tattered teeth. "And I must say, this here is the most excitement we've had for two, three months. You're a joy to look at, all you pretty people."

"Oh my . . . we're not pretty," Hannah Markham said. "We're wrapped up in all the worn-out coats and blankets we could find to bring with us."

Hannah was thirty-five or so, Emma thought, and even though the last year had been hard on her, she *was* a pretty woman, and spirited.

"Tell me your name," Hannah said.

"Margaret Wright. My husband here is named Franklyn. Y'all gather up around the fire, and Frank will add a few more sticks of wood. I'll see about cooking something. If the warmth makes you fall asleep, that's just fine. It'll take a while to get a stew going, and then I'll wake you up."

So Emma spread a double layer of blankets on the floor and sat close to the fire, but she left space for others to do the same. Joey, calmed by the warmth, did fall asleep with his head on her leg. Alexander was still docile and satisfied to stay close to his mother, but he had revived a little in the warmth and light. When Freddie tried to find a place somewhere near his mother, Julia pulled him close to her, and he was soon asleep as well.

Emma loved to see how tender Julia was with her brothers. For a seven-year-old, she had had little time to play with friends all this last year. She needed time to be a child, and Emma had no idea when that would happen. But Julia looked up at Emma, seemingly pleased to be warm and probably also to be of comfort to Freddie.

Emma took in the pleasure for a few minutes, and then she remembered what she needed to do. "Lord, I thank thee," she whispered.

◆

After a night of rest, warm food, and friendly treatment, the next three days were easier. But the little wagon train had arrived at the Mississippi now and the river looked ominously wide. It was frozen, as it usually was that time of year, but Brother Markham had spoken with Jonathan Holman, and the two were cautious.

Brother Markham told Emma, "I'm going to put Charlie in front and hitch him to the tongue of the wagon. Brother Holman can walk with him, and I can guide the wagon by moving the tongue back and forth. I'll tie up ol' Jim on the back to keep the wagon and the horses spread out a little more."

"Are you that worried about the ice breaking through?" Emma asked.

"Well . . . no. I just want to be careful. I'm going to ask you and the children to walk, not ride, and to stay back thirty or forty feet from the wagon. That will spread the weight even more."

Emma smiled. "I'm quite thin after what we've been through this winter. I don't think I weigh so much as a wagon."

He laughed. "I'm not saying that. But if the ice did break, and the wagon went under, I don't want it to pull you and your children in with it."

"What about you?"

"I told you, the ice will hold. I'm just being overly vigilant."

Emma hoped he meant the "overly" part. She had heard too many stories of people falling through ice during river crossings. "What about the other wagons?" she asked, aware that she may have seemed worried only about herself.

"After you make it across, I'll walk back and help everyone else. We'll just have to spread the wagons far apart."

"Oh, but it's such a long walk."

"It's only a mile or so."

Emma understood that, and normally a walk of a mile wouldn't have concerned her, but she pictured the waters, deep and frigid, moving under the ice. Still, she didn't mention her fears when she talked to her children.

"The ice is frozen hard," she told them. "Brother Markham will take the wagon forward, and we'll follow."

"Why can't we ride in the wagon?" Joey asked.

"We could, of course, but poor old Charlie and Jim are tired from all the pulling they've done. We want to give them some rest, don't we?"

Joey looked dubious about that. "Will the ice break?" he asked.

"No. Don't worry about that. The ice is thick."

Emma could see that he *was* worried. She wondered whether he had heard some of what she and Brother Markham had been saying.

So Emma waited until the wagon was well out onto the river to begin the walk, Alexander in one arm and Frederick in the other. Freddie was heavy to carry, but she knew it would be a long walk for him and she wanted to keep him close. Joey walked on one side of her and Julia the other. From the way they were clinging to her skirt, she knew that they were frightened. Joey's breath sounded strained, as though he were hiding his concerns. He often told Emma—especially after his father had blessed him to be courageous and strong—that he was no longer a little boy. But Emma wished he didn't have to feel such responsibility.

Emma and the children were wrapped in lots of clothes—all they had been able to bring with them. This was a way of transporting the clothing and, of course, an attempt to stay warm, but it made for extra weight now. What the children didn't know was that she had strapped a waistband under her skirt and buttoned it around her. From the waistband hung two cotton bags, each containing Joseph's papers. Most important was Joseph's inspired translation of the Bible, which enemies would certainly love to confiscate. She had been keeping Joseph's writings for months, sometimes hiding them away from her house, and finally, devising this protection under her skirt. She had become accustomed to the extra burden, but she hadn't carried the papers with babies in her arms and children clinging to her. She hadn't made it very far onto the ice before she realized how strenuous all that would become before she made the full trek across the river.

A wind was coming down the river, across the ice, stinging her cheeks and icing her nose. She knew that Joey, on her windy side, was also freezing, his coat, hat, and muffler hardly enough to protect him. But he didn't complain about the cold—probably because the fear of the ice breaking was occupying his thoughts.

Emma held her head down to keep the wind from her face, but also to help her think as little as possible about how far she had to go. Each time she glanced up she had the feeling she hadn't made any headway at all. The wagon was moving steadily ahead, no faster than she could walk, but the distance to the far bank seemed to stretch as she trudged ahead. She thought of handing Freddie to Julia, but he was too heavy for her to carry very far. He clung instead to Emma, his arms around her neck. She needed to put him down and let him walk for a while, but she couldn't bring herself to break him away from her. Gradually, the ache in her arms turned to numbness.

Emma kept taking steps, kept asking the Lord for strength, kept saying to herself that no matter the pain, no matter the fear, she would go on as long as she possibly could. She vowed, silently, "I'll take one hundred more steps and then I'll sit down and rest for a few minutes," but by the time she counted the hundred steps, the thought of sitting on the ice seemed worse than walking, and she hated to extend the time the crossing would take. So she counted another hundred steps, and then another, and another.

She kept up her pace, and her distress turned into a dazed sense beyond pain. The journey never became tolerable, not exactly, but she continued to stride ahead by sheer will—and constant prayer.

When she finally reached the bank, with the wagon and horses just ahead of her, she allowed herself to sink into the snow. But she knew she couldn't do that for long. Julia took Frederick from her arms and talked to him about being a big boy before she set him on his feet. Emma struggled to get up with Alexander in her arms, but when she did, she made her way to a log on the ground, well back from the river. She sat down and waited for Brother Markham, who was working with Brother Holman to harness the horses onto the wagon. Once that task was completed, Brother Markham drove the wagon away from the river toward a bluff out of the wind. Then he came back and walked Emma to the wagon, carrying the baby for her.

"Get in and stay as warm as you can," he told her. "Cover up with all your blankets and I'll head back across the river. I need to get all our people across, and then we'll look for a place to stay tonight."

But those words troubled Emma. She knew their location was somewhere in the vicinity of Quincy, Illinois, and she knew that some of the Saints had traveled there earlier. But she didn't know whether they were camped outside in wagon boxes and tents or whether they had found places where they could get inside. Everything was so unsettled. She was glad to be across the river, glad to have some of the ache in her arms and legs at an end, but at least while she was crossing, she had been able to concentrate completely on surviving that ordeal. Now what? A much longer nightmare might be ahead. She and the Saints had escaped the constant threat of death in western Missouri, but now they had no Zion, no place to gather, no idea what their next course would be.

Emma finally let herself consider her other fear. Joseph was two hundred miles away, still held in jail and unlikely to be acquitted by courts that were against him. He had told her that he would survive and return to her, but she wondered whether he was only saying what she wanted to hear. The fact was, she knew—and had known for a long time—that he could easily be murdered, and she would be left to raise her children alone. She prayed again, asked for help for Joseph and for all the Saints. She had learned to live with constant uncertainty, but she longed for peace, a house to live in, and her husband at her side.

CHAPTER 15

Sam Tillery did not return with his chains. In fact, he did not return at all. Other jailers brought food—which the men were allowed to eat upstairs—but after each meal, the jailers commanded the prisoners to climb into the dungeon. The guards allowed no visitors and offered no candles. As one day followed another, a deadness settled into Caleb's body and mind. His only solace was to give up on hope, even thought, and he slept as much as he could. The men talked very little as they lay in the straw. Everything, it seemed, had been said. No topics for discussion, no questions, not even any words came to Caleb any longer.

But there was one matter Caleb couldn't force from his mind: he hadn't heard from his family, and he had no idea whether Nancy and his children had left Far West. He kept envisioning all his daughters, especially the little ones, out in the cold, and it was that mental picture that haunted him. He also saw an image of the lovely young woman he had met in Cleveland so long ago: refined, accomplished, and certainly capable of marrying a better provider than he had been. Nancy had seemed delicate then, slender and neatly dressed. Now she was most likely slogging through snow and mud like a work horse, all the while loaded down with fear for her children.

Caleb wasn't angry any longer. He was simply defeated, and he knew the other men were just as resigned. But when they ascended to the upper room for their meals, he noticed a change in Joseph. He wasn't talkative, but when he blessed the food, Caleb heard prayers of a kind he had never known in his life. It was as though Joseph were continuing an ongoing conversation. His tone was respectful but familiar, and he offered his will. He didn't request a release, didn't ask to survive, didn't even plead for protection for the refugees from Far West. What he asked of the Lord was that the members of the Church, including his brothers in the jail, understand what was being required of them and find the strength to move forward. What struck Caleb most forcefully, however, was Joseph's expression of regret for his pride.

Caleb tried to take on the same willingness to accept, not resent.

After ten days or so, the jailers became less strict about sending the prisoners back to the dungeon after meals. In fact, they gradually fell into the old pattern of allowing them to stay in the upper room during the daylight hours. Tillery also showed up. He didn't mention the chains or the escape attempts, and he was reasonably cordial. In fact, one afternoon, as he waited for the men to finish their supper, he asked, "Are you fellas holding up all right? You don't look good."

This would normally be the sort of comment that would draw a humorous response from Joseph, but he didn't laugh. He only said, "You've won, Sam. We have no fight left in us."

Tillery clearly didn't know how to react. He picked up a stick of wood, opened the stove, and placed it on the fire. "I hope you get out of here before much longer. That would be good for all of us."

All the men knew, however, that whenever a hearing finally took place, the jury in Gallatin was not likely to exonerate them, which meant they very well might be returned to Liberty. Caleb had heard Doniphan speak of requesting a change of venue that might move the men to a county where opinions were not set against them and where a jail might not be so primitive. But Caleb had no reason to expect a motion of that kind to be granted. Judge King had stated that the Daviess County hearing would be held in March, and March was coming soon, but the last time Doniphan had visited, he had been skeptical that officials were in any hurry to get started. So the prisoners were likely to spend many more days in this jail.

After their evening meal, the men descended into the darkness. This time, Tillery had given them a candle, which at least sent a yellow glow out from the center of the room. Joseph sat against his wall, very still. Quietly, he said, "This has been good for me."

No one asked him why. They waited.

"I've gotten used to the members of the Church treating me like a king. But I'm a man, through and through. I'm like a rough stone rolling down from a mountain. It seems like the only force that rubs off any of my corners is to bump against the forces that work against me. God knows that, and he tries to smooth me. These last weeks, since the day we were caught with the augers, have been the hardest of my life . . . and maybe the best. The Lord knows that the humiliation of this jail—and the loss of all my worldly power and importance—is what I needed."

Caleb had not felt the same satisfaction—or benefit—but he was moved by Joseph's words. If Joseph had needed this dark time,

Caleb was willing to accept his own suffering as a sacrifice for the prophet, his brother.

"Maybe this experience will prepare you to lead the Church even better than before," Hyrum said.

"I'm not thinking only of me, Hyrum. The whole Church is facing the same test—the same humiliation. Down here in the dark, I keep imagining our people trying to make their way to cross the state, out in the snow and weather. I wonder how many are dying. All of us here in this jail have young children, even babies, and I picture what they're suffering. When the cold lets up, the mud will be just as hard to travel through, and who knows what kinds of mobs will continue to attack them?" He hesitated, and no one spoke. But then he asked the question Caleb sometimes asked himself. "Are we really that evil, brethren? Am I? Do we deserve this . . . *abandonment*? I keep asking myself when the Lord will say, 'It's enough.' But then the answer comes to me: 'Not my will, but thine be done.' Accepting that has given me more peace than I've ever known in my life."

◆

The days continued as before; nothing changed. And yet, Joseph had become more conversant, more willing to discuss his thoughts about spiritual matters. That helped Caleb, but he also heard in Joseph's insights about the eternities a seeming acceptance that his life might end before much longer. When March came, the days warmed enough to make the nights less miserable, and without thinking much about it, Caleb had become accustomed to the smell, the dampness, even the dirtiness of his own body.

Doniphan and Burnett had visited and said that a hearing was being planned, but that they doubted it would happen before

April. Word of conditions in Far West—or of the wagon trains crossing to Illinois—was hard to come by. Porter Rockwell was no longer allowed into the jail, and Brigham Young had been forced to head east himself, the locals having become aware that he was now leading the Saints with Joseph confined to the jail. But a few visitors did make their way to Liberty with reports of some of the prisoners' families. They learned that Emma had left with a few wagons led by Steven Markham, and that Mary and Mercy and some others had begun the trek not long afterwards. But no one seemed to know much about the families of the other prisoners. One brother had told Caleb, "The last I knew, Sister Nancy and your children were still in Far West, but I can't say that they still are."

Caleb hoped they were well on their way and would soon find some safer place to live. "If they're still in Far West," he asked, "are they still being harassed?"

"Not as much. Loudmouthed scoundrels come around, but they just bellow and bawl; they don't pull down houses and all that sort of thing, not the way they did at first."

Caleb tried to believe that Clark would be able to manage the situation, and that others would help. But, in truth, he had no idea whether that was true.

There was more sunshine now, longer days, but there was also rain, sometimes strong thunderstorms, and that brought on increased worries. But finally, on March 19, David Rogers arrived from Quincy with letters: one from Emma to Joseph; one from Bishop Partridge; and ones from Don Carlos and William Smith addressed to Hyrum and Joseph. Joseph read Emma's and Edward's messages, and he handed the other two to Hyrum. After they had read the letters silently, Joseph passed Emma's note to Hyrum and asked him to read it out loud.

Emma's letter began:

Dear Husband

Having an opportunity to send by a friend I make an attempt to write, but I shall not attempt to write my feelings altogether, for the situation in which you are, the walls, bars, and bolts, rolling rivers, running streams, rising hills, sinking valleys, and spreading prairies that separate us, and the cruel injustice that first cast you into prison and still holds you there, with many other considerations, places my feelings far beyond description.

She went on to describe the "scenes of suffering" she had witnessed as she and other Saints had made their way across Missouri in response to the order of the governor, an order she denounced as "fraught with as much wickedness as ignorance." In spite of all that, she was now living safely in the home of Judge John Cleveland and his wife Sarah.

"We are all well at present, except Fredrick, who is quite sick," she said. "Little Alexander who is now in my arms is one of the finest little fellows you ever saw in your life; he is so strong that with the assistance of a chair he will run all round the room."

She praised the people of Illinois, who were very kind to the refugee Saints, and she expressed her hope for better days ahead. She closed by offering her respects to the other men in the jail and by saying she was ever Joseph's, affectionately.

Hyrum then read his brothers' letters, and the news was much the same. All the Smiths had reached Quincy, and they had found housing that was adequate for the present. As Hyrum finished the letter, he and Joseph looked across the room at one another and nodded. Caleb saw the emotion, and relief, in their eyes.

Joseph then looked at the other men. "I'm sorry there's no

news for you brethren," he said. "I hope you hear something soon. But what we've learned today seems hopeful for all of us."

Don Carlos had mentioned in his letter that the governor of Missouri would soon release the Mormon prisoners. But such rumors often spread about. Caleb didn't want to make too much of that. He had tried not to hope in recent days, but he found himself feeling a little surge of optimism that his own family would find a safe place to live in Illinois.

Caleb noticed that Joseph had shut his eyes, bowed his head a little. Caleb suspected that he was speaking to the Lord, expressing his gratefulness.

Joseph didn't say much that night in the dungeon, but before the candle burned down, Caleb saw him leaning against the wall with that same distant look on his face. Late in the evening, he asked, "Are we contrite? Are our hearts sufficiently broken?"

No one answered until Hyrum said, "I don't know, Joseph. Do you think we've learned enough?"

"I believe so," Joseph said. "Words are flowing into my mind and spirit. I'm understanding things, seeing things I never grasped before, and seeing far into the future. The Lord is opening me up, filling me, changing my heart."

Caleb longed for the same knowledge. He wanted to hear what Joseph could reveal now. But Joseph offered nothing more that night. On the following morning, however, before the men were invited to climb upstairs, Joseph said, "Alexander, I want to write a letter—to all the Church. I need you to scribe for me. Will you do that?"

"Of course I will," Alexander said.

So once breakfast was cleared, Joseph and Alexander sat across from one another at the table, Alexander with sheets of paper before him, an inkwell, and a dip pen. Joseph didn't start immediately, but when he did, his words rushed fluently. He addressed Bishop Partridge and the Saints, then said, "Your humble servant Joseph Smith Jr., prisoner for the Lord Jesus Christ's sake and for the Saints, taken and held by the power of mobocracy under the exterminating reign of his excellency the Governor Lilburn W. Boggs, in company with his fellow prisoners and beloved brethren, Caleb Baldwin, Lyman Wight, Hyrum Smith, and Alexander McRae, send unto you all greeting."

Caleb couldn't help smiling at Joseph calling Governor Boggs "his excellency" and referring to his "exterminating reign." There was a hint of humor in that, and Caleb was glad to hear it. The other men also smiled, but Joseph remained intent on his task. His words seemed ready—as though in his mind just waiting to be voiced.

He continued, "Therefore, dearly and beloved brethren, we are the more ready and willing to lay claim to your fellowship and love. For our circumstances are calculated to awaken our spirits to a sacred remembrance of everything and we think that yours are also, and that nothing, therefore, can separate us from the love of God and fellowship one with another, and that every species of wickedness and cruelty practiced upon us will only tend to bind our hearts together and seal them together in love."

Caleb felt a surge of relief. He thought of Joseph's angry letter written in December. Now, it was good to hear Joseph speak of love, not retribution. Caleb also noticed strength in Joseph's voice that had been missing for many weeks. Emma's letter might have had much to do with the tone he was taking, but something more than that had clearly happened. Caleb was certain that Joseph had not slept all night and that he had been receiving these words, not composing them.

When Joseph decried the treatment the Saints had suffered,

Caleb heard no anger but only sympathy for the members. Then his language changed entirely. He posed his own question, the one all the men had been facing, and he asked it with pleading in his voice.

"O God, where art thou? And where is the pavilion that covereth thy hiding place? How long shall thy hand be stayed, and thine eye, yea thy pure eye, behold from the eternal heavens the wrongs of thy people and of thy servants, and thine ear be penetrated with their cries?"

Caleb saw the pain in Joseph's face, but Joseph's question seemed more of an invitation than a complaint. He was welcoming the Spirit back into his life, trusting that the Lord had an answer for him.

The emotions that Caleb had been unable to feel in recent days now flooded back, and tears filled his eyes.

Joseph's voice pinched off with emotion for a moment, but then he continued his questions, this time on behalf of the members of the Church. "Yea, O Lord, how long shall they suffer these wrongs and unlawful oppressions, before thine heart shall be softened towards them, and thy bowels be moved with compassion towards them?"

Joseph reiterated to the Lord the belief that he had expressed from time to time: that public opinion was turning in favor of the Saints and toward indignation for their oppressors. But then he spoke of the misery of the jail they were kept in and expressed gratitude for the friends who supported them.

Caleb was struck by the beauty of Joseph's language when he said, "One token of friendship from any source whatever awakens and calls into action every sympathetic feeling. It brings up in an instant everything that is passed; it seizes the present with a vivacity of lightning; it grasps after the future with the fierceness of a tiger;

it retrogrades from one thing to another until finally, all enmity, malice, and hatred, and past differences, misunderstandings, and mismanagements be slain victims at the feet of hope, and when the heart is sufficiently contrite then the voice of inspiration steals along and whispers . . ."

Joseph paused to let Alexander catch up to him, and as he did, Caleb could only think that this was a new Joseph. He finished his thought:

". . . whispers my son, peace be unto thy soul; thine adversity and thy afflictions shall be but a small moment; And then, if thou endure it well, God shall exalt thee on high; thou shalt triumph over all thy foes. Thy friends do stand by thee, and they shall hail thee again with warm hearts and friendly hands. Thou art not yet as Job; thy friends do not contend against thee, neither charge thee with transgression, as they did Job. And they who do charge thee with transgression, their hope shall be blasted, and their prospects shall melt away as the hoar frost melteth before the burning rays of the rising sun."

All this was piercing Caleb's own mind and heart. The words "thine adversity and thy afflictions shall be but a small moment" came to Caleb as powerful relief. The "small moment" wasn't over; Joseph still must endure. But the promise was given and Caleb was comforted, as he knew Joseph was.

Joseph continued for a time before Alexander said, "Joseph, I can't keep up with you, and my hand is aching. Maybe you need a little rest yourself. Could we just—"

"No, I don't need rest. I need to continue now, while the words are being given to me." He looked at Caleb, who was sitting behind Alexander near the stove. "Brother Caleb, can you scribe for a time?"

"I'd be honored to try," Caleb said, "but I don't write so well as Alexander does."

Joseph didn't respond to that. Alexander stood up and Joseph motioned for Caleb to come to the table. So Caleb took the chair and picked up the pen. He dipped it in the ink and waited. Joseph's tone changed again at that point and focused on a larger perspective. He spoke of the test the Saints must pass, and then he said, "The things of God are of deep import, and time and experience and careful and ponderous and solemn thoughts can only find them out. Thy mind, O Man, if thou wilt lead a soul unto salvation, must stretch as high as the utmost heavens, and search into and contemplate the lowest considerations of the darkest abyss, and expand upon the broad considerations of eternal expanse. He must commune with God. How much more dignified and noble are the thoughts of God than the vain imaginations of the human heart."

Caleb was struck by the thought that he and his friends in the jail had begun to think so much about the daily challenge of surviving that they had stopped considering the "dignified and noble" thoughts of God. The Lord was telling them, through Joseph, to remember the eternal meaning of their experience and not only the food they hated or the smell of their dungeon. Caleb had been struggling to cling to loftier perspectives, and had usually failed, but he felt the power of receiving guidance directly from the Lord.

Caleb was astounded then as he wrote down some of the most beautiful language he had ever heard: "How long can rolling waters remain impure? What power shall stay the heavens? As well might man stretch forth his puny arm to stop the Missouri river in its decreed course, or to turn it up stream, as to hinder the Almighty from pouring down knowledge from heaven upon the heads of the Latter-day Saints.

"What is Boggs or his murderous party but wimbling willows upon the shore to catch the flood wood? As well might we argue that water is not water because the mountain torrents send down mire and riles the crystal stream, although afterwards renders it more pure than before; or that fire is not fire because it is of a quenchable nature by pouring on the flood, as to say that our cause is down because renegades, liars, priests, thieves, and murderers who are all alike tenacious of their crafts and creeds have poured down from their spiritual wickedness in high places and from their strongholds of the divine a flood of dirt and mire and filthiness and vomit upon our heads. No, God forbid, hell may pour forth its rage like the burning lava of Mount Vesuvius or of Etna or of the most terrible of the burning mountains and yet shall Mormonism stand."

Since November, everything Governor Boggs and the attacking mobs had done had filled Joseph and the others with resentment, but all that seemed gone now. The Lord was telling Joseph that those who attacked the Church were powerless. The members could—and would—move forward.

Finally, Caleb wrote Joseph's closing to the letter: "Our respects and love and fellowship to all the virtuous saints; we are your brethren and fellow-sufferers and prisoners of Jesus Christ for the gospel's sake, and for the hope of glory which is in us. Amen."

CHAPTER 16

Caleb was tired—not from his brief stint at scribing, but from the energy he had expended in taking in all that Joseph had revealed in the extensive letter. At times Joseph had spoken as himself, connecting to the brothers and sisters of the Church, and in other parts of the letter he had spoken as a prophet, in the voice of the Lord, revealing insights that Caleb wanted to remember and ponder.

Caleb sat back, took in air, accepted a new reality. When he looked at Joseph, he saw the change in his face. Joseph had received a clean set of clothing from Heber Kimball a few weeks back, but he looked depleted with his straggly hair and beard, his pale skin. Still, his eyes were alive in a way they hadn't been for months.

"Thine adversity and thy afflictions shall be but a small moment," the Lord had told Joseph. Caleb could only think that the ordeal for Joseph and all the prisoners might soon be over. He didn't have to know how that would happen; he felt sure this was the Lord's promise. Caleb scanned the paragraphs he had written until he came across the further pledge that no force, not even the "burning lava of Mount Vesuvius or of Etna," could stand against the forward march of the Restoration. Zion, ultimately, Caleb told himself, would not be lost.

Now that Joseph had ended his dictation, a detachment came over him again. It seemed obvious that he was contemplating what he had received, but as Joseph continued the day with the same distant look in his eyes, Caleb wondered whether new thoughts—new revelations—were filling his mind. His way of moving about, taking his meals, looking at the other men, was familiar to Caleb. But a new softness was in his voice, as though he were overwhelmed with gratefulness. And all evening, in the dark, he remained quiet.

The next morning, Caleb awoke feeling as though he really hadn't slept. Joseph was not only awake but sitting up, leaning against the logs of the wall. He didn't say anything until Alexander began to stretch his long arms and legs.

"Alexander, I have more to say to the members," Joseph said. "Words have been coming to me all night. When we climb to the upper room today, I need you to scribe for me again."

"I'm happy to do that," Alexander said, and then he added, gently, "The Lord is with you, Joseph."

"He is," Joseph said, but his tone expressed more confidence than his simple words.

The morning wait began. When the door eventually opened, the men climbed up the ladder and ate everything placed before them. Once the guard was gone, Joseph asked Alexander to ready himself. Caleb moved to the place where he often sat on the floor near the stove, with Hyrum beside him. Lyman was too restless to sit very long. He liked to pace about, approach the stove—much too close—and then walk away from it. But this morning, he sat at the end of the table near Joseph and Alexander, who were across from one another.

Joseph's first pronouncements contained practical advice to the members. "We continue to offer further reflections to Bishop

Partridge and to The Church of Jesus Christ of Latter-day Saints, whom we love with fervent love," he began. And then he discussed the proposal of Isaac Galland to sell the Saints land in both Iowa Territory and in the area around Commerce, Illinois. He also advised the members to remember that in all choices made for the Church, decisions must "be discussed with a great deal of care and propriety lest you grieve the Holy Spirit, which shall be poured upon your heads." And he admonished them to listen to "principles of righteousness that are agreeable to the mind of God."

He also offered guidelines for such decisions: "Remember those who are in bondage and in heaviness and in deep affliction for your sakes, and if there are any among you who aspire after their own aggrandizement and seek their own opulence while their brethren are groaning in poverty and are under sore trials and temptations, they cannot be benefited by the intercession of the Holy Spirit, which maketh intercession for us day and night with groanings that cannot be uttered. We ought at all times to be very careful that such highmindedness never have place in our hearts but condescend to men of low estate."

Caleb was astounded by Joseph's articulation, the steady confidence and fluency of his voice. He also understood why Joseph concerned himself about the manner in which members treated one another. Too often, in spite of attempts to live the law of consecration, some Church members had sought to raise themselves above others and forgotten those who were struggling to get a farm started or who suffered from illnesses and setbacks. The Lord was asking the Saints to make a stronger attempt toward a higher law: a deeper spirit of unity and concern for one another.

And then Joseph's words—the Lord's words—struck with force, describing an attitude that Caleb knew he needed to rise toward:

"Behold, there are many called, but few are chosen. And why are they not chosen? Because their hearts are set so much upon the things of this world, and aspire to the honors of men, that they do not learn this one lesson—That the rights of priesthood are inseparably connected with the powers of heaven, and that the powers of heaven cannot be controlled nor handled only upon the principles of righteousness. That they may be conferred upon us, it is true; but when we undertake to cover our sins, or to gratify our pride, our vain ambition, or to exercise control or dominion or compulsion upon the souls of the children of men, in any degree of unrighteousness, behold, the heavens withdraw themselves; the Spirit of the Lord is grieved; and when it has withdrawn, Amen to the priesthood or the authority of that man. Behold, ere he is aware, he is left unto himself, to kick against the pricks, to persecute the saints, and to fight against God. We have learned by sad experience that it is the nature and disposition of almost all men, as soon as they get a little authority, as they suppose, they will immediately begin to exercise unrighteous dominion. Hence many are called, but few are chosen."

In December Joseph had railed against the men who had witnessed against him, but now the Lord was teaching him that the "traitors" had given way to a tendency—the "nature and disposition" of all people—to become prideful when granted authority. What Caleb perceived—and he was certain Joseph did too—was that they could no longer view all their troubles as caused by enemies. They had to look more to themselves and their own weaknesses.

Joseph continued to speak, looking past Alexander, but he pronounced his sentences as though he were reading them—or hearing them. "No power or influence can or ought to be maintained by virtue of the priesthood, only by persuasion, by long-suffering, by gentleness and meekness, and by love unfeigned; By kindness, and pure knowledge, which shall greatly enlarge the soul without hypocrisy, and without guile—Reproving betimes with sharpness, when moved up by the Holy Ghost; and then showing forth afterwards an increase of love toward him whom thou hast reproved, lest he esteem thee to be his enemy; That he may know that thy faithfulness is stronger than the cords of death. Let thy bowels also be full of charity towards all men, and to the household of faith, and let virtue garnish thy thoughts unceasingly; then shall thy confidence wax strong in the presence of God; and the doctrine of the priesthood shall distil upon thy soul as the dews from heaven. The Holy Ghost shall be thy constant companion, and thy scepter an unchanging scepter of righteousness and truth; and thy dominion shall be an everlasting dominion, and without compulsory means it shall flow unto thee forever and ever."

If Joseph had suddenly floated from his chair, Caleb wouldn't have been surprised. Caleb was on a solid floor, his back against a hard wall, but he felt as though *he* were floating, caught up in not only the words but the spirit of what he was hearing.

And there was more to come, more assurance: "If thou art called to pass through tribulation; if thou art in perils among false brethren; if thou art in perils among robbers; if thou art in perils by land or by sea; If thou art accused with all manner of false accusations; if thine enemies fall upon thee; if they tear thee from the society of thy father and mother and brethren and sisters; and if with a drawn sword thine enemies tear thee from the bosom of thy wife, and of thine offspring, and thine elder son, although but six years of age, shall cling to thy garments, and shall say, My father, my father, why can't you stay with us? O, my father, what are the men going to do with you . . ."

This, of course, was Joseph's story. All this had happened to

him. He had been dragged from his house with little Joey clinging to him. But it was the conclusion of the account that touched
Caleb: "If the billowing surge conspire against thee; if fierce winds
become thine enemy; if the heavens gather blackness, and all the
elements combine to hedge up the way; and above all, if the very
jaws of hell shall gape open the mouth wide after thee, know thou,
my son, that all these things shall give thee experience, and shall be
for thy good. The Son of Man hath descended below them all. Art
thou greater than he? Therefore, hold on thy way, and the priesthood shall remain with thee; for their bounds are set, they cannot
pass. Thy days are known, and thy years shall not be numbered
less; therefore, fear not what man can do, for God shall be with
you forever and ever."

Joseph's voice broke and tears coursed down his face. Caleb was
weeping too. He repeated the words that had struck him hardest,
whispering them out loud: "All these things shall give thee experience and shall be for thy good." The promise was to Joseph, but
Caleb knew that the same was true for all his brothers who had
suffered for the sake of the Lord.

Would Caleb ever become thankful for these months in jail?
The men had been promised recently that their pretrial hearing
and eventual trial were not far off, and Caleb knew very well that
a death sentence was not only possible, but probable. And yet, the
Lord had told Joseph—and Caleb thought the message might ap-
ply to him as well—that his days would not be "numbered less."
That seemed to mean that his death was in the hands of the Lord—
not in the hands of the judge and jury he would face, or even in
the hands of the mobs that might wait outside.

Joseph sat for a time, as though he also needed to consider the
words that had been given to him, but then he sat up straighter
and addressed some practical matters: mainly decisions the leaders

of the Church would have to make. He asked the members to write down the depredations they had lived through and to seek redress from the federal government. He added a promise that wherever the Saints gathered, they would welcome people of all faiths to live among them. Caleb knew that this was his way of saying that they would not reject and mistreat people in the manner that the old settlers in Missouri had rejected the Saints.

Joseph then closed the letter a second time with his testimony to the members—and to the world. "We say that God is true; that the Constitution of the United States is true; that the Bible is true; that the Book of Mormon is true; that the Book of Covenants are true; that Christ is true; that the ministering angels sent forth from God are true; and that we know that we have an house not made with hands, eternal in the heavens, whose builder and maker is God."

He sat back after that, as though to catch his breath. He looked around the room and focused on each of the men, one at a time. "Anything you would like to add?" he asked.

"No," Hyrum said. "It's of God. It's not for us to change a word."

Joseph looked down at the table for a time, and everyone waited. "This *is* of God," he finally said. "I'm only sorry that I couldn't hear the Lord sooner."

"We'll all be better men for this experience," Alexander said. "I knew when you spoke those words that they were true. I felt my whole body change, not just my mind."

"The body and spirit are not so separate as we think, Alexander. I'm glad you know that now." Joseph slowly stood. "Are you all willing to sign this letter with me?"

They all said they were, and without correcting or changing anything, they gathered about and each signed.

Caleb continued to watch Joseph. He seemed taller—or maybe just returned to his full height—and even though his new suit was already soiled and covered with bits of straw, Caleb saw him for what he was: dignified.

CHAPTER 17

More than two weeks had passed, but finally Caleb walked through the double doors of the jail and down the steps to a waiting wagon. Hyrum, Lyman, and Alexander had boarded the wagon ahead of him, and Joseph came last. It was April 6, the ninth birthday of the Church, and it seemed an appropriate day to be set free—at least for the moment—and finally travel to Daviess County for the promised pretrial hearing. Sheriff Hadley and several guards, all on horseback, were waiting near the wagon as the men climbed onto it. Joseph, standing at the back of the open wagon, called out, "Sam Tillery, you run a fine establishment here in Liberty, but I hope you won't mind if we take our leave."

Tillery laughed. "You've been decent guests—except for the holes you drilled in our wall. I fear you marred the appearance of such a fine facility."

"I suggest you daub some mud in the holes," Joseph said, "and no one will notice any difference."

Sheriff Hadley and the guards laughed, the anger over the prisoners' attempted escape now forgotten. Or maybe the sheriff and all the jailers were merely relieved not to be responsible for the men any longer.

A few locals had gathered to watch the prisoners depart. They weren't calling out this time, probably because the sheriff was there. But Joseph laughed and said, "Goodbye, my friends. Sorry we didn't get to know one another better."

One of the men mumbled that he didn't want to get acquainted, but most of the men smiled, clearly surprised that Joseph would joke with them.

Caleb loved to hear Joseph return to his good-humored self, but he also noticed that since Joseph had written his letter to the Saints and received the Lord's reassurances, he seemed milder, more reflective, and yet more confident. He had been talking more than he had for the last few months, and most of his talk was about the future of the Church and the aims he now had for taking the gospel to the world.

As the contingent set out with Peter Burnett and Amos Rees—defense lawyers and partners of Alexander Doniphan—on horseback alongside the wagon, Caleb thought about how long he had imagined this moment. He knew it was possible that he and his friends would be sent back to Liberty after the hearing, and he had little hope that the judge in Daviess County would dismiss their charges, but merely to be out in the spring weather for a few days was a relief. Joseph's regained optimism had also restored Caleb's trust that somehow, things would be better now.

The group headed north toward Clinton County. The day was pleasant, but there had been rain recently and the road was muddy in low areas. There were also streams to pass through that required a hard pull by the two big draft horses. But the hills were green and redbud trees were blossoming in the woods. Blue jays were screeching and cardinals singing high in the red oak and locust trees, and the willows along the Platt River were golden. It was a world that Caleb had almost forgotten, everything so alive and full of light.

"What are you thinking, Brother Caleb?" Hyrum asked. He

was facing Caleb on the opposite side of the wagon. "You haven't stopped smiling since we left the jail."

"I'm thinking God did a fine job when he made this world. It's good to know it's still out here."

Joseph was also smiling. "But, Caleb," he said, "what if you created your own world, would you change anything?"

"No, I like this one just fine . . . except maybe I'd get rid of lice and mosquitoes." He thought for a moment. "Oh, and one other thing. I'd change the smell of straw when it rots so it has a nice aroma to it, something like baking bread."

None of the men would miss the reek of the jail in Liberty, but Lyman said, "I'm afraid that's not a good plan, my brother. The smell of bread would only make a fellow hungry, and we've had enough of that."

Joseph chuckled, but he said something Caleb didn't expect. "I'm thinking we'll all have a chance to create worlds in the future. And what a fine experience that will be."

"What do you mean?" Alexander asked.

"I'll only say that much for now. But I'm starting to see the eternities in their vastness, and I'm just beginning to comprehend it all. I'll reveal more when the Lord grants me further knowledge on the subject."

Caleb was astounded by what Joseph had just said. Even more, he realized with joy that "Joseph, the Prophet," had not only returned but was reaching for greater understanding.

———————◆———————

The day passed agreeably for the most part, but the bouncing and jostling of the wagon became tiring and Caleb was relieved to hear that the party would stop for the night in a settlement called

Plattsburg. They had put about twenty-five miles behind them by late that afternoon, but they had a long day of travel ahead. Sheriff Hadley had already warned them that it would take part of a third day to reach Gallatin.

As it turned out, the quarters in Plattsburg still required the men to sleep on floors, but there was no rotting straw, and the prisoners received the same food as the guards—not fancy but generous and well-prepared. They spent the second night near Far West and continued the following morning into Daviess County, where Sheriff William Morgan took custody of the men and allowed Sheriff Hadley to turn back. Morgan was probably surprised when Hadley wished the men good luck as he rode away.

It was almost noon when the wagon rolled into Gallatin, where most of the burned log buildings had been rebuilt. A group of men had collected in the tiny town, apparently to gawk at the prisoners.

"They think we're zoo animals," Hyrum said. "Alexander, stand up and tell them you're a redheaded giraffe. I'd wager they'll believe you."

"At least they don't seem armed for hunting," Alexander told Hyrum. "I was afraid they might fire at us when we showed up."

What surprised Caleb was that few insults were cast at the men, and they were provided with a good meal before the wagon moved on to a home south of town. There, they were informed that the hearing would take place at the home of the city treasurer, Elisha Creekmore, and that this was also where they would sleep each night.

"We don't have no courthouse," Morgan told the prisoners. "You men burned to the ground the one we had, and that's one building we ain't rebuilt yet."

Caleb didn't look back at Morgan. He hadn't been one of those who had burned the courthouse, but some of the men in his militia company had started that fire. Even though Morgan was speaking civilly to the men, it seemed obvious to Caleb that if a trial eventually took place in Daviess County, there would be no hope of an acquittal.

As the wagon approached the Creekmore place, another gathering was waiting outside. These men were louder than the ones in Gallatin. They shouted profanely, vowing: "You ain't going to leave here alive. Don't even think about it."

Caleb didn't look directly at any of them. He tried to cling to the hopefulness he had felt during the ride north. But this crowd was frightening. He wondered whether he and his brothers would make it inside the house without being attacked. When the wagon stopped, Joseph stood and raised his hand to get the mob's attention. The response was intense and loud, the throng moving closer to the wagon. But Joseph shouted above the insults, "Could I say something to all of you?"

"You can speak your last words," someone yelled. "We got a tree out here. And a rope. Say what you want before we hoist you up by the neck."

This brought on roaring approval.

A ruddy, bearded man dressed in deer hide stepped toward Joseph and pointed a finger at him. "It's because of you that my brother is dead. Don't think you can get away with that."

That made no sense to Caleb. Most of the killing had been done by the Missourians. One old settler had been killed at Crooked River, but Caleb didn't know of any other deaths—except of the Saints. More than twenty members had been killed or wounded at Haun's Mill. All the same, the man was in a rage.

William Peniston, Deputy Sheriff in Daviess County, was shouting above the clamor. "If Joe wants to say something, let him do it. I'd like to hear what he wants to tell us."

The crowd did actually quiet. Joseph smiled and thanked Peniston. "Gentlemen," he said in a cheerful voice, "I appreciate this welcome. It was kind of you to come out to say hello."

Most of the men looked baffled, though a few smiled.

"I don't know about you fellows, but to me, there's nothing more agreeable than a beautiful spring day in this part of Missouri. The dogwoods are in blossom and the birds are chattering. We're all tired of winter, aren't we, and the sun feels good to us."

Now all of the men in the crowd were staring.

Someone shouted, "We ain't here to listen to no birds," but he sounded as though he doubted his own ferocity.

"Let him continue," Peniston said. "I think this must be the way a prophet talks—all about birds and springtime."

The men around Peniston laughed and so did Joseph.

"Actually, there is something important I want to tell you." Joseph paused and then announced, "We are in your hands. If we are guilty, we do not refuse to be punished by the law."

"Ain't no 'if' about being guilty," the man in deer hide growled.

"Wait a minute," Peniston said. "Joe makes a good point." He looked around at the other men. "Yes, gentlemen, these men are in our hands. Let us not use violence, but let the law have its course; we shouldn't disgrace our county by taking the law into our hands."

"If the law don't take care of it—"

"Stop right there." This was from William McKinney, a well-known enemy of the Saints. "Will Peniston is right. The law will surely convict these mongrel dogs. We don't need to act like wild men. They'll pay for the stealing and murdering they did."

A grudging acceptance prevailed among the crowd then, and the prisoners were ushered inside the house, where they were able to sit down and consult with their lawyers. The house wasn't spacious, but it was clean, and there was one bed available. The problem was, the prisoners, the defense lawyers Burnett and Rees, and several guards would be sharing the same quarters. That meant they'd sleep on the floor wall-to-wall, and the guards were unruly characters. As the evening came on, they passed around jugs of homemade liquor, and they became raucous and profane.

Caleb was tired and wanted to get some sleep, but the guards kept up their wild talk and drinking all night. Still, Joseph got along with them quite well. He joked with them and seemed not at all uncomfortable.

"So tell me, Joe," one of the guards slurred, "what makes you a prophet? How does a fella get a job like that?"

Joseph laughed and said, "Well, I didn't go looking for that line of work, and I have to tell you, it doesn't pay well."

The grisly man stepped closer to Joseph and peered into his face. Caleb wondered how Joseph could withstand the smell of his breath. "You don't look like a prophet to me," he said. "I think you're cheating all them people out of their money and doing just fine for yourself."

"I can understand why you might think that, sir. But I've paid a dear price for my calling, never having accumulated any wealth at all. And I take exception to your assessment of me as not looking like a prophet. I think I'm a fine-looking man, and frankly, sir, you look like a good fellow too—handsome as a shaggy old buffalo."

The man took in the words for a moment, and then he broke into bellowing laughter. So did the other drunken men. They didn't quiet after that, and the night was long, but Caleb was relieved that Joseph had avoided a confrontation. The guards kept slapping Joseph on the back, telling him that he was not what they had expected, and they even offered him a pull at their jug. Joseph did take one big swallow, which pleased the men immensely.

On the following morning, the same men who had guarded them turned out to be some of the jury of their peers. Most of them were still drunk, or if they had sobered a bit, they were tired and uninterested.

Caleb whispered to Peter Burnett, "Do you think these jurors like Joseph enough that they'll acquit us?"

Burnett shook his head. "No, I don't. They liked that he told them he'd submit to the law, and they liked laughing with him, but don't expect mercy. Some of these jurors—three, at least—were part of the pack of wolves who shot down your people over at Haun's Mill. They dragged a little boy out of the blacksmith shop and shot him through the head."

That brought a clearer perspective back to Caleb. The frivolity the night before was not likely to change anything. And as the hearing moved forward, that reality became increasingly obvious. Thomas Burch, the judge, had been a prosecutor during the Richmond court of inquiry, and the foreman of the jury was none other than William Peniston. Both of these men, Caleb had no doubt, wanted nothing more than to give Joseph what he asked for: justice before the law. Or at least what passed for justice in their minds.

The first day of the hearing was mostly taken up by descriptions of the hostile actions of the Mormons, and especially the attack on Gallatin. Burnett and Rees made no attempt to counter the accusations, having previously told Joseph and the other prisoners that their only hope was to be granted a change of venue to a county that wasn't so set against the Saints. Caleb understood that, but it was frustrating to sit in the confined little house and to hear the throng muttering assent to the accounts offered by the witnesses—at least when they weren't snoring or being carried out of the room, insensible.

And yet, when night came and the whiskey was passed around, these same men laughed and drank through most of the night again. Two preachers showed up at the house in the middle of this bedlam and set out to debate Joseph about his religion. Joseph sat on the floor with them, and Caleb was amazed at Joseph's ability to offer insights to the men, not in the spirit of argument but merely as an appeal to common sense. The preachers, almost in spite of themselves, granted his points. After a couple of hours—and when some of the wild behavior of the drinkers was quieting a little—Joseph asked, "So what do you think, my friends, would you like to enter the waters of baptism and join with the Saints in building Zion?"

The preachers were not sophisticated. Caleb could see that they were doubting their own assumptions about the nature of God and the purpose of life. Still, one of them, a slight little fellow with few hairs on his chin and fewer on the top of his head, said, "Well, no." He looked at his partner. "You weren't thinking of . . ." He hesitated.

"No, not at all," the bigger man said. "Of course not." But he didn't sound sure of himself. He stood up. "It's getting late. We better get along. But it was most interesting to talk to you, Mr. Smith."

Joseph stood and shook hands with the men. "Think about all we've said," he told them. "I don't know where I will settle once the Lord delivers me and my friends from our confinement, but look for us—probably in Illinois. You deserve better doctrine and a larger vision of things than you've been taught so far. We would welcome you into our fold."

The men thanked Joseph again but seemed in a hurry to get

away. When they were gone, Joseph looked at Caleb and said, "That's the trouble with the truth. It can be frightening." And then he laughed.

———◆———

The next day was mostly more of the same, except that Sampson Avard appeared as the main witness and related his version of the events of the "Mormon War," as people had started calling the recent conflicts. Avard's testimony was nothing new, but Caleb noticed one difference: Joseph listened to Avard, but not as intently as he had in Richmond. After the testimony, as Avard worked his way through the thick crowd of men in the house, he passed close enough that Joseph was able to say to him, "When you're ready to repent for what you've done, let us know. God still loves you."

Avard surely heard Joseph, but he didn't look toward him, and he hurried on out. What was striking to Caleb was that Joseph seemed to mean what he'd said.

It was during an afternoon recess in the hearing that one of the jurors, a man a little more respectable than most—or at least one who had stayed awake all day—spoke to Joseph. "Mr. Smith," he said, "we understand you're good at rassling. How about taking on one of our boys, just to show us if you're as strong as people say."

"Well, sir," Joseph said, "I might have done a little wrestling in my life, but remember, I'm a minister of the gospel. It might be taken as inappropriate by men of good breeding, such as yourself, if I were to engage in such sport." But he was smiling.

"Not at all," the man said. He too was smiling. "It would only be for a bit of entertainment. We wouldn't wager any bets, mind you. We have a little fella here who's known to hold his own with just about any man. We thought you might show him not to be so proud of himself. That's one of the teachings of Jesus, as I remember—not to be proud."

"You make a good point, but this fellow might be twice as proud after he betters a man like me. I doubt I could put up much of a fight against him. I've been through some hard months and I've lost weight—and, no doubt, muscle." Joseph looked around, the glint still in his eyes. "But let's go outside and see if I can stand up to him for a round or two."

Caleb laughed. He had seen Joseph wrestle several times, and no one had come close to besting him.

So the whole crowd moved outside. No one seemed to worry whether the prisoners would try to escape. The man introduced as Joseph's foe, John Brassfield, was built like a plow horse, with wide shoulders and a thick girth. He and Joseph each took off their coats and then shook hands. Joseph pretended to be injured by Brassfield's grip; he let out an exaggerated groan. "Oh, Mr. Brassfield, I should concede now. You're a man of might; I perceive that already."

The two men squared off, hunched forward, arms ready. But then Joseph dove forward and caught Brassfield with a quick grab behind his knee—and dumped him on his back. This brought a huge roar of laughter and approval, but Brassfield jumped up and said, "Wait just a minute. I wasn't ready."

So Joseph nodded, and the two addressed one another again. They sidestepped, circling each other in the ring formed by the crowd of shouting men. Suddenly Joseph bulled straight ahead and grabbed Brassfield. For a moment they seemed the equal of one another, each clinging tight, but Joseph twisted and pulled his opponent off balance, then tossed him to the ground.

Caleb was tempted to shout, "Well done," but he decided he

was better off not to take a chance on offending anyone in the crowd—especially any of them losing a bet.

And so the bout continued. They went at each other for five rounds and Brassfield ended up on the ground each time. In the end, both men were laughing and Brassfield was saying, "You're the best I ever faced. You're quick as lightning and strong as an ox."

Someone shouted, "It wasn't fair, Joe. You called on God to help you."

"No," Joseph said. "He thinks I ought to stick to my preaching and not enter into such lighthearted behavior."

Caleb looked around and saw the admiration in the eyes of the men who had come to Gallatin full of hatred for "Joe Smith."

Still, the hearing didn't change. A few witnesses for the Saints appeared, including Stephen Markham, who had returned from Illinois. He described the massacre at the Haun's Mill settlement, but that was met with growls from some of the jurors—probably those who had done the murdering.

In the end, when it was clear that the prisoners would be bound over for treason, Burnett and Rees carried out their strategy—the one they had planned with Alexander Doniphan. Amos Rees addressed the judge and said, "The defense moves at this time for a change of venue before a trial is held. This is the place where many of the events in question occurred, and it is doubtful that a fair judgment could be issued here. It also seems self-evident that you, as a previous prosecutor in this case, should recuse yourself."

"And what venue do you recommend?" Judge Burch asked.

"We request that the trial be held in Marion County."

Judge Burch replied immediately. "I grant your motion for a change of venue, but the trial will take place in Boone County, and the accused men will be carried there and held without bail in the jail at Columbia."

This response almost seemed too easy. Burnett whispered to Caleb, "The judge knew ahead of time that we planned to introduce this motion. I don't think he wanted to try you up here. He's glad to get rid of you."

That sounded good to Caleb. He looked at his brothers, and they all looked pleased.

But the jurors were not so accepting. Caleb later learned that some of them caught up with Stephen Markham outside the building and beat him badly. Still, they made no attempt to accost Joseph or the other accused men—as they had vowed they would do.

What satisfied Caleb was that the site of the trial was being moved from this hostile county, and he could now hope for a better jail.

CHAPTER 18

Something was happening that Caleb didn't understand. Not only had Judge Burch been quick to grant a change of venue, but he had assigned only five men to guard the prisoners during their transfer to Columbia, Boone County, which was 150 miles from Gallatin. Always before, the prisoners had been transported in wagons guarded by a posse of men. This trip did start out somewhat that way, except that the guards seemed less vigilant than others had been. William Bowman, who had bought Lyman Wight's home in Daviess County and was on good terms with Lyman, oversaw the guards, and Sheriff William Morgan was assisting him. John Brassfield, the wrestler who had come to like Joseph, was also a guard, along with William McKinney and a man named John Pope.

The travel to Columbia didn't really start until two days after the hearing. The guards chose to travel northwest, not south, and to stop in Adam-ondi-Ahman. This, they explained, was a chance for the company to obtain some needed provisions. For Lyman, a return to the two-story house he had built and once lived in might have been awkward if Bowman hadn't been so accommodating. The men slept in beds that night and on the following morning, with rain falling hard, Bowman delayed a full day. The prisoners ate well and were allowed a chance to bathe before setting out the following morning.

All this was pleasant, even restful, but Caleb wondered what it meant. Was an ambush waiting for them? The friendliness and delay could be part of a plan to let that happen.

The guards arranged for Joseph and Hyrum to buy two horses, which they were able to do by trading clothing and promissory notes, since they had little money. The plan was to get by without a wagon, but that meant the prisoners would have to take turns walking and riding the horses, and that led to considerable disorder. With the five guards all riding horses, there seemed no good way for the entire contingent to stay together. That was a curious way to transport accused "traitors and killers." Caleb feared it could be a way to separate Joseph from the others so that he could be assassinated.

"What's going on?" Caleb whispered to Joseph as they traveled that first day. "They aren't treating us like prisoners."

"I've been told certain things," Joseph said. "I don't think they want us to arrive in Boone County. I'm sure we'll find out about that in the next couple of days."

"What do you mean? Do they plan to kill us?" Caleb asked.

"No, brother, I'm certain they won't kill us. More than anything, they want us to leave the state before they have to put us on trial. My guess is, Missouri leaders don't want to give us the chance to testify to our treatment in their state."

Caleb hoped Joseph was right, but he found himself watching the woods and wondering whether someone might be waiting around a bend in the road. He wanted to trust Joseph's opinion and he hoped it was inspired, but fear had been part of Caleb's life for so many months that it was hard to believe that mobs weren't lying in wait to take Joseph's life—and probably his life as well. The

Lord had promised that Joseph's days would not be "numbered less," and Caleb had told himself he could accept whatever number that was, but he did long to see his family again.

As it turned out, the party only traveled to Millport that first day, a distance of about seven miles. The guards seemed in no great hurry to exert themselves. That night they stayed in the home of Josiah Morin, one of the other men in Daviess County who had become a friend to the Saints. Once again, Morin's hospitality made the stay comfortable. After a winter in the Clay County jail, the food, the beds, the friendliness, all seemed too agreeable to imagine.

But Caleb remained wary.

The next day, the contingent covered a few more miles and spent the night with a family of Mormon-haters who didn't show the same kindness. And on the day after that, the guards finally became serious about making some headway, traveling nineteen miles. But it was a disjointed system of travel. At one point, Caleb and Sheriff Morgan became separated from the other men, and the two spent more than an hour in friendly conversation. Caleb told Morgan about his experiences in the War of 1812 and even described the first time he had heard Parley Pratt preach the gospel of the restoration of all things. The Spirit had told him almost instantly that he had finally found the truth he was searching for. Morgan listened with considerable interest, even asked a few questions about Mormon beliefs.

The travelers located one another before the day was over and they decided to camp by a stream called Yellow Creek, which was, as Caleb reckoned, about seventy miles southeast of Gallatin. Caleb knew that the group would have to turn directly south before long to get to Columbia, but he also sensed that something new was happening.

When the men gathered to eat dried meat and bread around a campfire, Lyman presented a jug to the guards. "I bought this along the way," he said. "I thought you men, after making such a long trek today, might like a little refreshment."

The guards were overjoyed, and they immediately passed the whiskey around. It didn't take long for them to show signs of drunkenness—and sleepiness. Three of the men decided they would bed down for the night. Morgan and Bowman had imbibed their fair share, but they remained at the fire.

"Listen, men," Sheriff Morgan said, "Judge Burch told me never to deliver you to Boone County. Let me show you something." He got up and walked to the saddlebag he had laid by his bedding. When he came back, he said, "Look at this mittimus. It's not signed and it's not dated, and that's not an accident."

"What does it mean?" Alexander asked.

"I'm not legally bound to deliver you anywhere," Bowman said. "I know you want to find your friends and families in Illinois, and as for me, I want to get back to my own people at home."

Sheriff Morgan chuckled and said, "I'm going to take one more good drink of grog, then bed down, and you men can do as you have a mind to."

With freedom within reach, Caleb found he was locked in place. This is what he had prayed for, dreamed of all winter, but he still couldn't resist the feeling that it was too good to be true, that a trap was being set. If the prisoners left, the sheriff could claim the Mormons had tried to escape and he had had no choice but to chase them down and kill them.

Joseph said, "Thank you, gentlemen. You've been fair with us. We won't forget it. And we'll pay you for the horses. Some of the Saints are still in Daviess County. I'll try to get money to them and on to you, or you can seek us out. I'll pay you however I can arrange it. Don't worry about that."

"I'm not worried," Bill Bowman said. "But John Brassfield might worry. He procured those horses for you. He—or one of us—will be on your doorstep one day, wherever you end up, and we'll expect cash in hand."

"Yes. And you'll have it." Joseph laughed. "I wouldn't want to wrestle with John again. I was lucky that first time."

"I doubt John will be eager for another fight," Bowman said, and he laughed too. "But we know you'll pay."

Bowman stayed to help the men saddle their horses, and then he followed Morgan's example and rolled up in his blankets. The five prisoners collected their few belongings and then stood in a little circle and discussed how they would travel. Their plan was to trade off riding and walking and to keep together as best they could.

"We can't follow the main roads," Alexander told the others. "I think there's a good chance that someone will come looking for us."

"That's right," Hyrum said. "And we can't use our own names, no matter where we are. We don't look much like ourselves after all these months, but people know our names—or at least they know mine and Joseph's."

"All right," Joseph said. "Choose a name and don't forget it."

"Robert Brown," Alexander said. "So be sure to call me that."

They all chose names, plain ones—and they laughed as they tried them out on one another. But then they knelt in the dark near the horses and Joseph called on Hyrum to say a prayer.

Hyrum called on the Lord to guide them to their families and to safety. "Lord, we thank thee for delivering us and acknowledge thy hand in all that has happened," he said, his voice full of emotion.

Gratitude overwhelmed Caleb in the silence following Hyrum's prayer. But still, haunting him was a sense that their delivery was not yet accomplished.

With no road to follow, travel was difficult, and the men had to reckon by the stars to be certain they were heading east. It was also difficult to keep together in the dark.

Joseph took a turn walking first, and he admitted later that he had been too hasty in pulling his boots on. With his feet muddy, he had failed to work his boots on fully. By the time he had walked all night, he had worn a nasty blister. When the men stopped in the morning and watered their horses, Joseph took off his boots and found the inside of one of them soaked with blood. Caleb's feet weren't blistered, but they certainly hurt. It had been too long since he had walked any distance at all.

The men only rested a short time and then set out again in the daylight. They wanted to get as many miles behind them as they could before word got out of their "escape." Caleb and Joseph took a turn at riding the horses that morning, and as they traveled alongside one another, Joseph said, "Well, Brother Caleb, it's a fine thing to be free, wouldn't you say?"

Caleb did enjoy the clear spring day and the good air to breathe, but he said, "I'd feel better if we were across the Mississippi and away from this state."

"I agree, brother. Entirely. But I feel certain the Lord is in this."

"Is God telling you that, or is it just what you're hoping?"

Joseph laughed. "It's always the same," he said. "People ask me for reassurance, and then they want to know whether it's just old Joseph talking or whether Jehovah is speaking out of the cloud on Mount Sinai."

"But you feel sure he's speaking to you now?"

Joseph's head, his whole body, was bouncing with the strides of the horse. It seemed for a moment that he was nodding, but Caleb realized, he was thinking. "It's never quite that simple," he said. "I wish God would hit me in the chest with a big hickory stick, and say, 'All right. Listen now. This is coming from me.' And I will say, it sometimes happens almost like that. I've known pure truth to come in words that are not mine. That happened with the letter—this last one I wrote to the Saints. But other times I merely feel the peace of the Comforter, and that's what I feel now. I trust that we'll make it to our families. All the same, we have to use our heads and act with caution."

"I wish I had heard from Nancy," Caleb said. "I don't know whether she and the children have made their way out of Missouri."

"I can't advise you on that, Brother Caleb. But I know this. Sister Nancy is as strong and unwavering as you are, and Clark will be at her side, helping with all your children. Beyond that, there's something else I know. I've seen the vision of it. You and I may not live to see it, but the kingdom of God will someday roll forth to all the world."

"I believe you, Brother Joseph."

"Thank you for saying that. It's been a dark winter, my friend, but we've lasted it out together, haven't we?"

Caleb recognized the honor he was being granted to spend this time with the prophet—even to have suffered degradation with him in the jail.

------◆------

Later that morning Caleb walked again, and he was beginning to relax. But in the afternoon, as the men were crossing a field, Hyrum looked around, then suddenly stopped.

"Someone's coming up behind us on a horse," he said. "And he's riding fast."

"Spread out!" Joseph ordered. "Go different ways. Hide where you can."

Caleb darted to his right into a little thicket of hazel brush. He stretched out on the ground and waited, but he heard nothing. He thought of looking out to see what was going on, but he decided, for now, he better hold still, take no chances. And all the while, he wondered, was the rider a scout for a posse? Were they finally being chased down?

Caleb kept waiting, but when his fear began to subside, his exhaustion took over. The next thing he knew, he was waking to find the sun much lower in the sky. He waited for another minute or two and then looked out of his hiding place, but he could see no one—not his friends and not the horse and rider. He decided to set out in the direction he and the other men had been traveling, but walked at least a mile and caught up with no one. He wondered how long he had slept and whether anyone was looking for him. He chose to keep walking east. If he didn't find Joseph and the others, he would end up at the Mississippi in a few days, where all of the Saints were heading. But it was unnerving to be alone, not to have his friends around him.

As it turned out, Caleb walked the rest of the day and then made a decision to keep going all night. The truth was, he was frightened to be on his own, and he wanted to get Missouri behind him. Even though his body was weary—especially his feet—he kept moving forward, walking hard. By morning he had given up hope of finding the other men, and he thought of curling up somewhere for the daytime hours and then traveling by night again, but he still didn't feel like sleeping.

When he came to a farmhouse, he was desperately hungry.

He knew he couldn't keep up his pace without eating, so he approached the house and hoped whoever lived there would offer him some food, even if he had to work for it. He stepped to the door and knocked. The door opened to reveal a kindly looking man dressed in rough farmer's clothes. But he looked more like a schoolteacher than a man of the soil. Caleb was stunned when the man said, "Ah, you must be Mr. Baldwin."

For a moment Caleb couldn't think what to say, but when he glanced beyond the man, he saw the last thing he expected: Joseph, Hyrum, Alexander, and Lyman sitting at a table, all looking up from their breakfast plates.

Alexander got up and hurried to the door. "George," he told the man of the house, "you're exactly right. This is our traveling companion—the one we lost—Caleb Baldwin." He reached forward to grab Caleb's shoulder. "I rode a horse back to find you, but I couldn't see you anywhere. You must have taken a different path from us."

"I fell asleep," Caleb said, and he laughed at himself.

This brought on a laugh from all the men. But Hyrum called out, "Alexander, bring him to the table. He needs to eat."

Harris was laughing. "From all appearances, he needs a hearty meal."

Caleb looked again at Alexander.

"But aren't you Robert Brown?" he asked.

Alexander grinned. "No," he said. "We don't need those names here. Brother Harris is a member of the Church. I thought you must have come here knowing that."

"No. I had no idea. I was planning to ask for a meal."

"Well, he's a brother. Joseph knew where he lived, so we came here on purpose. No question, the Lord *led* you here."

Caleb sat at the table and ate well. The men rejoiced to be

back together. According to George, they still had three hard days' travel to reach the Mississippi, and he invited them to rest for a day. But the men all agreed; they had to keep moving forward. It was hard to say how people in Gallatin might have reacted when Sheriff Morgan and the others returned with a report that the prisoners had escaped—which they were sure to claim. By now, a posse could be riding hard, trying to track them down.

"Caleb," Joseph said, "we didn't know what to do when we lost you, so we decided to keep heading east and we hoped, somehow, that our paths would cross again."

"We also prayed," Hyrum said. "We asked the Lord to lead you back to us. And he did."

"It's like I told you," Joseph added. "The Lord is looking after us."

Caleb was happy to believe that again.

CHAPTER 19

The days that followed after leaving the Harris home were not easy. The Harrises had packed two loaves of bread and a hefty square of cheese for the men to take with them. That hardly seemed enough for five men to get by on for three days, but Joseph told the others that they would have to make the food last as long as they could. He was still wary of seeking help from farmers they didn't know.

"I believe the Lord is with us," he said, "but we can't be foolhardy. I don't want to get to the very gates of freedom only to be hauled back."

So the men ate little the first day and slept in a wooded area that night, and the next morning they shared small rations of the bread and cheese again. They continued to avoid roads. Late in the day, however, Hyrum said, "Joseph, I don't think we can keep up this pace without more to eat. I can see a house up ahead. It seems to me we'll have to take our chances. Let's ask the people who live here for a place to lodge—in the barn if nothing else—and see whether they won't offer us a meal."

"I have a little money," Alexander said. "We could offer to pay for food."

Joseph hesitated. "All right. I'll accept the inspiration you two are receiving. Let's see what happens. But don't anyone use our real names."

The men walked across a pasture in which cattle were feeding on the early-spring grass. The setting was pleasant with the small log farmhouse silhouetted in the evening light with smoke rising from a chimney. It was a nice evening, but the night before had been cold, and Caleb didn't want to sleep on the ground again.

As the men approached, the farmer stepped outside and watched them walk toward him. When he finally spoke, it was with a Swedish accent. "And what, may I ask, are you fellas doing wandering about on such an evening?"

Hyrum walked ahead and spoke first. "It is a fine evening, sir," he said. "But cool. We're looking to get inside for the night. Would you have a suitable place for us to sleep—and perhaps a little food we could purchase from you?"

"It's possible. But who are you, may I ask, and what is the purpose in your travels?"

"This man is my brother, and these others are my friends. We've been in the west, seeking a place to settle and open new farms. We're heading back to our families in Illinois now." Hyrum had apparently thought of a story he could tell the man without deceiving more than necessary.

"I don't know why you'd be going about with no provisions. What sort of settlers are you, with no more sense than that?" The question was apt, but the man laughed, as though he considered Hyrum and the others unwise, not dangerous.

"We started out with all we needed," Hyrum said, "but folks in the west of this state turned out to be less than accommodating. We were robbed of most everything we had carried with us."

Caleb recognized that Hyrum had chosen again to tell a subtle version of the truth, rather than an outright lie.

The man nodded. "Yes, it's what I hear. Are they still fighting with the Mormons out there?"

"Not that we saw. But the Mormons have mostly retreated and scattered to other places."

"Are they as bad a lot as some people say, these Mormons?"

"No, sir. Our impression was, they are people of good character."

"Well, sure. I hear it both ways. But people, for the most part, are just people. I don't know why such warring has to go on." He looked back toward his home. "We have a room on the back of the house. There's no bed or nothing like that, but we could maybe find a few blankets for you to share. And we can surely find something for you to eat."

"We have a little money," Alexander said. "We're willing to—"

"No. I don't need your money. But let me talk to my wife before I bring you all in. She'll want to know that you're good sorts, not rascals, so tell her a little more about yourselves and see what she thinks of you."

The man walked inside and was gone several minutes. He then motioned for the men to come inside, and once they were all gathered in the little log house, he said, "Now tell my wife your names and how you ended up out here in the middle of nowhere with nothing but the clothes on your backs."

"And shabby clothes at that," Joseph said. "But tell me your names first."

"We're the Bengtssons. My wife is Astrid and I'm Oscar."

Caleb listened as Joseph gave an accurate account of himself—except for all the parts he left out, such as his real name. He told of his four children, his wife living near Quincy, and his desire for nothing more in life than to have a fine farm of the kind these people had established. The couple was put at ease almost immediately, and the others introduced themselves by their chosen names, keeping their descriptions brief.

"My wife and I have seven daughters and two sons," Caleb told them. "My first two are married, and we have two grandchildren, one born only a few weeks ago."

"Seven daughters!" Astrid said. "That's a gaggle."

"They do set up plenty of chatter," Caleb said. Then he couldn't resist saying, "But I can't wait to see them again. We've been gone longer than I like."

"I wager you're a fine papa," she said, seeming satisfied. She offered a sleeping place for the night with more than a few blankets, and for dinner she cooked a veritable feast with beef roasted over a fire, along with potatoes and carrots.

The worst part was keeping up the ruse all evening. What Caleb wanted to do was teach these people the gospel. But he followed Joseph's lead, and Joseph was still being careful not to be identified.

After the hearty dinner, the men slept well and Astrid fed them again in the morning. As they were preparing to leave, Alexander got ready ahead of the others and he and Oscar walked out to look over the farm. The other men had just stepped to the door when the two returned, with Alexander bent over and moaning. The much shorter Oscar was holding him around the waist and trying to help him to the door.

"He's taken sick," Oscar said, "all in an instant."

"What is it, Robert?" Lyman asked. Then he glanced at Oscar. "Mr. Brown ate the same things as the rest of us, so it surely wasn't the food."

But now Alexander began to stretch his body skyward. "It's passing now," he said. "I think I'll be all right."

Caleb sensed that something wasn't quite right in this. But Oscar retrieved a jug from a cabinet and poured out half a cupful.

"Drink this. It's corn mash," he told Alexander. "It will fix what's wrong with you faster than anything."

"You mean liquor?" Alexander asked. He surely knew the answer to that question, but he seemed to be stalling long enough to make a decision.

"Sure thing. I make it myself."

Caleb knew that Alexander had promised himself not to drink alcohol, but either to keep his story straight or perhaps desiring to taste whiskey again after such a long time, he drank the cup down in a single draft, then shook himself and said, "That's powerful stuff, sir." Caleb thought Alexander looked a little too delighted.

But Oscar now insisted that the other men share in the corn mash to protect them from whatever Mr. Brown had experienced. So they used the same cup, each poured a little, and took their medicine whether they wanted to or not.

It was only later, when they had set out walking again, that Alexander told the whole story.

"We were enjoying a fine chat," he said, "until Oscar said, 'Now tell me your name again,' and for the life of me, I couldn't think of it. So I doubled over—you know, like I was in terrible pain—and I said, 'Something's just struck me. I'm sick to my stomach.' When you men called me Robert Brown, I knew it was time to recover."

This brought a burst of laughter from the other men, and all the rest of that day they took turns referring to Alexander as "Mr. Brown" and asking again and again, "How's your stomach feeling now, Mr. Brown? Do you need another dose of medicine?"

The men reached the Mississippi in another day—with the help of a sack of provisions Oscar and Astrid had sent with them. They slept in the woods a mile or so from the river that night, and then, early in the morning, Joseph and Caleb took their turn on the horses and rode ahead. No one seemed to be pursuing them, but as they drew nearer to the river, Joseph slowed his horse and told Caleb, "If someone is looking for us, they will be watching the ferries. Let's not play into their hands."

He dismounted and walked his horse slowly ahead as he surveyed the area up and down the river. Caleb saw a few people waiting at the dock, but he noticed no one who seemed suspicious. Still, Joseph said, "Someone could be hiding in the trees nearby. Let's wait until the ferry arrives and then hurry down and get on quickly."

They stayed in the wooded area and watched for the ferry, which arrived after twenty minutes or so. Once it did, Joseph walked fast toward the river, still leading his horse, but he told Caleb, "If anyone comes out of the woods—or maybe up from the riverbank—we'll jump back on our horses and ride west, but not on the main road."

"Shall we split up or—"

"Let's stay together." He kept walking and no one interfered, so they led their horses onto the ferry.

Caleb let out a big breath of relief, but Joseph said, "We'll have to watch as we get off. That might be where they would plan to intercept us."

That seemed unlikely to Caleb, but he understood Joseph's caution. They were so close now, and their families might not be far away. It was dreadful to think that all they had hoped for could still be lost.

The crossing didn't take long. Once they'd arrived on the

Illinois shore and walked their horses off the ferry, they waited for a moment and looked again for anyone who might appear suspicious. They saw no one, and Caleb breathed easier again.

"Do you have any idea where to go from here?" he asked.

"Quincy is close, I'm told," Joseph said. "Let's ask someone to be sure. But let's stay with the names we've chosen."

Caleb was about to reply when he noticed a man approaching. Joseph ducked his head and pulled down the floppy brim of his old black hat. He whispered to Caleb, "You do the talking. Just be careful what you say."

But the man walking toward them suddenly called out, "Joseph, is that you?"

As the man drew nearer, Caleb saw that it was Dimick Huntington, a brother in the Church. Joseph raised his head and said, "Brother Dimick, it's such a relief to see you. Are you sure it's safe to use my name?"

"Yes, of course," Brother Huntington said. "You have no need to worry here. We're well accepted. I only knew you by your frame and the way you moved—you're a ragged lot, the two of you. Your boots look like they're about to fall off." He laughed and reached to shake hands with Caleb. "All the same, you're a beautiful sight, and the members will rejoice to have you back."

"How did you happen to be here?" Joseph asked.

"Emma sent me. We heard a few days ago that you had escaped and would be heading this direction. So Emma asked me to come and watch for you."

"Where is she?"

"She's still staying in Judge Cleveland's house, east of Quincy. She's comfortable there, and your children are well. She wants me to bring you to her. It's several miles from here, but I have my horse tied up nearby. We can haste there now unless you want to see your mother and father first. They're staying directly in Quincy."

"No. I would shock them with the way I look. Let's go to Emma. After I clean up, I can see others."

"What about *my* family?" Caleb asked. "Have you seen Nancy and my children?"

"I haven't. If they've made it here, I'm not aware of it. But we can ask if anyone else has seen them."

So the men set out. As they passed through Quincy, they saw others who recognized Joseph. He greeted everyone, but he didn't stop to converse. He told Dimick and Caleb that he didn't want to spend time telling the story of his release over and over. He just wanted to reach Emma.

Caleb asked a few more people about his family, but no one had seen them.

"They were on their way a few days ago," one brother told him. "The last time I saw them, they was traveling on the main road from Chillicothe. They all seemed well enough, but most was walking, and the old team of oxen that was pulling your wagon was making slow progress. If you head back across the river, I think you'll find them not too far away."

"It would be better to wait for them, Brother Caleb," Joseph said, "and not go back into Missouri."

Caleb knew Joseph was right, but he didn't want to wait. Still, he continued on with Joseph and Dimick. He felt he had to clean up as best he could so he wouldn't look too haggard when Nancy finally saw him.

As they rode east, Brother Huntington pointed at a house up ahead and said, "That's the Cleveland place."

The words had barely left his mouth when Caleb saw Emma step from the front door. She was looking toward the men as they approached. As they drew closer, Caleb made out her features and saw her face brighten in recognition. By the time Joseph dismounted and walked to the front gate, she was running toward him.

"Oh, Joseph," she was saying. "Oh, Joseph."

"I'm sorry I look so terrible," he told her.

"No. You look wonderful." She threw her arms around him. And then the children came running: Julia, Joey, and Freddie. And a woman, whom Caleb assumed was Mrs. Cleveland, stepped to the door holding little Alexander. The children wrapped their arms around Joseph's legs.

Caleb knew that Joseph and Emma had imagined this moment for many months, and he saw in their faces, heard in their voices, how grateful they were. Emma sounded mostly relieved when she said, "Joseph, I've worried so much these last few days. I thought maybe you had been hunted down and . . ." She didn't say the word.

"The Lord has brought me back to you," Joseph said, "and now I have much to do. But I never want us to be separated again."

Caleb was moved by hearing them and seeing the joy in the children as they took turns hugging their papa. It was the very thing Caleb had been thinking about for such a long time, and now he wanted to be the one surrounded and embraced by his own family.

Emma asked to hear the entire story: how the men had gained their freedom and made their way across the state. But she posed questions faster than Joseph could complete his answers, and finally he said, "I'll tell you all about it. But first, I'd like to have a bath, if that's possible. And I need to shave."

"Do you suppose I could do the same?" Caleb asked.

Mrs. Cleveland had approached by then, and she handed

Alexander to Joseph. The little boy looked dubious about the rough-looking character who was holding him and telling him how glad he was to see him, but he didn't pull back.

Mrs. Cleveland assured the men that she would start heating water, and while they waited to bathe, they could eat. Caleb hesitated to take too much time, but he knew he needed food, and above all, he needed that bath. When Mrs. Cleveland said she would try to find clothing that would fit the two men, that was more than Caleb had hoped for.

It was almost midday when Caleb was finally fed, washed, clothed, and ready to head out. Joseph had accepted that Caleb could not be deterred from seeking his family.

"Take the horse," Joseph told him, "and that will hurry you along. But be watchful. Don't let anyone catch you back in Missouri."

Caleb agreed, shook Joseph's hand, said goodbye, and walked toward the front gate. But then Joseph hurried after him, turned him around, and embraced him. "Thank you, my brother," he said. "You helped me through a terrible time."

"We all helped each other, Brother Joseph."

"But I despaired at times, Caleb. I fear that I wasn't the strength to you that I should have been."

"That's not how I remember it, Joseph. You tried to lift us in the midst of your own despair. I'll consider it an honor all the days of my life that I spent these months with you, side by side."

Joseph's eyes filled with tears. "It's good of you to say that, Brother Caleb. The Lord gave us *experience*. That's what he told us, didn't he? And it *will be* for our good, just as he promised." Joseph glanced back at the house, then hesitated for a moment before he said, "I'm thinking I should go with you. I need to help you find your family."

"No, Joseph, you can't do that. You have to stay out of Missouri now. I'll find my family, and you stay with yours."

Joseph looked solemn, but then he nodded his agreement.

Caleb was moved by the sense of brotherhood he felt with the prophet. There in the jail, especially during the overwhelming blackness of the nights, they had been brought—both of them, all of them—to a depth that few people would ever understand.

The two embraced again, and then Caleb mounted his horse. He was worried about crossing the river and riding back into Missouri, but he had to find his family, then find them a place to live.

CHAPTER 20

As Caleb rode back through Quincy, he learned from the ferryman that Hyrum, Lyman, and Alexander had crossed the river. Caleb was relieved to know that, and he hoped they had located their families. He felt some trepidation about returning to the place he had longed to escape, but he knew he wouldn't feel content until Nancy and his children were with him. He rode for a couple of hours and knew he would soon have to let his horse rest, but then he spotted a wagon pulled by two oxen plodding toward him.

It took another minute or so before Caleb recognized his family for certain. Nancy was sitting in the wagon, but all the children were walking. Clark was out front, guiding the oxen.

No one noticed Caleb at first. They were looking down to watch their steps in the muddy road. Nancy was holding little Elmina and the baby's head was bobbing with the sway of the wagon. She seemed half asleep.

Then eleven-year-old Abigail looked up. She stopped, stared, and cried, "Papa!"

Soon all the children realized who was riding toward them, and Julie and Ellen were running toward him. Caleb dismounted and grabbed the girls, who had wrapped their arms around his legs. He hoisted little Ellen into his arms and hugged and kissed her.

"You've grown since I saw you last," he told her, then kissed her again.

"I'm big now," she said. She was only four, but she did seem older than when he had left her. Her clothes were muddy and strands of lifeless hair were sticking out from her limp bonnet. Even so, she looked beautiful to him.

"Yes, you are big. Do you know that Papa loves you?"

"I love you too," she said. "But why did the men take you?"

He realized she still remembered that dreadful day. He wished that she didn't. And he wished that he had an answer for her.

"It doesn't matter now," he told her. "We're all together again." He put her down, then picked up Julia, kissed her, and held her tight for a time. He looked to see Nancy watching from the wagon. "Are you all right?" Caleb asked.

"Yes, yes. I'm just so . . ." But she couldn't complete her sentence. She was sobbing.

"I love you," Caleb said. "I . . ." But he ran out of words. He had imagined this moment, had even thought of things he might say, but there was too much to tell her. They needed time together so he could somehow help her comprehend how much he had missed her. She looked as bedraggled as everyone else, but he saw the Nancy he had married, the beautiful woman she still was, not hidden at all by a layer of grit.

Elmina was twisting by then, looking at her papa. But when Caleb reached for her, she pulled back, clearly frightened by someone she didn't know. She was only a year-and-a-half old, and she hadn't seen him since just after her first birthday. Caleb understood her fear of him, but it pained him all the same.

"She'll know you soon, Caleb," Nancy said. "She's a loving little girl."

Caleb looked around at his older children and hugged Abby,

who was crying. She had made a smudge on her cheek where she had tried to wipe away her tears, but she was as pretty as her mother.

"A man told us you were out of jail," she said, "but we didn't know where you were. Every day we've been praying we would find you."

"I know. I've been saying the same prayer." He hugged her a second time, and now he was crying unabashedly.

He turned to Mary Ann. She looked taller to him, but she was terribly thin, and her skin looked gray. He hated to think what she had been through. "You seem more grown-up, Mary Ann," he told her.

"I'm sixteen now," she told him. "I had my birthday this week."

All winter Caleb had tried to think of his children, to imagine himself home with them. It was wonderful to be home with his family, but he regretted not remembering Mary Ann's birthday. In his mind, she had been a little girl, and now she was changed. He hoped she would soon regain her color.

Eunice had been waiting all this time. She was older, eighteen, and she had always been willing to let the younger children have attention ahead of her. Her blue eyes were watery, but she was looking composed. Caleb stepped to her, hugged her.

"We were so worried about you all winter," she said, and then she let go and cried.

"It's over now," Caleb said. But Eunice didn't look her best either. Her face was almost skeletal, and the dress and cloak she was wearing were faded and worn.

James had been waiting stolidly, as though to prove he was a man and not the twelve-year-old he was. But Caleb motioned for him to draw near, and he hugged his son too. James didn't say a word. Caleb could see in his eyes that he was on the verge of crying and that he didn't want to embarrass himself.

Ann, by then, had walked to Clark, and the two were standing near the oxen. Caleb went to them and embraced them both. Clark, when he had stepped back, smiled. "We have something to tell you."

Caleb knew what it was, heard it in Clark's voice. He looked at Ann, who nodded happily.

"Next fall," she said without waiting for the question. Another grandchild. Nothing could have pleased Caleb more, but it also raised another question. What about his daughter Maria and her husband, Morgan? Where were they?

"Didn't Maria and Morgan travel with you?" he asked.

"They came ahead of us," Clark said. "They should be in Illinois by now. We got held up for a time in Far West. We didn't have a wagon until our leaders brought one back to us, and then, after that, we got bogged down in a storm. So we're behind most of the people."

"How did you know how to find us?" Ann asked.

"I crossed the river into Illinois and learned you weren't there, but a brother told me you were on this road, so I came back to find you."

"You shouldn't have," Clark told him. "We've been getting along all right. Isn't it dangerous for you to be in Missouri?"

"Maybe. We do need to move on. Let's get to the river and across, and then we can take our joy together."

That was wise advice, but it wasn't taken very seriously. Everyone wanted to have Caleb's attention, tell him something of their trials, or whisper to him again how happy they were that he was all right.

Caleb also felt a need to say something more to Nancy, and

by then, she must have felt the same. After handing Elmina to Eunice, Nancy climbed down from the wagon. Caleb finally had his chance to hold her in his arms. He put his arm around her and they walked together, side by side.

"I didn't know if this time would ever come," she said. "I feared they would take your life. The soldiers around Far West kept telling us they would."

"I know. We heard that over and over. Sometimes I believed it, no matter what the Lord whispered to me."

"We'll be all right now."

"I don't know where we'll live, Nancy. Most people, from what I heard in Quincy, have found places, but there won't be many houses or sheds or barns that aren't taken up by now. We may have to—"

"No, Caleb. Don't fret about that for now. We'll find a way. Let's just be thankful we're all alive."

And the reality finally did strike Caleb. He had passed through his ordeal, and the Lord had delivered him from the dungeon he had hated. Now he would cross the river to safety. It was what he had prayed for—pleaded for—almost half a year now. He had known all winter that he would welcome the hardships of a farmer's life if only he could be with his loved ones again.

"I know, Nancy. You're right. What we need to do, before we push ahead, is pray together."

So Caleb called his family around him, and they knelt in a grassy spot by the side of the road. He pronounced a father's blessing on everyone, and he thanked the Lord even for the difficulties that lay ahead.

The family walked on then and crossed the river on the ferry. The Saints—and the people of Quincy—welcomed them, fed them, and helped them find shelter. Everyone Caleb talked with wanted to hear his story. He told them a few things, but he wanted to dwell on the future, not the past. Above all, he didn't want to talk about those nights in the dungeon, where even God had seemed walled off and out of reach.

CHAPTER 21

It didn't take long for word to spread that Joseph had arrived, and Church members soon made their way to Judge Cleveland's home. Joseph greeted everyone, and he met for short discussions with the Church leaders, who told him the apostles were not in Quincy. They had left to travel back to Far West in order to commence their missions from the temple site on April 26, as Joseph had prophesied they would. Emma heard the joy in Joseph's voice when he responded to the news, even though he expressed his concern for his brethren. She knew what it meant to him to know they were moving forward—and still believed in his prophecies.

Emma soon moved away from the hubbub created by all the visitors; she retreated to the bedroom that she would now share with Joseph. Sarah Cleveland had taken the children from the living room where the visitors had gathered so Emma could stay with Joseph and the others. But Emma had wanted time to be with her husband, and it soon became obvious that she wouldn't have that chance. She realized that she should have foreseen what would happen when people learned he had arrived, but that didn't change how she felt.

After a time, however, Joseph opened the door and stepped in. "There you are," he said. "I've been looking for you."

She was sitting in a rocking chair near the foot of the bed and didn't want to appear unhappy, but she could see in his face that he understood her disappointment.

"I'm sorry," he said. "I didn't feel that I could send people away too abruptly. But they're gone now."

"Everyone wanted to see you," Emma said. "I recognize that."

Her words clearly registered with him. "But I can't give *all* my time to the members anymore, Emma. I plan to be careful about that from now on."

"Joseph, you belong to God—and to the Church—not to me. I've known that for a long time." Emma had been well aware, even before she had fallen in love with Joseph, that he had been called to serve the Lord. And yet, in those early days of their romance, she had never truly understood what that would mean. Still, it was wrong to be jealous of God; she knew that.

"I'm going to be different now, Emma." He walked to her, then sat on the bed facing her, their knees nearly touching. "I've tried to lead the Church too much on my own, but I won't do that now. We have good leaders. I can rely on them and clear out more time for you and the children."

Emma smiled. "Joseph, you're alive, and I've worried all winter that your life would be taken. I'm not going to complain if Church members love you and want to be near you."

"Yes. Today. But in coming days, I won't—"

"It's all right. Don't make promises you can't keep." She hesitated, waited until his eyes engaged with hers. "But Joseph, please learn to be careful. There are still people who want to kill you. Crossing the river doesn't mean they will all go away."

Joseph bent forward and put his hand on her knee. She touched her fingers to his. "I don't think Boggs will come after me, Emma. We didn't *escape*; our guards let us go. I think the governor is happy to have us out of his state. And Illinois is different. This is a place where we can start over and win the respect of the people."

Emma took a breath. She could hear it already: Joseph's optimism returning. But how long before new troubles would begin? "Joseph," she said, "Bishop Partridge thinks we shouldn't start our own city again. It's when we gather to one place and become too numerous that local people fear we'll take over. I know we want to build Zion, but—"

"I understand what he's saying." He straightened, considered, and Emma heard his attempt to sound judicious when he spoke again. "Emma, Zion isn't my idea; it's the Lord's. We can't give up on the gathering. We are to build a center place, then spread the gospel out from there to all the world. Still, we don't have to separate ourselves from local citizens. From what I've been hearing today, the people of Illinois feel kindly toward us, so we can build friendships. If we start a new city, we'll welcome everyone who wants to live among us. That never happened in Missouri. The people rejected us without finding out that we could all live together."

"Joseph, we *tried* in Missouri. But people don't like the way we live. They don't think a city and a religion should be mixed up together. They end up believing you're a dictator. Over and over, they say the same thing about you: that you're a fraud and a tyrant, that you're claiming to be a prophet so you can take advantage of your followers."

Joseph was nodding. "I know. You're right. But we need, this time, to show people who we really are—and who I am. At our hearing in Gallatin, the men there wanted to kill me when we first arrived, but they ended up getting along with me just fine. It's all a matter of finding a way for them to understand that we're not fanatics, that we're normal people."

We're not normal people, Emma was thinking, but she didn't say that to Joseph. Instead, she asked, "Are you going to buy the land that Mr. Galland wants to sell you?"

"I'm not sure yet. We need to learn more about the offer, and I need to see the lands he—and some others—want to sell us. But it looks promising. The place they call Commerce is in a big bend in the river, and from what I'm told, once we drain the wet areas, it will be a perfect site for a city."

Emma knew already that it would happen. She had seen Joseph get excited about such prospects before, and she knew it would not only be useless to discourage him, but wrong. He was a prophet, even if he was her Joseph, and if he received an answer from the Lord, she would accept it. But she still wondered whether gathering into one place again would lead to more troubles. She feared that the Saints would never be accepted. She longed for peace, and she wondered whether it would ever come.

The two were silent for a time. Joseph was joyous to be released from jail, joyous to be with the members—and admittedly, joyous to be back with Emma and the children—but she admitted her fear in a whisper: "Someone will always want to destroy you, Joseph. It's been that way from the beginning."

Joseph nodded solemnly. Emma already wished she could take the words back. She had fallen in love with an enthusiastic young man who wanted more than anything to do the work of the Lord. It wasn't his fault that people accepted the worst rumors about him. She knew that some members of the Church had become disillusioned and turned against him, but in her mind, that was mostly because members wanted him always to be a prophet, not a man—never to make a mistake.

"I suppose there will be those who want to rid the earth of me," Joseph said, "but I'm confident the Lord will protect me so long as I have work to do." He took a breath, then added quietly, "But I've known for many years that I wasn't likely to have a long life."

Emma stood and walked to the window. She looked out toward the woods. It was a nice day, April 22, and spring had changed the look of the gaunt, leafless trees she had seen when she had arrived in February. But she didn't feel the sense of rebirth she had hoped for. "And if you're taken, what about me? And what about our children? We own nothing. I would have to live off the charity of others."

"Yes, and that concerns me." He joined her at the window and put his arm around her shoulders. "This winter I thought many times about the life you would have to lead if I'm taken. It's the first matter I need to resolve. But I honestly believe all the Saints can prosper together—and you and I can prosper with everyone else—if we live righteously and accept the Lord's guidance."

Emma told herself to believe that promise, to trust. But she had seen mostly heartbreak in her life with Joseph, and after the tragic end to their Kirtland years and the disastrous time in Missouri, it was not easy to convince herself that the future would be different.

"Let's walk outside," Joseph said. "I want to know what it's like to walk about as a free man."

"If people see us, they'll—"

"We'll walk into the woods."

"Didn't you get enough of that these last few days?"

"We were worried that someone might be chasing us, so we didn't yet feel free. I just want to stroll about with you for a time and feel a sense that my dark night is over."

Emma felt a surge of joy, just hearing that he wanted this time with her. So she spoke with Sarah Cleveland and asked her to look after the children while she and Joseph walked out for a short time.

"Of course I will," Sarah told Emma. "The boys are playing, and Julia is staying close. You needn't worry about them."

Emma thanked her, and then she and Joseph slipped out the back door and into the nearby woods.

Emma took Joseph's arm as they followed a little path along a creek. The sound of the water, along with the breeze in the trees, was soothing. Emma breathed in the loveliness of the warm air. She noticed fancy patterns of light as rays of sun filtered through the tree limbs and colored the ferns with splotches of brighter green.

Joseph was quiet too as they walked slowly and let the peace settle into them. Eventually he said, "It's hard to tell you how different this all feels—after those gloomy months in jail."

"It's new for me, too. I've been jailed with you, even though it may not seem so to you."

"No. I do understand. I think I know what you've suffered. I didn't realize before, not fully, but I've felt it today. I can hear your pain when you tell me about your worries."

"I won't talk that way again, Joseph. I'll look ahead, not back. I need to learn that from you."

Joseph didn't respond at first. He stopped at a place where the path angled close to the creek, stood still, and looked into the water. "Did you read my letter, Emma?" he asked. "My last letter to you and the Saints?"

"Yes. Of course I did."

"One question was, 'How long can rolling waters remain impure?' I think of that when I look at this little stream. The gospel *is* going to reach the entire world. It's not my opinion; it's what I know. I also know we'll face more opposition—but resistance to the Restoration will be like rocks in a river. There's no power that can stay the heavens. That's what the Lord told us."

"I remember those words. And I do believe them." But what

she still feared was that the "opposition," as he called it, could be monstrous boulders that would test the utmost power of the Saints.

Joseph was still watching the water, seeming to see more in it than she did. "I have to look beyond the obstacles in the stream and keep my eye on the plan that's being carried out. Our trials are not over, but the Lord will direct us."

"I'm glad you can say that now. You told me once that you felt abandoned."

"I know. But the Lord needed to break off some of my rough edges. When I was first confined in the jail, I was angry that my brothers in the gospel had denounced me—the man called by God to be their leader. But in that dungeon one night—when I was so sick that I thought I would die—I saw clearly that my resentment was part of my pridefulness and it was keeping me from hearing the voice of the Lord. Even after that, though, I tried to break out. I still saw the jail as my impediment. But the Lord wouldn't let me escape *myself* that easily. I had to accept his will and truly humble myself."

"Joseph, you're human. Of course you were angry; of course you hated that jail. You needn't take so much blame on yourself."

"Yes, I'm human. But I can't be petty and bitter. The Lord expects more of me than that. After I heard from you and knew you were safe here in Illinois, I was filled with gratitude, and all my anger was taken away. I could finally hear the Lord, and I could write the letter I needed to write—offering the members the words the Lord gave to me. My heart had been set too much on the things of the world and the honors of men. Those were his words, and I've said them over and over in my mind since then. In the jail, I had to accept my own powerlessness. Once I accepted that frailty, the Lord let me understand more than I had ever perceived before."

Emma desperately wanted to know more, wanted to know

everything Joseph had learned, but she also understood that she couldn't push him to say what he wasn't prepared to tell her.

"There are doctrines we don't yet understand, and there is growth beyond anything we can imagine right now. What we need to do is keep our hearts pure, our minds focused on the things that matter." Joseph looked from the stream up into the trees and the rays of light. "If my life is cut short, the work will go forward, and it's the work that matters, not me."

Emma gripped Joseph's arm. He turned to her and embraced her. He held her for a long time, and she basked in the enveloping tenderness she felt. He kissed her, lovingly, slowly, and then he said, "Let's walk back to the house now. I want to spend some time with the children, all of us together. It's what I longed for day and night while I was in the jail."

It was what she had longed for all these months—not to be alone anymore. The two walked back to the house, and Joseph gathered the children around him, Julia on one side and Joey on the other, Frederick and Alexander on his lap. Alexander was still hesitant at first, but he seemed to accept Freddie's example and settled in against his papa.

It was a perfect picture to Emma, Joseph and the children together. She sat close and watched them, heard Joseph talk to them, laugh with them. Emma could only think that the family had not only survived an agonizing test of strength, but that something new had come to them. Joseph was not the same man who had been dragged from their home and locked up in jail. She heard a new gentleness in his voice, saw it in the warmth he showed the children. She sensed a refinement about him and was certain that his spirit had been touched by the hand of God.

AUTHOR'S NOTE

Some readers will wonder whether I invented some of the events in this book. Did Emma Smith really visit Joseph three times while he was in the jail? Did Joseph actually wrestle a juror during a break in his pretrial hearing? Did guards transporting the prisoners in fact allow them to go free? Did Alexander McRae forget his pseudonym and then pretend to be ill? The answer is, yes, all those things happened. But what kinds of conversations did Emma and Joseph enter into on her visits? What were the details of the wrestling match? What did the guards have to say as they released Joseph and the other men? What were the details of the scene in which Alexander faked his illness? Such scenes I had to fictionalize. I only knew the anecdote about McRae forgetting his name, faking an illness, and drinking liquor as a "cure." I had to imagine the event, create dialogue, and in the case of the farmer, I had to invent him and his wife entirely.

What becomes more complicated for me is that, at times, more than one version of an event has come down to us. That's the case with the release of the prisoners at Yellow Creek. I had to choose one of the versions since I can't report variations in available accounts the way a historian can. There is, however, little doubt that the men were released and didn't escape. Only the details of exactly how it took place are in question.

I always think that it's useful to read historical fiction along with scholarly history. The power of fiction is immediacy—a sense of "being there." Readers often report that they come away from a historical novel, if it's written well and accurately, with a sense of time and place, along with an emotional connection to the characters. The power of scholarly history is that it provides a higher level of objectivity and thoroughness than fiction ever can. Some readers who are interested in the history of a period or event choose to avoid fictional versions. Others read fiction but take no interest in scholarly books. In my mind, both approaches are valid and worth experiencing, and studying the two together can lead to a more complete understanding.

I always hope that my works of fiction will stimulate readers toward further study, not serve as an end in themselves. I read more scholarly history than I do historical fiction, partly because I'm often doing research toward writing another novel, but also because I crave the carefully gathered information and insights historians offer. One great blessing for all of us is that information about Latter-day Saint history is now available as never before. The Joseph Smith Papers have provided a greatly expanded availability of important documents. And *Saints,* the updated history of the Church, has borrowed from the narrative style of fiction to create a story everyone can enjoy reading.

Having said that, one of my challenges in writing *Liberty* was that information about the incarceration in Liberty Jail is not as readily available as it is for some historical events. Joseph didn't keep a journal during the months he was incarcerated or engage a scribe to keep one for him. This rare break in his records was perhaps caused by the conditions for writing in the jail and perhaps by the depravation and tedium of the experience. Hyrum Smith wrote a few passages in a journal toward the end of his stay, and some letters from him and others have survived, but much of what we learn about that abysmal winter confinement has come down to us indirectly: from visitors to the jail, retrospective accounts, affidavits, family histories, etc. Historians have also found added information in recent years, and I tried to track down all the documents, letters, and other sources available.

For those seeking further knowledge on this subject, a good source to start with is *Saints, Volume 1: The Standard of Truth, 1815–1846.* The account of Joseph's time in jail is brief, but you will find context to comprehend more about the so-called "Mormon War" that led to the jailing of Joseph and other Church leaders. Use the footnotes or study the "Sources Cited" section at the end of the book to discover many publications or documents for further study.

The Joseph Smith Papers offer an exhaustive source of valuable information. For study of the period of 1838–39 in Missouri, read the introduction to part three in *The Joseph Smith Papers, Documents, Volume 6: February 1838–August 1839.* This is an up-to-date, careful account that I used not only for information but as a guide to further sources. The letter that contained the material published in Doctrine and Covenants 121–123 is called, "Letter to the Church and Edward Partridge, March 1839," and for those interested in reading it in its entirety, it can be found in *The Joseph Smith Papers, Documents, Volume 6.*

No historian has chosen to write an authoritative book on Joseph's months in the jail, but there are many articles or references in books on the Missouri era of Church history. Information about the jail, the prisoners, the written letters, etc., can be found with online searches, but I'll offer a warning. Many of the articles, though interesting and often well written, pass along out-of-date information and even the myths I spoke of in this book's preface. Leonard J. Arrington's classic essay, *Church Leaders in Liberty Jail* (BYU Studies Quarterly, Volume 13, Issue 1, 1973) was a seminal, valuable essay for its time, and it postulated the concept that Joseph's experience in the jail gave him time "to ponder his course, to synthesize ideas, to formulate goals." Subsequent historians have built on that theme. The essay was written early, however, and further research has brought to light added details and insights.

The preeminent scholar of Latter-day Saint history in Missouri is Alexander L. Baugh, professor of Church History and Doctrine at Brigham Young University. His book *A Call to Arms: The 1838 Mormon Defense of Northern Missouri* (originally a Brigham Young University dissertation, and since reprinted) remains the most authoritative history of the Mormon War. It does not deal extensively with Joseph's confinement in Liberty Jail, but it describes fully the events that led to the Church leaders' arrests and custody, including the court of inquiry in Richmond, Missouri.

For the purposes of my book, some of Professor Baugh's more recent research has been especially useful. In an interview with Casey Griffiths ("Myths and Facts about Liberty Jail - Interview with Alex Baugh," produced by Doctrine and Covenants Central), he makes the case that the prisoners could stand up straight, that they spent their daytime hours in the upper room, that there was a stove upstairs, that Old Major was in the jail for a period of time, and that a guardhouse existed outside the jail. He also made a good case that the men held in the jail never were served human flesh and were probably not poisoned, as the prisoners themselves believed.

Professor Baugh also wrote an important essay: "'We Took Our Change of Venue to the State of Illinois': The Gallatin Hearing and the Escape of Joseph Smith and the Mormon Prisoners from

Missouri, April 1839," originally published in spring 2001 in *Mormon Historical Studies*, volume 2, number 1, pages 59–82. This is a detailed account of the hearing in Gallatin, the release of the prisoners, their trek to Illinois, their finding each other at the home of George Harris, and the humorous incident of Alexander McRae forgetting his name.

Early on, as I gathered information, I asked myself how Joseph found a place within himself—during perhaps the darkest time of his life—to write some of the most beautiful ideas and language he was inspired to compose. This book is my attempt to imagine that process. What I believe is that the words in that March 20–21 letter were revealed to him, but that he had to reach a state that prepared him to receive that revelation. The process may not be exactly as I imagined it, but I do think it's useful to place ourselves in that jail with him and to look for those answers.

I appreciated a telephone chat that I had with Professor Alexander L. Baugh—a very congenial and informative one in which I asked a number of questions. But while I acknowledge and appreciate his help, I blame none of my mistakes or misperceptions on him.

My editors at Deseret Book, Kristen Evans, Celia Barnes, and Laurel Christensen Day, have been patient and kind as they've guided me—once again—through many much-needed revisions.

It's sort of perfunctory to thank one's spouse under the heading of "acknowledgments," but in my case, Kathy has been my partner, not my proofreader. She reads multiple drafts, and as I have mentioned in previous publications, she never hesitates to tell me the truth about the weaknesses she perceives. Believe me, I listen. It's really true that I couldn't write a book without her.